GETTING AWAY WITH **MURDER**

Joy Wood

To Vicki
with thanks
Joy Wood
x/x

A CIP catalogue record for this title
is available from the British Library

Dedication

To my dear husband, John.

My life's biggest security is not just in
loving you, but in knowing that you will always
be there to love me back no matter what.

Chapter 1

Claire

A profound, dark sensation wrapped itself around her, like a heavy thick cloak weighing her down. Something horrendous was going to happen, she knew it. She'd experienced the exact feeling of doom clenching at her gut once before – the day her father died.

She stood in front of the huge bi-fold doors which, when opened, almost brought the garden into the house, and savoured her morning fix of filtered black coffee in her favourite, *World's Greatest Mum*, mug. Normally she loved the tranquillity of early morning before anyone else had risen, but today she felt unsettled. While her gaze focussed on two beautiful collared doves scrambling around for scraps on the lawn, her tummy contracted with melancholy. Inevitably, thinking about her dad, the tears threatened . . . it was still incredibly raw. Only months earlier on a bleak February morning, her father had been hit by a car as he cycled home from a night shift. Initially the medics thought he was going to be alright, but the bleed in his head had caused his brain to swell and twelve hours later, the sixty-two-year-old giant of a man, was gone.

Devastation didn't come close to describing Claire's loss. Her GP had been sympathetic and offered a prescription for some mild tranquilisers but she'd declined them. Yes, they'd no doubt *lift her mood* as he'd said, but she didn't want to rely on them. At the end of the day, she wasn't depressed, she was grieving, that's what it was.

An image sprang to mind of her beloved dad holding her hand with his pale skin blending in with the stark white hospital sheets. If ever the saying 'Daddy's girl', applied to anyone, it was to her. She'd had to watch him become weaker and weaker, and between shallow breaths he'd mumbled his final promise that he'd watch over her forever. A familiar salty tear rolled down her cheek. She couldn't stop it as she recalled his last words before succumbing to the induced coma he never woke up from. *"Never forget, darling . . . those we love don't go away, they walk beside us every day."* She swallowed the urge to sob out loud – she'd done all her crying, surely?

Her maudlin thoughts were interrupted by her husband strolling in the breakfast area which they'd had converted to a state-of-the-art kitchen with comfortable seating at the back of the house, overlooking the huge and impressive expanse of garden. She hastily wiped the tear away on the sleeve of her robe. Max looked like a walking mannequin for menswear in his Armani business suit and his carefully chosen designer tie. It was ironic that his purpose-built dressing room in their exclusive house was filled to capacity, much more than hers as a female, which was unusual in any household.

He handed her a leaflet. "Someone's going to be upset," he said making his way towards the burbling coffee maker she put on religiously each morning. She glanced down at the flier which he must have picked up from the front door as he came downstairs.

Missing since Wednesday, Tiny, my Yorkshire terrier. He escaped from the garden and won't be able to fend for himself. I'm begging everyone to check their outhouses and garages please. I'm offering a substantial reward if he's found.

My mobile number is 07810 170338.

The photo on the poster was cute and she hated the thought of someone losing their much-loved pet. As a child, her family had a faithful dog, Bess. Pleasant childhood memories flooded back as well as the sadness when the little thing died.

She put the flier down, hoping it wasn't a child's dog and headed towards the cooker to make a start with breakfast. As she cracked eggs into a bowl and whisked them together, she glanced at her husband who had taken up prime position at the long kitchen table and was flicking through the sport in the Daily Mail. She inwardly tried to shrug off the feeling of gloom and chastised herself for being silly. Nothing bad was going to happen. Why would it? It must be just worry, as there had been a lot going on in her life the last few months. The upheaval of leaving London and settling into their new home in the prestigious Sandbanks area of Poole, and her mother's recent stroke had knocked her out of kilter again. Thankfully, the stroke was only mild, but it had upset her and made her anxious. She'd lost one parent, she couldn't face losing another. Maybe the feeling of doom was more to do with having two strikes of bad luck in the space of months, and the old wives' tale of bad luck coming in threes?

She took the plate she'd been warming from the microwave and slid the cheese omelette she'd made onto it, alongside a dollop of her homemade hot tomato relish, and placed the food in front of her husband.

"Aren't you having anything?" he asked tossing the newspaper on the adjacent unit.

"I might in a bit when Freddy comes down."

He ground some pepper onto his food, "What time are you picking your mum up?"

"Around eleven. The ward sister said they'd be a while sorting her tablets out so to leave it until late morning."

"Right, well, I'm afraid something's come up and I won't be here for the next couple of nights but that should give her a chance to settle in and have some time with you and Freddy."

The plate of toast she'd buttered for him landed on the table with more of a slam than she intended. "You said you'd be home this week."

"I know I did, but I have a bit of an issue I need to deal with and I have to be in the office."

"What, for two nights? I thought this place was supposed to be your office. Isn't that why you spent so much money on it, so you didn't have to keep commuting to London?"

He forked a mouthful of omelette into his mouth and exaggerated his enjoyment. "This is good, Claire, no-one can make an omelette like you."

She widened her eyes, "Cut the flattery and answer the question, am I right?"

"Yes and no," he said munching on a bite of toast, "I've wanted to live here ever since I can remember, but I need to earn the money to pay for it. You know that."

"Yeah, but you said all along that once the house was done, you'd cut back." She took a seat next to him at the table, "And I thought you were going to put the London flat up for sale?"

"I did say that," he reached for more toast and mopped the oil and melted cheese around the plate, "and I will when the market is a bit more buoyant. Right now, I don't think I'd get what it's worth, so it makes sense to hang on a bit."

"But that wasn't the plan. We both agreed we needed to leave London," she rested her hand on his wrist and

4

squeezed it gently, "the move was supposed to be for us all. It's no fun for Freddy and I being here while you're in London all the time."

"You do exaggerate. It's not all the time, it's only while I wind things up. Come September, I'll be doing most of the work from home. I tell you what, I'll just make it an overnighter tonight, I'll come back tomorrow, how about that?"

"You'll have to," she said firmly, "we have parents' appointments at six tomorrow."

"Oh yeah, you did say, I forgot. Okay, I'll be back tomorrow afternoon, I promise. Hey, have you got hold of that woman who does the mock eleven plus papers? Time's marching on and Freddy should be doing them now, he needs plenty of practice if he's going to get a chance of passing the entrance exam."

She hadn't done anything about it. If Max spent more time with his son he'd soon realise Freddy wasn't an academic. But she couldn't face going over that again. "No, I haven't."

"Well make sure you do, love. I want him to start on the papers sooner rather than later. He's lucky he's going to get help. I never did when I sat the exam."

No and she hadn't either. She may well have benefited from practice papers as she'd failed the eleven plus miserably and gone to a comprehensive school. But she'd done okay in life, she'd worked hard and got a degree, and she'd been happy, which was all that counted.

"Yes, well, maybe that's not a bad thing. You got into a grammar school on merit as you were bright. I'm not sure it's right to be tutoring kids to pass the exam. They'll only end up struggling with the academic work afterwards."

"Rubbish. Don't be such a defeatist. Give the woman a ring, or I will."

He stood up to leave the table with his glass of orange juice in his hand. "Oh, and don't forget that gardener bloke, Adam, he's starting today."

"Another reason for you to be here, then."

He ignored her and downed the juice in one gulp, "We'll have to see how it goes with him. I'm still not sure about having a convicted murderer around Freddy."

She screwed up her face, "I wouldn't label him that, as such."

"And what do you call it when you punch the living daylights out of someone and he dies?" He wiped his mouth on his napkin, "In my book that's murder."

"It wasn't quite like that. It was a fight which led to an accident. And he's been to jail and served his time, so now needs to rebuild his life. I'm glad we're the sort of people who have the grace to help him on his course of rehabilitation. And anyway, there's no point in bleating on about it now, let's not forget who gave him the job."

"Only because I was leant on by his father."

"Well you will be part of that secret society that spends it's time scratching each other's backs."

"Yeah, that might be the case," he acknowledged, "but remember his background and maybe not be quite so friendly with him. I know what you're like fussing round with cakes and tea. He's paid help not a friend of ours."

"Oh, for goodness' sake, have you heard yourself? We aren't living in the eighteenth century," she scoffed, "paid help? He's a gardener and will be *allowed* a coffee break while he's working."

"All I'm saying is, don't forget he's the gardener. We'll be paying his wages and he works for us. End of. And I don't want this jailbird inside the house," he warned, "I'm just doing this as a favour. He's only a young bloke so with a bit of luck he'll be off after a few weeks. I've only said until the end of August anyway so he can start and sort the gardens out. Seemingly before his brush with the law, he studied landscaping so he might actually be an asset. Keep him in the garden though whatever you do and don't let him near Freddy."

She rolled her eyes.

"I mean it, Claire, I don't want him around the house."

"Okay, okay. You say he's young, how young?"

He shrugged, "Late twenties, no more than thirty that's for sure."

"Will he even know what you want the gardens to look like?"

"Yeah, I've told him. He knows exactly what I want, so leave him to it. I'll speak to him if he needs instructions, he's got my number. You stay clear."

"Right, oh great one. Are there any other restrictions you want to put on me?"

There was a time when he would have thrown some kinky remark back about tying her to the bed, but not lately. Project managing the house had been all consuming alongside his London business. Trying to get used to a much less attentive husband was hard; she prayed daily the old one would resurface soon. Hopefully, once he'd cut all ties with London, he might start to relax and settle into the life they both wanted and planned for.

He kissed her gently, "I'll see you tomorrow afternoon. Good luck with your mum."

Their nine-year-old son staggered into the kitchen in his pyjamas and his usual just got out of bed look. Max ruffled his blond curly hair, "I've got to dash, son, work hard at school."

"Ah, at last," she smiled affectionately at her precious boy, "come and get some breakfast." Freddy climbed on a chair at the table and she placed a bowl of his favourite cereal in front of him.

"Have you put Jake's present in your school bag like I asked?" she said, pouring the milk on his cereal, "remember, don't give him it until you get to his house for the party."

"I won't."

"I've told school you are going home with Jake's mum. I'll come and get you at seven from their house."

He munched on his cereal. "Jake's dad's going to be at the party and is sending out for pizzas." She knew by the tone of his voice what her son was implying. His dad had missed his ninth birthday with yet another *important meeting* he couldn't get out of. His apology was an over the top present and the usual promise he'd make it up to his son which had really narked her. He needed to do better with his tenth birthday when it came up.

"Great," she smiled tenderly at her much-loved son, "you love pizza."

She poured herself another coffee. The doom and gloom anxiety cramps were still there, but she was going to have to try to ignore them. The overwhelming feeling of dread she'd experienced first thing was probably nothing more than hormonal.

Nothing awful was going to happen. Why would it?

Chapter 2

Claire

The doorbell rang interrupting her as she applied her lip-stick in the downstairs cloakroom. She continued, hoping it was a door-to-door salesman who'd eventually go away. She fluffed up her short, cropped hair, always grateful she didn't have to fuss with it. She'd been blessed with thick dark hair and a long neck. She smiled back at herself in the mirror thinking about her mother's sentiment that she *had the right shaped head for short hair.* The chime of the bell a second time made it difficult to ignore. She made her way to the front door and the second she saw a silhouette of a male torso, she remembered who it would be. She reached for the door and opened it. A slender and toned man, much taller than her, lifted his head and held out his hand, "Mrs Maric?" he smiled, his vibrant green eyes crinkling at the edges, "I'm Adam. Adam Bishop, the gardener."

"Oh, hi," she took his calloused hand and gave it a weak shake, "my husband said you'd be coming today, welcome."

"Thank you. He did say not to disturb you but I just want-ed to say hello," he shuffled awkwardly as if he was wishing he hadn't, "before you spotted me around the gardens."

"I'm pleased you did," she smiled reassuringly, "you're okay? . . . I mean, you know what you're doing?"

"Yeah, absolutely. I've got a list of jobs and priorities

from Mr Maric, which is good, and it's a long one so that'll keep me busy."

She screwed up her face, "I hope he wasn't too overbearing, he can come across as a sort of project manager type."

"Not at all. He's clearly a man who knows what he wants and I'm happy to follow his instructions."

"That's good then. I'm sorry I missed you when you came. I was visiting my mother in hospital when you got the garden tour."

"No problem at all. Is your mother alright?" he tilted his head slightly, "sorry, I didn't mean to pry."

"No, you're not. It's kind of you to ask. She's actually coming home today . . . in fact," she glanced at her watch, "I'm just going to collect her from the hospital. She's staying here for a while until she's back on her feet."

"I'll let you get on then. That'll be nice for her I'm sure," he looked towards the garden, "I can't think of a better place to stay, it certainly is a beautiful house and in a prime spot."

"Thank you. We love it. But it has been quite a project and the gardens are the last bit. Max wanted to wait until every last digger and cement mixer was out of the way before they were tackled."

"I don't blame him," he smiled displaying the most perfect set of white teeth which were natural unlike those cosmetically enhanced ones everyone seemed to be going for.

"Right, I'll make a start, shall I?" he asked.

"Yes, thank you. You've got keys to the outbuildings, haven't you?"

He held up a bunch of keys.

"Great. I'll only be gone for a while this morning. There's a fridge in the workshop with some cold drinks and bottled water, and a toilet adjacent to that. But if there's anything else you need, please knock and I'll try and help if I can. My husband is away on business so won't be back until tomorrow."

"Sure I will, but I'm pretty self-sufficient, so I don't think I'll need to bother you. And as I said, your husband has told me exactly what to do."

She couldn't help but take in how attractive he was. He had thick collar length brown hair, not styled in a formal way, just wavy and doing its own thing flicking out at the edges, and the few days' stubble suited him, but it was his eyes that defined him. They were such a beautiful green it actually looked like he was wearing eye liner. The dark curled eye-lashes would be an asset to any female; they'd certainly negate the need for lashings of mascara.

"Oh, before I forget," she was about to invite him in but remembered Max's warning, "just a moment." She made her way into the kitchen and found the flier about the dog and took it back.

"Would you mind having a scout around for this dog? I can't imagine it's here as I'm sure we'd have heard it barking, but if you could have a look, I'd feel better."

She noted his hands as he read the leaflet. It was evident from the old scars and calluses they were working hands. "Poor thing, it will be anxious if it's locked in somewhere. I'll do that now. If I find it shall I ring the number and take it back?"

"Oh, yes please do. There's a reward . . ." she blushed, why was she rambling on about a reward as if he was some sort of pauper, "you know what I mean. You might as well have it if you do find the dog."

He nodded, but there was something about his pained expression which made her feel she'd embarrassed him.

"Be lovely if you did," she smiled kindly, "I'll perhaps see you later then."

She closed the door surprised at how tanned he looked considering he'd just been released from jail. As she picked up her handbag and car keys, she thought about how pleasant on the eye he was for a gardener. He was certainly rocking the shorts and tee shirt look with the mustard coloured desert boots and his muscular long legs.

* * *

Claire eventually returned home with her mother after a delay with her discharge from hospital, and led her into the downstairs guest bedroom which overlooked the outdoor swimming pool. There was a nice comfy chair in the full-length window that her mum could slip off to if she needed some quiet time.

"You have a lie down, Mum and I'll fetch you a cup of tea. I've been to your house and got you some clothes and things which I've put away, and there are plenty of toiletries in the bathroom."

"Thanks, love, I think I will, I am a bit tired. Hospitals are supposed to be for rest and recuperation, but quite honestly, I'm glad to be away from that ward. It was so noisy during the night."

"Yeah, I bet. Hopefully you can get some rest now, there's nothing spoiling here. And remember what the ward sister said, no rushing about for a few days."

She piled the pillows up for her mum and she rested against them.

"I won't get into bed, I don't think, I'll just have a rest on top for now."

"Okay, if you're sure. I won't be long." She made her way to the bedroom door.

"I want to be able to do things while I'm here, love, you know . . . normal stuff. Don't turn me into an invalid, will you?"

"Course I won't. You can do as much or as little as you like. I'm just glad to have you here with us for a while so I can look after you."

"Me too."

She watched her mother's eyes getting heavy as she gently closed the door. She'd leave it for half an hour before she took her some tea so she could rest. It was a huge relief to finally have her home from the hospital. Time was what she needed now to make a full recovery. Her stroke had been a dreadful shock. Life without her dear mum didn't bear thinking about, not with the loss of her dad still so terribly raw.

Chapter 3

Annabelle

Her naked body fitted perfectly in his arms where she'd shuffled in and rested her head on his shoulder. She felt his breathing slow down. He'd drifted off to sleep. Max had made love to her like a man possessed. It had been days since she'd seen him, two agonising days where he played happy families with his clingy wife and kid. She inhaled his fragrance. She'd give him time to rest, knowing when he woke up, he'd want her again. And she'd want him too. She savoured every moment until he had to leave and she'd be alone again, waiting until the next time. How in the space of a few months had she become so needy? It was alien to her. Even during her brief marriage, she'd never felt anything like it for her husband. She'd never experienced such overwhelming love for any man. But she loved Max Maric, desperately. If only she didn't have to put up with all the crap that came with him.

He took a deep breath, which indicated he'd opened his eyes. She lifted her head so she could see his handsome face. "Hey, old man, you fell asleep on me," she smiled lovingly.

"That's 'cause you wore me out, you witch," he kissed her head.

"Do you want to eat?" she asked, hoping he wouldn't as she was content lying with him.

"That'd be great. I haven't eaten since lunch." He swung his legs over the edge of the bed and she couldn't help but admire his lean naked torso as he headed towards the en-suite. He certainly was a fit bloke for forty.

She reached for her housecoat and made her way to the main bathroom to freshen up before heading for the kitchen. Earlier, her housekeeper had put together an antipasto platter of salami, mozzarella and blue cheeses, olives, tomatoes, and balsamic vinaigrette. It was just a question of taking the gourmet delight out of the fridge, cutting up the French bread and pouring the wine.

Max devoured food. The expression *the way to a man's heart is through his stomach,* certainly applied to him. She loved watching him eat. The food was far too calorific for maintaining her perfect size ten so she picked at it, content to sit and watch him. Their time together was precious so she savoured every single moment.

He forked the last piece of cheese into his mouth. "That was something else, Annie," he placed his knife and fork together and leant back in his chair, "you are talented in the kitchen department," his eyes glistened, "as well as every other department."

She smiled inwardly, *yeah right.* She loved him calling her Annie, nobody else did. He'd reckoned Annabelle was too stiff and formal for a sexy woman like her. So Annie had stuck and she loved it, especially when he made love to her and breathed it in her ear over and over again.

He shuffled slightly in his chair and his demeanour stiffened. She sensed she wasn't going to like what was coming next. She could read him; he was building up to saying something. He took a large mouthful of the wine she'd poured him which she'd wager would be for Dutch courage.

"Do you want the good news or the bad news?" he asked licking the excess wine off his lips.

Her heart sunk, she'd been right. "Er . . . bad first," she screwed her face up, "I think?"

"I've only got tonight." His face looked pained, and so it should. She had plans for them both the following evening. He'd said he would be there for two nights.

"I'm sorry, sweetheart," he reached for her hand, "I've got to go home tomorrow. Freddy has a parents' evening I have to attend. I'd completely forgotten."

"Parents' evening?" Her voice went up an octave, "He's only nine, isn't he? What on earth's so important in his academic life? He's hardly at a crucial stage of his education."

"I know but the school encourages parents to attend and I'd already said I would." His expression was apologetic, "It's one of those things I really can't get out of. And I do want to be included in my son's education."

"But what about me, what about what I want? We discussed this when we first agreed we wanted to be together. I said then I wouldn't be your bit on the side. Someone to visit when you're at a loose end. I told you when we spoke about our feelings for each other; I'm not waiting around for you to visit whenever you can fit me in."

"It's not like that and you know it," he said, "I love you, and I want to be with you."

"You say that, but when? I keep making allowances, but quite honestly, I'm all out of them right now." She injected some force into her voice, "I've already said I want children of my own before I'm too old. You say you want more kids, too. So we need to make a life together, I'm not getting any younger. I don't know why you just can't tell Claire it's over. People split up all the time, she'll get over it."

"I know that, but right now it's hard. She only lost her father a few months ago, and her mother having a stroke has thrown her. She's been backwards and forwards to the hospital trying to support her. What sort of a bloke tells his wife their marriage is over while that's going on?"

"Okay, I get that, but didn't you say her mother is coming to recuperate at your house? That must mean she's getting better, right? Surely it's best to tell Claire now and you can be out of there. Otherwise you'll be saying next you can't speak to her while her mother's in the house. Or maybe that is exactly what you are thinking?" She glared at him. *Please deny it.*

"Look," he ran a hand through his hair, "it's been a difficult few weeks. I am going to tell her, but I've thought of something I wanted to run by you first. Claire's fortieth is in August, there's a massive party planned, her brother is coming over from Canada. How about I get that over with, then I'll tell her and leave finally."

"August! But that's two months away," she glared at him, "there's no way I'm carrying on like this for months waiting around until you can get away for a snatched few hours, no way at all, Max."

"Look," his eyes were pleading, "you're gonna have to cut me a bit of slack. I'm going to leave my whole life to make one with you. It's a massive undertaking and one that needs planning. I don't want her to throw a wobbler and get rid of the house. I need to tread carefully."

"But it's highly likely you will lose the house," she said, "Claire's not going to let you have it."

"She will eventually. I don't even think she likes it that much. Once the divorce is out of the way, I'll buy her another one somewhere close by. After the dust has settled, of course . . . it might take a year or two."

She shook her head, "I can't see any of this working out. She'll get a solicitor and you'll be screwed big time. I think you need to write that house off. We can get another."

"I don't want another house, I want that one. It's been in my family for years. It was my father's house, Claire knows that. And she doesn't have a spiteful bone in her body, so I know eventually she'll want out and let me have it."

Her tummy knotted. She disliked him talking kindly about his wife. She wanted him to hate her, and to get her well and truly gone from their lives so they could be together and have their own children. She'd been waiting thirty-six years for the right man to come along. A man she could truly love. Two months were going to be unbearable having to wait for him. And there wasn't a cat in hell's chance she was living in that house either. No point in telling him that now though, that would come later. And she wasn't leaving London either, no way at all.

He reached forward and cradled the back of her head, pulling her towards him. He kissed her slowly. Every single time he did that, she loved him a tiny bit more. Nobody could kiss like he could. He broke away, "I really do love you," he breathed with conviction, "give me two months to sort everything out and I promise you I'll make a clean break and then we'll have the rest of our lives together. And I'll never let you down, just give me this time, Annie, please?"

There foreheads touched and she gently nodded. If she wanted him, then she knew she'd have to wait.

"Come on," he said, "let's go back to bed."

Her smaller hand fitted so nicely in his large one as he led her towards the bedroom. It was what she wanted for the rest of her life, her hand in his. She loved him like no other before him. He'd said he had good and bad news; she'd ask him later what the good news was. The bad news meant the next two months were going to be tortuous, but she'd have to be patient, then he truly would be hers. But waiting for what she wanted was alien to her. Patience wasn't a virtue she had.

Being wealthy saw to that.

Chapter 4

Annabelle

In her white Mercedes convertible, she made her way towards Claybourne Hall, the luxury health spa she'd inherited from her father. The journey only took thirty minutes from home and on a sunny day she liked to drive with the top down and the wind blowing in her hair. And each time she turned into the long, tree-lined drive that would take her to the main building, she experienced the same buzz. The business afforded her an opulent lifestyle. Success meant everything to her.

She was booked in for a treatment with Erin, one of the therapists, for a full body massage which she was desperate for since her previous evening with Max. Every muscle and sinew ached with tension since he'd dropped the bombshell and asked her to wait for over two months until they could be together. She wasn't in the habit of waiting for anything, and thoughts about his clingy suburban wife hanging on to him, rankled.

Thankfully, she'd already got her wedding planned, in her mind at least, which gave her something positive to look forward to. It now looked like it was going to have to be an autumn wedding. Not ideal, but she'd make sure it was sorted in the coming weeks. Focussing on that would kill some time, but having to wait didn't sit well, she never waited for anything in her life. However, choice wasn't a luxury she had if she wanted him, which she did, desperately. Waiting until after his clingy wife's fortieth birthday party would fester inside. Why the hell had she agreed to that?

She manoeuvred her car into her allocated parking space and cut the engine. The grounds of the house never ceased to amaze her. The views were spectacular from every aspect of the spa which overlooked neatly manicured vibrant green lawns stretching for miles. The infinity pool at the top of the building had a stunning aspect overlooking the extensive grounds. A prominent feature was the pond, almost as large as a lake, with flowering lily pads and a small wooden bridge that crossed the middle. Vibrant colour enhanced the gardens courtesy of an array of geraniums fuchsias, chrysanthemums, dahlias and daisies. It had taken years for the extensive gardens to mature into their current vista. Her father had wanted the grounds to be equally as inviting as the inside of the spa. His vision was that paying guests could not only take pleasure in the indoor recreation the facility had to offer, but also benefit from outdoor pursuits such as cycling, peaceful walks, and outside yoga in beautiful and tranquil surroundings.

She reached across the passenger seat for her designer handbag, carefully selected from her extensive range to match her charcoal Catherine Walker dress. Clothes and appearance meant everything to her. Her ritual for every moment of the day was making sure she looked like a model, which meant well-fitting designer clothes, eating little and often to maintain her perfect figure, and regular skin treatments. Right now her skin was fresh and wrinkle free, but she knew she'd eventually have to resort to surgical procedures to maintain her high cheekbones and plump lips. The only vice she did succumb to, far more frequently than she should, was alcohol. Somehow she never managed to control her desire for a fine alcoholic beverage.

Yegor, the resident caretaker, approached the car. He was one of those men that seemed to appear out of nowhere. Maybe he waited around for her, she wasn't sure, but he always seemed to be there to greet her each time she arrived at the spa. She wouldn't put it past him having a tracker of some sort on her such was his shadiness.

"Morning," he said in his usual gruff way.

"Morning Yegor, it's a lovely day, isn't it?"

"Sure is."

He held the car door for her to exit and she smiled appreciatively. Yegor looked smart in full morning attire of a black jacket and ornate waistcoat she insisted he wore. The spa was all about class, and image meant everything.

"Thank you," she nodded clicking the fob to lock the car, "have a good day."

She didn't do small talk with Yegor. He was an ex-Russian policeman, so he told her, but she deduced if that was the case, he'd most probably been booted out. She knew from personal experience he operated under the law.

She made her way to the opulent entrance flanked by elaborate pillars. The ornate sign, boldly displaying 'Claybourne Hall', never ceased to give her a kick. When her father started the business in the seventies, there wasn't a great call for leisure facilities, but gradually when women became more independent and gained more freedom, they concentrated on personal indulgences and the spa facilities grew.

"Good morning, Ms. Claybourne," Kimberly, the greeter with her cosmetically enhanced face smiled from behind the reception desk. It was vital all front of house staff appeared immaculate and a full face of carefully applied make-up was a must. The spa was one of elegance and giving the message to all women that they too can look refreshed and glamorous.

"Morning, Kimberly," she nodded, skirting past to make her way towards the lift so she didn't have to talk to her about the weather or some other mundane pleasantries. She knew her business manager and very dear friend, Anthony would already be in his office working. He was always there before her. If he was going for a train, he'd be on the platform an hour before it. Each Friday evening they had a regular dinner date together and he'd always be at the exclusive Simone's in Chelsea before she arrived, waiting patiently with a refreshing alcoholic beverage ready for her.

She tapped and opened the door to Anthony's plush office. He was sat at his desk facing the door with the telephone in his hand and speaking quietly, but she went in anyway. As she approached to take a seat, she noticed a slight flush on his skin as he hurriedly said goodbye to the caller.

"Sorry," she winced apologetically, "was that personal?"

"No, no," he said, "nothing that won't keep." His sheepish smile said differently. He was keeping something from her. Maybe he was organising something special for her birthday? Anthony was the kindest of men. Over the years, he'd spoilt her, and a life without him in it, didn't bear contemplating. But the biggest asset was the way in which he ran the spa efficiently and effectively. With him at the helm, she knew her business was in safe hands.

"I wasn't expecting you," he tilted his head slightly, "I thought you said you were tied up for the next couple of days?"

"I was." Her tummy knotted, *and I should have been but I've been bombed out,* "but my arrangements have changed. I'm going to have a massage so thought I'd call in and say hi."

"Do you want Angela to fetch you a coffee?"

"No," she glanced at her Rolex, "not enough time, I'm going down in five minutes. I just wondered if you'd heard anything about James Slater. Have we got a court date yet?"

James was a fitness instructor that they'd had to sack

along with his fiancée for stealing high end beauty products from the stock they sold in-house. Both had vehemently denied it and engaged a solicitor to challenge them for unfair dismissal.

"Yes, finally. I was going to ring you later and tell you as we aren't meeting for dinner as usual. It's next month, the sixteenth."

"Good, I'll be glad when that's sorted. Oh, I can now make dinner," she smiled, "can you ask Angela to ring Simone's for our table?" His demeanour was awkward; the penny dropped. "Unless you've got something on tonight, we don't have to have dinner."

"Not at all. I'll get Angela to sort it. Usual time?"

"Yes, if you're sure?"

"Course I'm sure. I'm glad as I've got something I want to discuss with you."

"Brilliant, me too. So we'll have plenty to talk about. Right, I'll leave you to it and see you later."

He stood and walked around the desk, leaning forward as she stood to kiss her cheek. There was definitely something different about him. She'd wheedle it out of him tonight.

* * *

Following her massage, Annabelle returned to her office feeling more relaxed physically, but she was still tense thinking about Max. His suggestion of her having to wait until August for them to be together had irritated her to the point of being angry. She didn't do waiting around. Her head pounded, which could have been the release of toxins from the muscles following her massage as the therapist had said, but it was more likely due to Max and his request for her to wait. Stress was a huge problem for her – it made her do stupid things. He wouldn't know about that, though. If he did, he would never have postponed leaving his wife. How had she even agreed to his suggestion? Two more months would be torture. She reached in her handbag for two aspirin to settle her headache. Removing two from the blister pack reminded her that she hadn't taken her prescribed medication that morning. It was unlike her to forget. Max's bombshell had thrown her routine completely. She should really go back home and take her pills. If she didn't, she could end up going back to the dark place she'd worked so hard to get out of.

She buzzed and asked Yegor to come to her office. Unlike any other member of staff, when she sent for him, he never came straight away. It was as if he purposely kept her waiting. But he was completely loyal and discreet, so even though it riled her, she let it go. No point in sweating over the small stuff. He always delivered on everything she asked him to do, which he should do as she paid generously. Their arrangement worked – he kept her one step ahead of the game, always.

Eventually he knocked on her door and opened it slightly.

"Come in, Yegor."

The giant man made his way towards her clutching a manila folder. The sheer size of him made all his movements appear awkward. It wasn't just his height, he was built like a man-mountain and the small chair opposite would look like a footstool when he sat on it.

"Did you get the information I asked you to?"

"I did." He placed the folder on the desk.

"Thank you. Take a seat."

She opened the folder and pulled out the file on Max's wife, Claire Maric. The small photograph of the stunning looking woman came as no surprise to her. She expected nothing less from Max – he wouldn't have a plain woman for a wife.

"Anything out of the ordinary?" she asked, closing the file. She already knew exactly what she looked like anyway as she'd seen her and their brat on Max's phone.

"Nope. Just routine stuff you'd expect about a married woman with a kid. Takes the kid to and from school and visits the hospital to see her mother. Seems a quiet life. She goes out to choir on a Wednesday evening. Her husband, Max Maric is Maric Fitness and Leisure," he raised an eyebrow, "but you probably already know that?"

"Yes, I do. That's fine, I'll look through it later."

"Do you want any further updates on her movements?"

No way. She'd handle Claire Maric herself.

"I'll let you know. Right now, I've got another job I'd like you to do."

He stared, waiting for her to speak.

"You know James Slater who used to work in the gym and his girlfriend, Kelly?"

"The couple you fired?"

"That's correct. They were stealing from us. Unfortunately, they've decided to take us to court for unfair dismissal and we've got a date. As you can imagine, I don't want that negative publicity."

"You want me to deal with it?"

"If you could. The last thing this company needs is to be dragged through the courts."

"I'll get on it right away."

"I want it to go away," she stressed firmly.

She unlocked the top drawer of her desk and handed him a large brown envelope stuffed with the cash she'd removed from the safe earlier. Cash was the currency she used. It couldn't be traced.

"As always," she looked directly into his eyes, displaying a stare that indicated she was in charge exactly as her father had taught her, "this is between you and I."

Yegor took the envelope from her and put it in his inside

jacket pocket. He wouldn't let her down, he never did. He stood up and made his way towards the door.

"Let me know when it's sorted."

He nodded. A man of huge stature and action, but diminutive on words.

Just how she liked it.

Chapter 5

Claire

She was sitting at the kitchen table having breakfast with her mum and Freddy.

"Is it choir tonight, love?" her mum asked taking a bite of toast.

"It is but Max says he might be late, so I'll give it a miss."

"No need to do that. I can look after Freddy, he's no trouble."

"Thanks, Mum, but you're not here to babysit, you're here to rest. You've only just come out of hospital. Maybe another week, we'll see, but not right now."

"How long are you staying for, Grandma?" Freddy asked between mouthfuls of Coco Pops.

"Until I'm fully better and can go to back to my house," her mum smiled lovingly, wiping her fingers on a napkin.

"What, like a month or something?"

"Maybe not quite as long as that, we'll have to see."

"Don't be rushing her off too soon, sweetheart," Claire interrupted, "you like having her here, don't you?"

"Yeah, but I like stopping at her house."

"Well, you will be able to do that again I'm sure, just not for a little while."

"Can I come at half term, Grandma?"

"If I'm better by then, of course you can," she said. "I like having you stay with me. And Mr Bradley from next door is always asking when you're coming again."

"I like his dog, Chum."

"I know you do. And Chum seems to like you too." Her mum stood up, "Just excuse me a minute while I use the bathroom."

Freddy waited until she'd left the room. A worried expression passed across his face, "Is Grandma really poorly?" he whispered.

"No, not ever so, but being in hospital has upset her, so she needs a bit of time to recover. You can get different types of strokes, some can be really bad, but Grandma's was quite a mild one, thankfully."

Freddy scrunched his nose up, "She's not going to die like Grandad, is she?"

Claire moved round to the table, wrapped her arm around his shoulders and kissed his head, "No, sweetheart, Grandma isn't going to die. She is doing well with her physio and taking the tablets the doctors have prescribed. But for a little while she needs a bit of extra help. That's why she's come here to stay, so we can look after her and spoil her. We just have to be patient with her, especially if she's a little ... hesitant with things. She'll be fine in a few weeks, you'll see. The old grandma is still in there, she's just got to get well. And the hospital said she will do, each day she'll improve. She just needs lots of love and care right now."

"Daddy doesn't want her to stay long," he said in all innocence, spooning another mouthful of cereal into his mouth.

"Did he say that?" she snapped, a little too quickly.

He nodded sheepishly.

"Well, he shouldn't have. That isn't nice."

"I like her being here."

"I know you do. I do too."

In her peripheral vision she spotted Adam, the new gardener, stood near the bi-fold door. He was clutching what looked like a red dog collar. She made her way towards the door and slid it open.

"Morning," he smiled.

"Morning." Her gaze moved towards the dog collar knowing it could only mean one thing. Fear snaked through her that Freddy was around and he was going to mention a dead dog. She stepped out of the kitchen area into the garden and slid the door closed, "Is that what I think it is?"

"Yes, but it's only the collar, no sign of the dog."

"Where did you find it?"

"Down the bottom of the garden stuck to a twig. I'm guessing it must have been loose and he's managed to wriggle out of it."

"Oh dear," she frowned, "I wonder if the poor little thing's still alive?"

He shrugged, "Who knows. Do you want me to take the collar back to the owner, the address is on the back, or do you think that might cause more upset?"

"I'm not sure. I guess they might want it as a keep sake?" She took the collar from him and turned the silver tag over in her hand, noting the name Tiny on the front and the address on the back. "It looks pretty expensive, maybe I ought to drop it off?"

"Yeah, maybe . . . if you're sure?"

"Yes, I am. I'll take it back later today. Did you have everything you needed yesterday? Sorry again for not being around."

"No probs at all, and yes, I did. Everything it just as your husband said. Did your mother settle in okay?" he paused, "sorry if I'm prying again. It's just with you saying she was being discharged from hospital."

"Yes, she's here . . ."

The sliding of the door made her turn. Freddy was looking puzzled, clearly wanting to meet the man his mummy was talking to.

"Ah, Freddy, come and meet Adam, he's the new gardener." Max had said to keep them apart but she had to at least introduce him. She couldn't have a man working in the garden that Freddy didn't know.

"Hi, Freddy," Adam grinned, "I like your hat. A man after my own heart supporting Man U."

Freddy's eyes lit up, "Do you support them, too?"

"Yep, I love them."

"Have you been to Old Trafford to watch them play?"

She cringed. Not much chance of going to see a live football match from where he'd been recently, locked up in a cell. Freddy carried on, "My grandad used to take me," his expression turned sad, "before he died. Daddy says he'll take me soon though, didn't he, Mummy?"

"He did," she nodded knowing full well that was unlikely to happen.

"You're lucky then," Adam smiled, "I've only ever seen them on TV."

"I've got a book of stickers with all the players," Freddy smiled eagerly, "I can show you, if you like?"

She remembered Max's warning so quickly interrupted. "Hey, come on, another time maybe. We'd best go and see how Grandma's doing and if she wants anything else for breakfast."

She smiled at Adam, "Thanks for the collar, and do yell out if there is anything
else you need."

He nodded, "Will do." He winked at Freddy, "See ya, buddy."

She walked back into the kitchen as her mother was coming through the door, her gait not quite as steady as it once was. "You okay, Mum?" she asked.

"Grandma," Freddy interrupted, "Adam the gardener supports Manchester United, too."

Chapter 6

Claire

She checked the house number again on the dog tag just to make sure she was stood in front of the right property. It was a decent sized detached house, probably built in the sixties, but appeared as if it had been modernised with sympathetic PVC displaying beautiful bay windows. She walked up the huge ramp to the front door, rang the bell and waited. It had an ornate name plaque next to the number elaborately engraved with the house name of Red Chimneys. She glanced at the roof, the plural indicated more than one chimney but she could only see the one.

It didn't appear anyone was in. She considered posting the collar through the letter box, but thought against it. That would be too upsetting for its owner to find. She checked her watch. Probably better to call again late afternoon on her way to fetch Freddy from school. As she turned to walk away, she heard someone approaching the door. It opened and her eyes drifted downwards to a young woman in an electric wheelchair. Her heart took a significant drop – if only she was delivering good news.

"Hi," she smiled, "I'm Claire Maric. I live around the corner and got your flier about your missing dog."

The woman's face lit up, "Have you found Tiny?"

"I'm afraid not." She wished she hadn't come, "Sorry."

The young woman looked crestfallen. She pushed herself to continue. "My gardener found this," she held up the collar, "which must belong to your dog. That's all though, no sign of him. I wasn't sure what to do to be honest. In the end I thought you should have it."

The woman turned a shade paler as she took the collar from her outstretched hand, "Yes, that's his," her eyes filled with genuine tears, "it's torture not knowing what's happened to him. I haven't been here long and I can't believe I've lost my little companion." The tears started spilling down her cheeks.

What should she do now? She couldn't just leave her.

"Are you alone?" Claire nodded down the hallway, hoping someone might be there so she could go.

"Yes, I live alone," the woman sniffed, "I'm okay though. It's just the realisation he's not coming back. He's only a tiny little thing, hence his name, he won't last long without his home comforts."

"I'm really sorry I'm the one to be bringing you his collar. I guess there's still a bit of hope he could be found."

The young woman smiled through her tears. "I doubt it, but you're very kind bringing the collar back, thank you. Could I invite you in," she moved the wheelchair slightly, "and offer you a drink or something . . . if you've got time that is? I do understand if you're busy."

Surely she could spare half an hour, rather than leaving her alone. Freddy was at school and her mum was comfortable at home, she had her mobile if anything came up.

"Yes, I've got some time. Thank you, a drink would be lovely."

A speck of light shone through the woman's tears as she wiped her nose on a tissue. "I'm Philippa by the way, Philippa Simmons, but people call me Pippa. Would you mind closing the door?" She waited until Claire did and turned the electric chair around. "Follow me."

Claire watched Pippa ably manoeuvre the electronic wheelchair down the laminate hallway and followed closely behind, keeping the conversation going. "I live round the corner at Brereton Place with my husband and my son, Freddy."

The hall was a square shape and dominated by a light wood staircase with a chair lift at the bottom. Pippa manoeuvred the wheelchair past the closed doors of the other rooms off the hallway and led into a beautiful open plan area at the back of the house. Not nearly as grand as hers, but a similar layout with a large living and combined kitchen area, and patio doors opening onto what looked like a stunning garden.

"Please, make yourself comfortable," Pippa indicated towards the luxurious leather seat occupying prime position in the window. She manoeuvred her wheelchair towards the adapted low kitchen units. "I've got a bottle of Rosé opened, can I tempt you with that, or would you prefer tea or coffee," she looked up at the kitchen clock, "it's after eleven, so in my book it's officially wine o'clock."

Claire was relieved the tears had dried up. "In that case, I think a glass of Rosé would be lovely. Just a small one though or I'll be asleep all afternoon. Can I help at all?"

"No, please, take a seat, I manage perfectly, I can assure you."

Claire sat down and glanced around her immediate area. It was a beautiful house, clearly adapted for someone disabled with the laminate flooring and the wide doorways. The garden appeared accessible for a person with limited mobility, with ramps and rails, and a secluded paved area out of the sun.

Pippa glided towards her in the electric wheelchair. There was a control on the right arm of it, and on the left, she'd attached a small tray with the two glasses of wine. "Here, can I give you these."

Claire took the tray from her, placing it on the coffee table.

"The gardens are stunning aren't they?" Pippa smiled which enhanced her already pretty face.

"They are. I guess there must be a regular gardener maintaining them?"

"Yes, he came with the house. I've rented it for two months and I get the gardener thrown in, which is great. He's elderly though so I hope it isn't too much for him. Seemingly he's been doing the gardens for years. The chap that owns the property is a paraplegic."

"Ah, I see, so the house was modified by the previous owner?"

"Yes, which was a major renting point for me. Adapted houses don't come up for rent that often. It's actually a bit larger than I wanted, it's got two bedrooms upstairs which I don't need. I think the chap that owns it must have a family."

"Did I see a stair lift though when I came in?"

"Yeah. The master bedroom's upstairs, but he's added a smaller extension downstairs with an en suite wet-room that I'm using, which is perfect. I'm only here a few days each week at the moment, but next month I intend to spend the whole of it here. I've got a good friend who's just completed gruelling chemotherapy so I'm hoping she's going to come and join me. She can have the upstairs to herself which will give her some privacy."

"That sounds ideal. Is your friend doing okay?" she asked sipping the refreshing Rosé.

"As well as she can be, going through all of that. We were booked on a month's Australian adventure together, but she was diagnosed with breast cancer so unable to go. Once we got a refund, I saw this property and thought it would be nice for me for a couple of months, and she'd benefit also."

"Well it's certainly a beautiful place for anyone to stay in for a break."

"Isn't it? I've been lucky to get it. What about you, you say you're round the corner. Have you lived here long?"

Claire rested her drink on the coffee table. "No, not at all, only a couple of months actually. We previously lived in London. We inherited our house over a year ago but have had it completely rebuilt and only recently moved in."

"How nice. Have you modernised it?"

"Oh yes, completely. It's nothing like the original. And my husband has built an office adjacent to the house and is hoping to be able to work more from home rather than commuting to London all the time. That's the plan anyway but typically he's busier than ever at the moment. That's business people for you I guess," she said, trying to keep the cynicism out of her voice.

Pippa nodded as if she understood and changed the subject, "How old is your son?"

"He's almost ten."

"Has he settled okay?"

"Yes, he's doing fine. He's going into the last year at primary in September so it was a wrench him leaving his London school friends, but the new friends he'll make here are the ones who he'll be going to secondary school with so I'm glad we've made the move now."

"That sounds sensible then. Great that he likes it."

Claire sipped her drink thinking how nice Pippa seemed. Curiosity was burning inside, wanting to know why she was in the wheelchair.

"Thanks for stopping by and sharing a drink with me," Pippa smiled, "much as I like solitude, sometimes it's nice to mix a bit."

"I know the feeling. I haven't had chance to make any friends here yet. I've just brought my mother home from hospital to recuperate from a stroke. She's absolutely fine on her own for a short while, like now, but I wouldn't like to go off for long."

"No, I can imagine. Is she doing okay? It must be a relief that she's home."

"Yes, it is. Thankfully, it was only a mild stroke and if you knew my mum you'd know it would take more than a stroke to keep her down," she smiled.

"My sort of woman, then," Pippa said, "it takes guts and willpower to push yourself on through adversity. I should know."

"Oh, yes, I can see it must be hard for you, too."

"It is, but I'm good. I had my accident a number of years ago now so I'm more used to being in a wheelchair than not being in one, if that makes sense."

Claire nodded. "What do you do the rest of the week? You said you weren't here all the time?"

"I have a part-time job."

"In London?"

"Just outside of it, actually." She was hoping Pippa would say more, but she didn't.

"Do you work?" Pippa asked.

"No. I haven't done for years. I tend to keep the ship steady at home, that sort of thing. My husband works long and unsociable hours, so I've always wanted to be around for him, and my son of course. I never wanted him to have to go to after-school clubs, or to a childminder."

"No, if I had kids, I'd be exactly the same. What does your husband do? You say he works unsocial hours?" Pippa frowned, "Sorry, it's like a million questions, I don't mean to be intrusive."

"It's fine," Claire reassured, "he owns a health spa. You might have heard of it, Maric Health and Leisure. It's in London and he's looking at expanding at some stage, maybe into Europe."

"Gosh, how exciting. No, I can't say I've heard of it, but then again, health spas and leisure aren't something I participate in."

Claire pulled a face, "Sorry."

"Don't be, honestly there's no need. And you must excuse my frankness. It's part of being disabled, you sort of put on a front which isn't absolutely necessary. Luckily, it's usually when I'm around people I don't know, but once I get to know them, I drop my guard." She smiled, "It's something to do with the old adage about being seen as a whole person, rather than someone in a wheelchair."

A movement in the garden caught Claire's eye, and she turned to see an elderly gentleman with a pitchfork. "Is that your gardener?"

Pippa craned her neck, "Yes, that's him, Ken. He looks like he's going to drop dead any minute, doesn't he?"

Claire laughed out loud, liking Pippa's humour. "He does a bit. How old is he do you think?"

"Oh, I don't know, maybe seventy."

"Seventy! I think you need to go to Specsavers. I reckon he's eighty if he's a day."

Pippa grinned, "You're probably right, I'm rubbish at guessing ages. Pity it's not a hunky twenty-year-old to bring a bit of brightness into the day."

"Oh you should come to my house, I've got one of those."

"Really," Pippa widened her eyes, "tell me more."

Claire smiled, loving the company of another female about her age. "My husband has just taken a chap on to sort out the gardens for a couple of months. He's only young but he has a degree in landscaping by all accounts. Anyway, he really is pleasant on the eye. My mother will be swooning over him as we speak."

"Lucky you. I wouldn't mind having a look at him. Anything's better than Ken," Pippa grinned.

"You can do if you like. You're welcome to come to my house for a drink. It'd be nice to reciprocate, and for my mother to see someone other than Freddy and I."

"That's so kind of you," Pippa glanced down at her wheelchair, "but it can be difficult. I get around fine, of course, as public places mostly have disabled access, but residential houses can't always accommodate an electric wheelchair, and," she widened her eyes, "I better not go there about the toilet situation."

Claire nodded, eager to portray she understood, when in reality, she'd never even considered how hard it must be for someone in a wheelchair visiting a residential house.

"You could bring her here though," she said eagerly, "I'd love to meet her, and for you to come again. It's great having a bit of company for a change."

Claire didn't need any thinking time, she liked Pippa and it would be nice see her again. "That'd be lovely, as long as you're sure?"

"Course I'm sure, I'd love it. Shall we say next week? Which day suits you best, Tuesday or Wednesday morning, I'll be here then?"

Apart from hospital appointments with her mother, she didn't have anything particular on. "Tuesday's good?"

"Fine, let's make it then." Pippa's eyes were drawn towards their empty glasses, "Can I offer you a top-up?"

"No, one's enough for me in the middle of the day, but thank you anyway. I'm glad you invited me in, it's been lovely to meet you. I'd better be making a move though."

Looking at her kind, friendly face, Claire couldn't help but feel a pang of sorrow for all the routine stuff she must miss out on. What an awful life confined to a wheelchair for someone so young. Yet there was an upbeat spunkiness about her which she found charming.

She picked up her handbag, already looking forward to seeing her new friend again. "I can see myself out if you want."

"Don't be daft, I can see you to the door, it's no trouble." She started to move forward in the wheelchair, "It's been so nice having you here, Claire, I'm so pleased you came in for a drink."

"Me too. I'm really glad we've met."

Considering how upset Pippa had been about her dog when she'd first arrived, it was reassuring she was much happier as she was leaving.

She'd done the right thing going in for a drink.

Chapter 7

Annabelle

She made her way through the restaurant to their regular Friday night table tucked away privately. Anthony, her trusted spa manager and dear friend was seated with their martinis ready. He stood up to greet her and kissed her cheek. "You look beautiful, Annabelle."

"Why thank you, kind sir, you don't look too bad yourself." And he didn't. He was an attractive man. Tall, with a great head of salt and pepper hair, and he kept himself fit, not an ounce of fat on him. She'd never seen him looking anything but immaculate from his well-cut suits, his designer jackets and his crisp pressed shirts with a perfect crease down the sleeves. She liked that in a man. Her father used to say *clothes maketh the man*, and she couldn't agree more.

She took her seat, smiling inwardly at his gracious compliment. Even though she was admired for her looks frequently, tonight she actually did feel quite beautiful. Two more months and she'd be with Max. He'd be leaving his clingy wife and they'd be together.

She took a sip of her refreshing martini. The barman at Simone's managed to mix the best drinks. They never tasted quite the same anywhere else.

"Shall we order first and then we can chat?" Anthony suggested, handing her a menu which both of them knew back to front. The chef would cook them anything they wanted anyway.

"I think I'll have a green salad to start with and then the sea bass."

"Sounds good to me, I think I'll have the same." He didn't even look at the wine list; he knew his wines probably as well as the sommelier. "How about a nice cool chardonnay?" he asked.

"Yes. It'll complement the fish beautifully."

"That's what I thought. Italian okay?"

"Perfect."

Once the waiter had taken their order, Anthony took a sip of his drink and cleared his throat. This would be about her birthday, she knew it. She also knew it would be some sort of made up story disguising the real event. Anthony would have something special planned. He always did.

He took her hand. "You know how much you mean to me, don't you?"

Over the last couple of years he'd asked her to marry him numerous times and she'd always said no. She loved him dearly, but not like that. She'd have to tell him about Max. She'd have preferred to wait until he'd left clingy, but what did it matter really?

"Of course I know, and I feel the same way about you. We've discussed this and nothing has changed, well not on that front, but I do need to tell you my news."

"In a minute," Anthony continued, "let me finish mine first. What you've just said makes what I'm about to say a bit easier."

"Go on."

"Well, without going over old ground and asking you to marry me yet again, even though that's my dearest wish, regrettably you don't love me, not in that way anyway." His eyes were sad as he continued, "I've always hoped you'd change your mind and we could be together. Catherine has been dead for almost three years and I've resisted getting serious with another woman as I've been holding out for you. But me wanting that isn't enough, it's not going to happen. So I need to move on with my life."

She sipped her drink. *Where the hell was this going?*

"I suppose what I'm bumbling around and trying to say is," he swallowed, "I've met someone."

She widened her eyes, "Met someone?"

"Yes. Her name's Fiona, she's quite a bit younger than me, and even though it's early days, I never expected to feel quite like this again."

Anthony had been married for years to his late wife and had been the doting husband during her long battle with cancer. After her death he'd thrown himself into work and never really let up. So this news from him was an almighty surprise.

"Sounds serious, then?" Where had that knife stabbing her tummy come from? She could have Anthony if she wanted him, he'd asked her enough times.

The waiter arriving with their salads gave her a bit of breathing space. She didn't want Anthony to be serious with anyone. He'd had other women, he was an attractive bloke, why wouldn't he? But he'd never discussed them with her before.

"How wonderful for you," she smiled encouragingly with an optimism she didn't feel, "where did you meet? Come on, I want all the details."

His face became animated. "I was after a cleaner as my lady emigrated to Australia to be near her son and grandchildren. I'd been pottering around doing stuff on my own, not that well I hasten to add, and was thinking I needed to contact an agency and get someone organised. But it was one of the things I never quite found the time to sort, and then I spotted a card in the newsagent's window. It was Fiona."

She frowned, "So Fiona's your cleaner?" The disparaging note in her voice was purposeful.

"Yes. Well," he flushed, "she's a bit more than my cleaner now."

"You're sure it's you she's interested in and not seeing pound signs?"

"No," he scowled, "contrary to what you think, other females do find me attractive."

She regretted speaking harshly and squeezed his hand, "I am sorry, I didn't mean it like that. It's just that I would have thought you'd require a bit more mental stimulation than a cleaner can provide?" She already had an image this Fiona would be providing him with much more than mental stimulation. *No fool like an old fool* sprang to mind.

"She's everything I need, which you'll see as soon as you meet her."

"When do I get to do that?" she asked, injecting a degree of positivity into her voice even though she really didn't want to be meeting Fiona-the-cleaner.

"Soon I hope. But before you do, I wanted to be absolutely certain about us. You know my belief is I could make you happy, but I can't wait around forever, I'll be an old man. And I want a life. So before I pursue things further with Fiona, you just need to say the word, because if you don't, after tonight, there's no going back."

The waiter arrived and removed their starter plates. She put as much love into her expression as she could. It wasn't difficult; she did love him very much. The stab of jealousy taking hold, reminded her how much. But she was about to embark on a new life. Soon she'd be married, and this time next year she could have a child of her own.

"I do love you very much, Anthony, you know that," she said, "I love you like a dear brother I never had. You mean the world to me and I want you to be happy. You deserve to be. And this is quite timely as I have some news too."

She took a sip of the wine and dabbed her mouth with the napkin. "While we're being frank with each other, can you believe I've met someone, too?"

His eyes regained some of their sparkle, and not a sign of jealousy. That showed what a gentleman he was. "You have? That's wonderful, Annabelle, when did this happen? I thought there was a bit of a spring in your step."

"I haven't been with him long, it's all happened rather quickly, but I have to say, he's most definitely the one. He reminds me of Daddy, he has all the qualities he had. I'm finding it hard to believe I'm going to spend the rest of my life with him."

"It's got that far, has it? He's actually asked you to marry him, then? And here's me thinking I'm rushing ahead with Fiona."

They paused while the waiter placed their main courses on the table. No need to mention Max was already married. Anthony would pour cold water on it. She'd tell him another time.

She raised her eyebrows, "Are you going to marry, Fiona?"

"I'm not entirely sure," he took a mouthful of food, "we aren't there yet. I've been holding back a bit until I had this conversation with you. But I think now, I can move on." He stared intensely at her, "If you're happy, then I'm happy. That's all I ever wanted. I promised your father I'd take care of you, that's why I hated it when you married Mark, he was never right for you."

"I know, and I'm not going to make another mistake. I married in haste, but this time, I know I'm marrying the right man. I even want children with him, which I never did with Mark."

"I'm pleased to hear that. You should have children, it'll make your life complete."

"What about you and Fiona, is that something you might want in the future? Have you got a photo of her?"

He rested his knife and fork down and reached in his jacket pocket for his phone. "Children are not high on my agenda, can't say they ever have been if I'm honest. And now I'm getting a bit old for all of that. Fiona has an eighteen-year-old, so I can't see her wanting to start again. But we haven't really discussed our future, only the here and now."

"Well, there's no rush is there? You can take your time."

He flicked onto Facebook and passed his phone to her. The photo was a blonde woman who looked to be about late thirties. She had her hair piled high on her head and was laughing. It looked like she was somewhere abroad judging by the colour of the sea behind her. Must be a holiday photograph? She was certainly attractive so she could see why Anthony was smitten.

"She looks lovely." Her eyes quickly scanned her surname to make a mental note of it before handing the phone back. "I'm so pleased for you," she lied. She wasn't at all. By the look on his face, he'd got it bad. She could tell how serious it was. And he was an attractive bloke so she knew he didn't spend all of his time in slippers and dressing gown sat in front of the fire.

"What about you and . . . what's his name?" he asked.

"You know him actually," she kept the tone of her voice light, "It's Max Maric."

Anthony wouldn't be happy at all. Maric Leisure was a rival chain. They all knew each other from the endless charity events and dinners they supported. Anthony's eyes darkened as he disparagingly turned the tables and repeated what she'd said minutes earlier.

"You're sure it's you he's interested in and not the business?"

"Touché," she tapped his hand playfully, "and no, he isn't."

"Forgive me for being cynical, but he has a reputation for

being ruthless in business and I'm sure it will have crossed his mind how lucrative a merger would be between Claybourne and Maric.

"Yes, well, I can assure you it isn't like that. We're deeply in love."

He didn't look terribly convinced, "When are you thinking of tying the knot?"

"There's no rush." How another lie slipped off her tongue. No need to mention he was married, she reassured herself again, he'd be free soon anyway.

"Please don't be coerced into rushing anything, my darling," Anthony's eyes were concerned, "I know you're much better now, but I still worry about you. Are you still attending your sessions with your therapist?"

"Yes of course I am, I'm seeing him Monday, actually."

"Have you told him you've met someone?"

"No, it's not actually come up to be honest."

"You must make sure he does know," he encouraged gently; "you're supposed to share everything with him. Are you still taking your medication?"

"Yes, of course. Can't you see that I'm a picture of health?"

"I can and I want it to stay that way. You must speak up if you feel things are drifting."

"Nothing's drifting, Anthony, that's all behind me now. I've a bright future to look forward to and eventually I hope, children."

"Then I'm delighted for you," he smiled kindly, "you have explained all . . . your past to him, haven't you? He knows about what happened?"

"Yeah," she lied, "he's a great support, you've really no need to worry."

"Good. I want to make sure someone is looking out for you. So," he lifted his wine glass, "maybe a toast to us both moving on."

"Yes." She clinked her glass with his, "Here's to us all being happy."

Anthony wiped his mouth, "Be nice if we could all meet up as we're going to be seeing a lot of each other by the sounds of things. How about next Friday instead of just the two of us meeting here, we bring them both along?"

"That sounds like a great idea." It would give her a chance to suss Fiona-the-cleaner out. "I'll check with Max that he hasn't got anything on."

"Yes, do that. If Friday's a problem, we can do it Saturday or Sunday. Whichever suits?" She couldn't tell him that Max would be with his wife at the weekend.

"Okay, it's a date. Now then, are we having a liqueur coffee for the road?"

Would Max be able to get away? She'd be furious if he couldn't. This was important to her. Anthony had to be included in any plans for the future. He was the most stable person in her life, which Max would realise once he got to know him.

It wasn't until she was settling down to sleep that evening she realised Anthony hadn't mentioned her birthday once, and yet every year without fail, he organised something special. Awareness kicked in that his mind was now on this woman, which meant her birthday was probably no longer his priority – it might never be again.

Damn, Fiona the bloody cleaner.

Chapter 8

Annabelle

She took her seat in the therapist's plush office decorated in creamy pastel colours, no doubt aiming to be *restful* on each client's eyes as they unburdened themselves of traumatic events affecting their lives. She'd never been one for such indulgence, preferring to sort out her own issues, but currently she had no choice and had to attend as her sessions were mandatory as stipulated by the judiciary a year earlier. All that palaver seemed a lifetime ago; her life had moved on now. The sessions were a load of rubbish as far as she was concerned, but she went through the motions as anything was better than a prison sentence.

George Grey gave her his *I'm here to help you look*. His name suited him, he was grey from his ashen skin tone, to his boring old-fashioned grey suit. He had a huge red birthmark around his left eye and she wondered why he'd never had it removed. They could do wonders with laser technology and she often itched to tell him to get something done. It was terribly unsightly.

"Ready?" he asked reaching to the coffee table that separated them and switching the microphone to record. He always started the same way, with her name and the date. Then he'd recap on where they were last time. He had paper notes in front of him but she knew that wasn't the main file he'd have on her. That would be pretty hefty and would flatten his knee in no time. The notes he had were most probably from their last session together. Not that he ever referred to his notes, he rarely looked at them. Maybe he did before their sessions though as he knew exactly where they'd finished at the end of the previous one.

Earlier, she'd made her mind up she couldn't face going over all the usual old nonsense. Now was the time to share how her life was going to change.

"Good morning, Annabelle, how are you?" he asked in the same boring way he asked at the start of every session.

"I'm fine, thank you," she smiled, "no, more than that actually, I'm really happy."

"I'm pleased to hear it," he said in his usual monotone, *encouraging her to say more*, voice. He never showed any emotion. She deduced that was part of the training. Never let your expression be anything other than straight-faced.

He raised one eyebrow – did therapists have special training for that? Most people's eyebrows raise together. Or it could be something to do with the hideous birthmark over his eye?

"Has something happened to make you feel this way, or is it just generally feeling good about life?" he asked.

"I've met someone," she told him confidently.

"I see."

"And he's asked me to marry him."

No change in the deadpan expression, maybe he thought she was making it up.

"And you've accepted his proposal, I take it?"

"Definitely."

"That certainly is exciting news. And a lot of planning to do, I would think?"

"Absolutely. So . . ." she put on a hopeful expression, "I'm wondering if we need to continue these sessions quite as frequently? I thought perhaps we could go to monthly or maybe two-monthly?" It was worth a try.

He didn't answer directly, but that was nothing unusual. He didn't do direct. It was all, *I see, would you like to elaborate,* and long pauses when he didn't interject but just sat quietly waiting for her to fill the silence.

"Tell me, now that your life appears to be taking a different direction, I'd be interested to know if you perceive the sessions have contributed to your current state of happiness?"

"I think they've certainly helped, yes, but I'm moving on now and getting my life back on track. I'm in a much better place than I was. For the first time in ages, I'm looking forward to my future."

"I'm delighted to hear it. But it would be remiss of me not to ask what strategies you are aware of now, that possibly you didn't have before, to cope when things get difficult." He peered at her from over the top of his glasses, "As they do in all relationships, which you know from your own past experience."

"Yes, but that was then, the key word here is the *past.* And that's precisely where I want to leave it. I've moved on now. I feel with my future husband by my side, I can cope with anything." She remembered his medical background, "And I have medication to control the mood swings and all the other stuff."

"So, if things are going that well, it could be the very reason to continue with the sessions as the court recommended." He raised his one eyebrow enquiringly, as if he was asking the question, but he wasn't, he was telling.

"Fine," she shrugged dismissively, "if that's what you think, I can still come."

"It's not about what I think, Annabelle, it's about you recognising you are in a much better place right now, so why stop the sessions?"

"Okay, I've said I'll carry on with them."

"Have you told your," he glanced at her ring finger which

was bare – an engagement ring was next on her list to sort, "husband-to-be about your past?"

"No," she shook her head, "I haven't told him."

He gave his usual supercilious look, "And what about the sessions with me?"

"No, he doesn't know."

"Why is that?"

She shrugged, "I will tell him, it just hasn't come up, that's all."

"I see." Why did he manage to make *I see* sound like a huge disappointment?

"It's no big secret," she continued, "I just haven't got round to it yet."

"Does he know you have a clinical diagnosis of schizophrenia?"

"No," she said more sharply than she intended, "but it's no big deal, I will explain it all. I'm fine now so there really aren't any concerns, and I haven't had any episodes recently." She looked at his enquiring face. His expression was one of, *go on* and she always ended up doing so. Years of social training from her parents, if there's a gap in the conversation, fill it.

"Look, I'm in a good place right now. I'm really happy. I don't want to blight all that with negativity. It's a new relationship, we're enjoying each other. For the first time in my life I've got a different future to look forward to. I'm planning children, which I still can't believe. Everything is much brighter. I was never happy in my last marriage, it was a mistake, but I know with Max, things are going to be totally different."

"It's positive then that you're happy. What type of work does Max do?" Typical therapist, trying to make out he's familiar with her life, she only mentioned Max's name once, and he's carrying on as if he knows him personally.

"He's in business, similar to me actually. It's health and

leisure. And before you even think it, he's wealthy and not after me for my money."

He tilted his head slightly, "I wasn't thinking that at all."

"Yes, well, maybe I can see the cogs going round in your brain."

No need to tell grey old George their future plans about the intention to merge their companies. He'd be thinking straight away that Max was after her business and not her. She wasn't daft, she could see how that conclusion could easily be drawn. But she was no dummy and Max would have underestimated her if he thought she'd be doing anything before they were married. Not a chance. She loved him very much, but not that much. The merger would only take place after they were married. She needed to secure her future and that of any children they might have together.

George Grey swiftly changed the subject, no doubt realising it was pointless pursuing it any further. "It's coming up to the anniversary of when your last episode occurred. When we finished our previous session, we were discussing how that date approaching made you feel. Shall we start there today now we've got your news out of the way?"

Oh, for God's sake, didn't the stupid man realise she made half the stuff up she told him? As if she was bothered about any anniversary. It was over a long time ago. She'd well and truly moved on. The quicker she got this baloney started, the sooner she'd be out of there. She was keen to get home and pamper herself for meeting Max later that evening. She'd spoilt herself with a new dress which was so revealing, she knew that he'd want to take off. The sexiness of it would ensure he'd come back to her house after drinks rather than heading home to clingy.

"Yes, I was a bit down," she painted on a woe-is-me expression, "it all seems such a long time ago, now."

* * *

She sipped cocktails with Max in the Gong Bar at the Shard which was a favourite of hers for early evening drinks. It offered incredible views across the city and she loved to unwind there with him and snatch a few hours. Thankfully she'd escaped from boring George Grey after her allotted hour and was able to go home and spend some time on herself, but not before he urged her to discuss her condition with Max. Well, he could get knotted. That wasn't happening.

She was delighted with her appearance that evening. Treatments at the spa ensured she always looked perfect. Image was important to her. She was a beautiful woman and she liked to show that off at all times.

"Can't you make it a midweek night?" Max asked, responding to her request about dinner with Anthony and his new girlfriend on Friday evening. She could sense the irritation in his voice, "It's easier for me to get away then."

"No. I nearly always have dinner with him on a Friday night at Simone's. It's a regular date." She glared knowingly at him, "He did suggest Saturday or Sunday but I thought that would be impossible." There was no way Max would be able to escape to London on a weekend, clingy wouldn't ever let him do that. "I do want you to meet him," she said firmly, "it's important to me."

"I have met him."

"Yes, I know, but that's socially. I want you to meet him properly. He's more or less family and I want you both to get along."

"I'd rather have waited until I've left Claire before we came out in the open about our relationship." He scowled, "Did you tell him I'm still married?"

"No, should I have done?"

"Not particularly, I just wondered if you'd told him, that's all."

"I can do. I've only just told him about you. It seemed appropriate as he was telling me about this Fiona woman he'd met."

"Maybe it's best you don't say anything yet, I really don't want Claire to get wind of anything until I tell her myself."

"Well, I hardly think Anthony is going to be in a social situation and conversing with your wife, do you?"

"You know what I mean. Chinese whispers and all that spring to mind. You only need one person who knows someone else, and it's all out in the open."

What's wrong with that? I wish it was out in the damn open . . .

His expression was pained. "Do I really need to meet him right now?"

"Yes, definitely. You will need to get him on your side eventually when we do decide to merge the businesses. And he's a big part of my life so I want you both to get along."

He sighed, as if resigned he was going to have to meet Anthony. "Yeah, well, he's not going to be such a big part when we're together, I hope." He reached for her hand and kissed it, "I'm not sharing you with him on a Friday night that's for sure; weekends are going to be just for us."

A warm glow spread through her. She loved it when he talked like that. As if she was his exclusively, which was exactly what she wanted to be.

"They most certainly will be," she smiled lovingly, "I promise you that. So, what do you think, can you make Friday? I really would like you to be there otherwise I'm going to feel like the gooseberry with the two of them."

"God," he rolled his eyes, "you a gooseberry, never. You're too beautiful to ever be a gooseberry." He glanced round the room, "Right now, every man here is jealous you're with me, and they're wishing you were with them."

She grinned, loving his playfulness.

He narrowed his eyes, "Has there ever been anything between the two of you?"

"Never. So you needn't worry about that. I told you, he's my father's protégé. He was the son he never had. Daddy loved him and Anthony was always loyal to him, as he is to me. He's been my rock."

"Well, hopefully when we're together, he'll become less important in your life and my name will be chalked on the rock then?"

She lifted her glass, "I'll drink to that. So . . . are we on for Friday?"

He took a sip of his drink, "I don't know," he grinned sexily, "I'll need an incentive."

She widened her eyes cheekily, knowing that look. Max was insatiable. "I'll have to see what I can do, then."

He watched as she slowly and provocatively crossed her long legs, displayed beautifully by the shortness of the dress.

"Are you heading straight home, tonight?"

He shifted his position in the chair. "Not now. Come on, drink up."

Chapter 9

Claire

She returned home from taking Freddy to school and as she locked the car, Adam was coming down the drive towards her rocking the shorts look again. For some bizarre reason, an excited ripple rushed through her.

"Morning, Adam," she smiled. He'd be the perfect catch for someone. He had it all, good-looking, tall, and those eyes of his were amazing.

"Morning, I just wanted a quick word." He looked concerned, as if something was troubling him.

"What is it, is everything alright?"

"Yeah, fine. I don't want to alarm you but at the bottom of the garden, you know where the fence is near the workshop," she nodded, "it looks like a panel has been kicked in deliberately. And the way the grass is flattened down, it seems to me as if someone's been standing there, maybe watching the house. You can see right inside from there."

"Oh, God, that's awful."

"It's probably kids with nothing better to do but I thought you'd want to know. There are a couple of cigarette butts so it's obvious someone has been there. I can easily fix it if you want to get a fence panel delivered."

"That's really kind of you. I'll have a word with Max. I'm sure he'll want that done straight away."

"Yeah, that's what I thought."

A shudder ran through her. What if they had binoculars or something? Her anxiety must have been obvious.

"Are you okay?"

"It just feels creepy that's all. Freddy and I are often on our own at night when Max is working late, and of course Mum's here now. It sort of makes me feel vulnerable."

His beautiful vibrant eyes appeared concerned, "I tell you what, there are some planks of wood knocking around, I'll stick something temporary up so you're not worried until we get it fixed."

"Would you? Do you mind?"

"Course not, I'll do it now. Leave it with me."

"Thank you so much, I am grateful. Mum's around this morning, I'm calling to see a friend. Why don't you knock when you're done? I've made some cakes and I'm sure Mum will make you a hot drink, it's the least I can do for your efforts."

His smile displayed his perfect white teeth, "Ah, well, if there's cake involved, I might just do that. I've got a weakness for anything sweet."

"That's good then as I always have cake . . . it's my secret weapon." She had no idea why she said that. She faked a small cough to clear her embarrassment, "I'll ring Max now and tell him."

"Yeah, I would do. Maybe see you later then," he nodded and walked away down the garden displaying the sexiest legs she'd seen on a bloke. Max was fit, but Adam was something else.

She hoped she would see him later and then inwardly chastised herself for behaving like a teenager.

She reached for her phone out of her bag and called Max, half expecting to get his answer phone, but he picked up. "Hi, love."

"Hi, darling, just a quickie. Adam's just stopped me when I came back from taking Freddy to school and told me the fence panel is down at the back of the house near the workshop."

"Yeah."

"He reckons it looks like it's been deliberately kicked down. He said if you get a fence panel delivered, he'll put it up."

"Did he? Okay, I'll have a look when I get back tonight."

She could tell by his tone he didn't like Adam advising on anything so certainly wouldn't be pleased with his initiative of putting something up as a temporary measure. "I asked him to put something up for the time being," she said, stretching the truth, "I was worried that someone might be, you know, spying on us."

"I hardly think anyone would be spying on us, love."

"You never know, you hear these things. And Adam did say the grass was all trodden down as if someone had been standing there. It might be kids, but you worry about people casing the house to see what you have. You know, like opportunistic criminals."

"Well, Adam would know all about those."

"That isn't nice." Max could be horrible sometimes and she hated that side of him, "He's working really hard for us."

"Yeah, well, let me take a look tonight."

"Okay, will do. What time will you be home?"

"About six. I'll have a good look then."

"Alright, see you then."

"Bye, love."

Her mum was flicking through the newspaper at the kitchen table when she went inside. "I thought I heard your voice, love, were you on the phone?"

"Yes, I was just speaking to Max." She reached in the

cupboard for a glass and filled it with tap water. Adam's suggestion that someone might have been spying on them made her feel unsettled. She took a large gulp of water to calm herself and forced a smile. "Shame you don't fancy coming with me today, you'll like Pippa, she's lovely."

"I'm sure she is, but I don't fancy making small talk with someone I don't know, not today. I didn't sleep that well so I'm going to have a lazy day. And it'll do you good to go on your own. You enjoyed it last week with her and I'm perfectly happy staying here with my book. It's going to be beautiful in an hour or two so I'll be able to sit outside and watch that handsome looking gardener you've hired, what did you say his name was?"

"Honestly, what are you like? It's Adam."

"Yes that's it, Adam. He is rather attractive, don't you think?"

"I've never thought about it, to be honest."

"What do you mean you haven't thought about it? You have eyes don't you?"

"Yes," Claire grinned, "and they are firmly fixed on my husband."

"That doesn't mean you can't look and appreciate," her mum laughed.

"Sounds like you're doing enough looking for both of us. Anyway, I've told him to knock for a cake this morning if you wouldn't mind making him a coffee, he's repairing a fence panel so I thought it was the least I could do."

Her mum widened her eyes playfully, "Let's hope he does, then."

"Don't get too friendly with him though," she warned, "Max isn't keen. He's only taken him on as a favour, so he's hoping he won't hang around for long."

"Oh well, if Max isn't keen . . ."

"Muuuum, we don't want to be going over all that again," she said wearily. She squatted down to look in the cupboard for a storage tin, more to stop her mother saying anything else. She wasn't Max's greatest fan. His brief affair three years previously had tainted her opinion of him. On hindsight, Claire wished she'd never told her, but they were close and she was hurting at the time. It was actually her dad who'd urged her not to give up on Max. He'd spoken about men making mistakes and not to throw everything away, but to try and repair the marriage and be patient. And she'd done just that. Her dad had been right. Her and Max had managed to get over it. Thankfully it was just a fling, a *few weeks of madness* Max had called it when he begged her forgiveness and vowed never to stray again. It still hurt after all this time, but she'd learned when it came into her mind to quickly think of happier memories so she didn't try analysing again.

She retrieved a tin from the back of the cupboard and tore off some kitchen roll to line it. Her mother looked over the frame of her glasses and Claire knew there was more to come.

"It does worry me, the time you spend waiting around for Max to turn up when he sees fit. It isn't good for a woman your age."

"I don't spend my time waiting around for him," Claire couldn't keep the irritation out of her voice, "he is my husband. He works all the hours God sends providing for us, and we have all this," she indicated the kitchen area, "we're lucky to have him."

"He does work long hours, I'll give him that. But it can't all be work. Is he avoiding being in the house because I'm here, or is there something he's not telling you about?"

"Mum, stop it," she snapped, "that was a long time ago. He's busy right now with work, that's all."

She couldn't listen to her mum going on about Max anymore. She hated her criticising him. It unsettled her, which wasn't difficult after Adam's discovery. "Anyway, I'm going to make a move, are you sure you're going to be alright on your own?"

"Of course I'm sure. I need to be thinking about getting back to my own house shortly, anyway."

"Yes, but let's wait until your physio's finished, then we can think about it." She placed four cupcakes she'd made the previous day in the tin. "I'll take these for Pippa although she doesn't look the type to be filling up on cakes. Her figure's really trim."

"I'm sure she'll enjoy one, everyone likes a treat every now and again. I know I'm looking forward to my elevenses. This Pippa sounds nice. Was she very upset about her little dog?"

"I thought she was, but once we got talking, she was fine. I'd love you to meet her while you're here."

"I will do, just not today. Why not invite her here for coffee next time?"

"Easier said than done," she closed the lid, "even if we could get her in the house with her wheelchair, there's still the toilet, which she did mention was a problem so I didn't pursue it."

"Oh, yes, of course, you're right. You just don't think of these things when you're able-bodied. Her life must be a constant struggle. The things we take for granted, eh?"

"Yeah, absolutely. It's probably best to call on her, or maybe we could go out for lunch. That might be nice?"

"Yes, we'll see. Did she say how she ended up in a wheelchair? Is it a medical condition?"

"An accident I think she said, but I didn't like to ask," Claire placed the tin in her bag and put her sunglasses on for the short walk round the corner, "but she's so lovely and doesn't know anyone in the area so I'd like to make a friend of her."

"Oh, you must, absolutely. It'll be nice for you both. You enjoy your coffee with her. And don't be rushing back, I'm absolutely fine."

"Okay, I'll see you later."

Chapter 10

Claire

"Well you certainly know how to make cakes, Claire," Pippa wiped her hands on the napkin, "that was bloody gorgeous. You should go on Bake Off."

"Oh, God," Claire rolled her eyes, "I don't think so. I'm not in that league, it's years of practice, that's all. Cakes are dead easy to do, and I actually find them therapeutic. I make them most days and have on occasions been known to be making them in the night if I can't sleep."

Pippa laughed, "Yeah, and I bet you're one of those women who can cook well too, am I right?"

"I suppose so. I've spent a lot of time over the years doing stuff. When Max was first starting out in business, I hosted functions and that sort of thing. Initially from home, but when the business grew I used to facilitate them in London. I loved overseeing anything like that."

"Don't you do any parties now?"

"No. He has an events manager and a fabulous chef, so I'm pretty much redundant on that front. But he doesn't do loads of that corporate stuff now that he's established."

"I see. Would you like to get a job?"

"No, I don't think so. I'm used to not working now. I'd be rubbish. Max doesn't want me to work anyway. He likes me at home."

"Oh does he? He's not one of those men that thinks a woman's place is in the kitchen, is he?"

"No, not at all." She thought for a moment, "He is a bit chauvinistic about certain things though."

"Aren't all men?" Pippa said with a touch of cynicism in her voice. Maybe she'd been hurt before?

"Anyway, enough about me," Claire said, "while we're on about work, tell me what sort of job you do?"

"Nothing that exciting. I work for an old eccentric historian. He went to school with my father, and his late wife was disabled so his house is accessible for me. I'm currently putting his library in order. It's boring stuff really, but I quite like doing it. And it's flexible which I prefer." Pippa glanced at their empty cups, "Was the tea enough, or can I tempt you with a glass of prosecco?"

"I'm fine thanks, but you have one."

"Nah," she shook her head, "not if you're not."

"What did you do before your accident?" Claire inwardly cursed herself for being too intrusive. The last thing she wanted was to come across like a nosy parker. "Tell me to shut up if you want to."

"No, it's fine, honestly. I've always done admin type work, boring stuff really. I'm good with figures and things like that. I'm lucky that now I have the funds to be able to work and retreat to the gorgeous Sandbanks when I want to. I got a really good compensation payout from my accident which should last me the rest of my life. I just fancied coming back for a while to reminisce on holidays I used to have here as a child."

"Have you got any brothers or sisters?"

"No, have you?"

"I have a brother, Philip, he works for a pharmaceutical company in Canada. He's actually coming over for my fortieth in August so it'll be nice for us all to see him."

"You, forty . . . never," Pippa frowned, "I can't believe that. You look amazing for forty."

"Now I know why I like you," Claire grinned, "but I did tell you the other day you needed to go to Specsavers. To be honest, I don't feel forty, I still feel about thirty in my mind."

"Me too. But you're as young as you feel, really. It's just a number."

"Yeah, you're right. What about you, how old are you?"

"Thirty-six."

"Gosh, well you don't look that either. I had you down as younger than that."

"You're only saying it about me because I said it about you," Pippa laughed.

"I only speak the truth," she smiled, loving their banter. "Oh, I meant to ask, I don't suppose there's any more news on your dog?"

"No, nothing." A wave of sadness passed across Pippa's face, "I can't bear to think foxes might have got him."

"Aw, it won't be that. I'm sure he's with a family right now, eating lots of treats and running round a garden playing with kids."

"You are sweet, Claire. I'd rather think that way too. Are you sure I can't tempt you to have another drink, I have plenty of nice wine?"

"No, honestly, I'll get off in a bit and make sure Mum's okay."

"Oh, how's she doing, still ogling the gardener?"

"Yes, I bet she will be. She'll be going back to her own home soon. I'll miss her when she does but it'll be nice to get back to normal. I might even get to see more of my husband."

"Is he still as busy?"

"Is he? I think half of it to be honest is he's avoiding Mum."

"Don't they get on?"

"Yeah, they get on. I just think like all blokes, they give the mother-in-law a bit of a wide berth." She wasn't about to share her personal life with a stranger, as easy as Pippa was to talk to.

"Do you have a dad? Sorry," she apologised, "that sounds a bit nosy. It's just with your mum staying with you after her stroke."

"My dad died a few months ago," Claire's tummy plummeted at the mention of her dad, "he was on his bike and was hit by a car."

"Oh, how awful, that must be still raw."

"It is. But I'm working through it. We were very close."

"Bless you. I'm sorry for mentioning it."

"Don't be. It's one of those things, you weren't to know."

That feeling of impending doom kicked in again and an overwhelming need to leave flooded through her. Something bad was going to happen, she was sure of it.

"Right, then," she smiled so Pippa wouldn't think she was leaving because of bringing up her dad, "I'd better be getting off. If I leave it too long, my mother will end up cooking lunch."

"Do you fancy meeting next week for coffee?" Pippa asked, "If you've got time that is. I don't want to tie you down."

The poor woman looked anxious, as if she might have upset her mentioning her dad.

"Of course. That'd be lovely."

"Great," Pippa smiled, the brightness coming back to her face, "I'll be away at the weekend, but back on Monday."

"Ah, Monday's tricky, I have to take Mum for her physio and then we'll have a spot of lunch out."

"Tuesday then?"

"Yeah, Tuesday's good, if you're sure?"

"Definitely. You can update me on your mother and the gardener. I could do with a bit of Lady Chatterley."

Claire laughed out loud, "That's tickled me. If you met my mother you'd know how funny that was. I think she's only ever been with my dad. She likes to look, though. And trust me, if you saw Adam, you'd see exactly why."

Pippa widened her eyes, "That nice, is he? Does your husband need to watch out?"

Claire reached for her bag and slung it over her shoulder, "I wouldn't put it quite like that, but I could see how he certainly would be a temptation to some women. It'll be one lucky lady that gets him that's for sure."

"Hey, you'll have to get a picture of him to show me. Is he on Facebook?"

"I have no idea," Claire placed their used tea cups on the kitchen unit and smiled, "and I'm not checking either."

"Spoilsport," Pippa laughed, "tell me his surname and I'll have a look."

"Bishop, Adam Bishop."

"I'll look tonight. I might even send him a friend request if I like the look of him."

"If you came round for a coffee, we could sit in the garden and you'll see him. I could introduce him to you."

"Oooooh, now there's an idea. That sounds very tempting."

It was only fun talk, but she couldn't somehow picture Adam and Pippa together. Maybe she was being judgemental. They were both single people, there was no reason why they shouldn't be friends?

But the truth was, she didn't really want them to be.

* * *

That evening, her and Max were in bed and she was talking to him about Pippa, but as always he was glued to his iPad.

"She's really pretty and has a lovely figure," Claire applied some hand cream to her hands, "can you imagine how hard it must be to be confined to a wheelchair? Yet, she's so jolly. She doesn't appear one bit, woe is me. She just seems to get on with it."

He didn't reply. It was evident he was barely listening. She reached in the bedside drawer for her Kindle to try and read some crappy chick-lit novel she'd started, but ended up reading the same sentence over and over again. Her mind just wasn't on it.

"Is everything alright?" she asked.

"Mmm," he grunted, his eyes not leaving the screen.

She reached across and put her hand over the iPad, "Can you put that down for a minute so we can talk?"

His irritated expression said it all. "Talk about what?"

"Us."

"What about us?" he scowled.

"I'm worried. We're hardly seeing you at the moment, all you're doing is working."

"How do you think all this gets paid for?" He gestured with his head around the room.

"I realise that, but I'd rather you were here than have all this. Wealth isn't everything, you know."

"It would be if you didn't have any."

"Well right now I'd rather have a husband and a father for Freddy. It's no fun being on my own all the time."

"You know the score, Claire, I thrive on work, I've never been any different. And right now, you're not on your own. You've got your mother for company."

"What's that supposed to mean?"

"Nothing," he shrugged.

"No, come on, out with it. What is it? You'd rather my mother went home to an empty house and fended for herself after having a stroke?"

"I'm not saying that at all. I'm busy at work right now and she's around when I get home. So it's hard to do much."

"So that's all it is, my mother being here? There's nothing else bothering you?"

"Nothing. Why would there be?" He leant forward and kissed her. "Stop worrying. As soon as your mum is ready to go home, things will be back to normal, you'll see."

She wasn't totally convinced but felt better from his reassurance. He caressed the side of her face, and pulled her towards him, kissing her passionately. This is what she wanted, proof of his love. The kiss deepened.

She lay in his arms. Max was a fabulous lover. It was the first time in ages they'd made love. She'd missed the affection between them both. Their lack of intimacy was another reason she knew he was working too hard. Max was normally a man that liked regular sex.

He cleared his throat, "Hey, before I forget, I've got a dinner I have to attend on Friday night. Can't get out of it, I'm afraid. So I'll stop at the flat and come home on Saturday."

"Dinner on a Friday night?" she frowned, "who with?"

"It's a charity thing I said I'd attend, completely forgot about it to be honest."

"Do you want me to come with you?" She leaned on her elbow to face him, "We could bring Freddy. I'm sure Marjorie would babysit, she's missing him since we left London. And we could do something in the city on Saturday. We could make a weekend of it?"

"What about your mother, you can't leave her, can you?"

"Mmm, there's a thought. She's getting better all the time though, so it could do her good to have a night on her own. Get her ready for going back to her own house. Maybe just have an overnighter then?"

"I reckon you'd be better off staying here. I'll just put in an appearance at the dinner, place a couple of bids on the raffle prizes to show willing, and be back for elevenish. No point in getting all your glad rags on for a boring dinner. It's not as if you'd know that many there, and those you do, you don't like."

"It's not that I don't like them, most of them are false, that's all."

"All the more reason for you not to come, then."

"You're probably right," she kissed his cheek, "Okay, long as you're sure."

"Yep, quite sure, I'll be fine on my own." He sat up and flung the covers back, "I'll use the bathroom and then we can get some shut eye."

She watched his naked backside as he headed for the ensuite. She felt better they'd been intimate together. Max was the epitome of masculinity. As soon as they started to plan for a child, she'd fallen pregnant straight away. Nine months later she'd given birth to their precious son, however, since then, despite not using any type of contraception, she'd never managed to conceive again. Max had always been extremely active sexually, but for some obscure reason, another pregnancy never happened. And as she was now approaching forty and fertility declining with age, it was unlikely it would.

They had undergone extensive tests, which gave no explanation. Both of them were fertile and should be able to conceive a child, there were no scientific reasons why not. They both loved Freddy and a brother or sister would have enhanced all of their lives, but she had to tell herself endless times, you don't get everything you wish for in life. She'd tried over the years not to dwell on it too much, hoping secretly that one day it might happen. In the meantime, she focussed all her efforts on her husband and dear Freddy. As her dad often used to say, *Don't spend too much time thinking about what's missing in your life – focus on what's currently filling it.*

Chapter 11

Annabelle

It was Friday evening and she'd been expecting Max much earlier. They could have had the afternoon together, but he'd annoyed her by arriving late so he had little time to get ready for the dinner with Anthony and his new girlfriend.

"Look, I'm here now," he leant forward and tried to kiss her.

She pulled her head away. "I don't think so. You know what that leads to and we haven't got time now."

He widened his eyes cheekily. "So you don't want to hoist yourself over the couch . . . I can be quick."

"I'll pass on that, if you don't mind," she pushed him playfully, "now, if you're really quick, you've got time for a shower."

"Okay spoilsport," he winked and made his way to the bathroom.

She checked her watch. She had a car arriving in thirty minutes to take them to Simone's. She'd made a special effort with her appearance, wearing her Donna Karan's palazzo black pant suit, with Christian Louboutin zebra print shoes and matching clutch. It was important to look her best in front of Fiona-the-cleaner. What the hell Anthony was doing with his domestic help, she had no idea. He was an attractive man, articulate and well-read, he could do so much better. Typical bloke with his head in his trousers. She'd play the part tonight of a dutiful friend of Anthony's, but she was going to have this woman checked out. She couldn't allow him to become ensconced with the likes of her, for God's sake.

I bet all her Christmases had come at once when he showed up.

* * *

The service at Simone's was extra special that evening. Anthony had asked for a private room with a small seating area they could relax in and enjoy their aperitifs prior to seating at the table that had been set for them. Harry, the usual sommelier, had her and Anthony's martinis ready and Max said he fancied the same. Fiona had asked for a lager and lime which seemed about as crass as she was. Simone's had every cocktail and spirit in the world and she wanted lager. *Did they even do lager?*

The maitre d' appeared and went through the chef's recommendation for that evening. While they perused the menus, Max lifted his glass. "Here's to new friends," he looked directly at her, "and to happy endings." As they raised their glasses, she smiled tenderly back at him, loving him a tiny bit more for making such an effort.

Anthony turned to Fiona, "Would you like me to order for you, darling?"

His gentleness with Fiona kicked her hard. She didn't like it one bit.

Fiona smiled gratefully back at him with doe eyes, "That would be nice, thank you."

She covertly watched Fiona out of the corner of her eye while pretending to peruse the menu. *No doubt she'd be clueless as to what half of the dishes were.* Her drab outfit, which most probably came off the rack at Marks and Spencer, and the do-it-yourself nail job, confirmed exactly what she'd thought initially when Anthony told her about meeting the cleaner, she wasn't right for him at all. He deserved someone far more sophisticated. She recalled reading a funny greetings card once which immediately sprung to mind, *You can put lipstick on a pig, but it would still be a pig.*

"What are you having, darling?" she whispered to Max, loving the kick it gave her when she thought about going home together and spending the night with him. Yes, she definitely needed to fake some sort of headache when they'd eaten so they could leave and be alone. They could make love leisurely into the night instead of the frantic afternoon sessions. And they would wake up in the morning together and repeat it all over again.

"I think I'll go for a fillet mignon. What about you?"

"Fish, I think. It's divine here."

She took a sip of her drink. The alcohol was hitting the spot and beginning to relax her. Tonight had sealed Fiona-the-cleaner's fate. She had to go. She'd be doing Anthony a favour. Fiona wasn't right for him. Tonight she'd play the part, but tomorrow she'd start the ball in motion to get rid of her. The same as Max's clingy wife, she wanted them both gone. Yegor would sort it.

"Anthony tells me you have a son, Fiona," she smiled, "is he local?" She didn't give a damn about Fiona's family. The objective of the evening was for Max to get to know Anthony.

"No unfortunately he's in Scotland. He's at Edinburgh University so I don't see as much of him as I'd like to."

"Oh yes, lovely part of the country but quite a journey. What's he studying?"

"Computer science." She laughed nervously, "He's one of these IT nerds, I'm afraid to say."

"Hey, don't knock it. He's always going to be in work, that's for sure, a bit like a plumber."

Fiona smiled, she was quite attractive. It was easy to see why Anthony was smitten, "Yes, although I must say, I never thought of it quite like that."

"You don't have children?" Fiona asked, knowing quite well she didn't. Anthony would have briefed her.

"Not yet, no, but I'm hoping to in the future. Max and I would like a large family."

"That's nice," Fiona smiled, "I'd have liked more children. Sadly, my husband and I split up when my son was young so it didn't happen. I've been on my own since then," she smiled adoringly at Anthony who was hanging onto her every word like a love-struck puppy . . . "until now."

Anthony squeezed Fiona's hand and Annabelle felt her gut tighten as she witnessed the adoration in his eyes. She disliked the woman already. Anthony needed someone completely different.

The waiter interrupted her thoughts advising them dinner was ready to be served. Their starters had been placed on the table and they were each directed where to sit. Once they were seated, the four waiters, simultaneously lifted the cloches off the starter plates. "Bon appetite," they said in unison before leaving the room.

"This looks too nice to eat," Max smiled politely, keeping the conversation going, "Did you tell me you have a regular table here with Anthony?"

"Yes. We come here most Fridays," she turned to look at Anthony, "we catch up a little about work, but it's become more of a social thing, hasn't it?"

"It has," he agreed. "But I don't see why we can't all enjoy a meal here together occasionally."

She didn't answer but caught Fiona looking adoringly at him as if to say, anything you choose is fine by me.

Anthony then turned to Max, "What about you, Max, do you have children?"

"Yes, I have a son, he's almost ten."

"How nice. Do you get to see much of him?"

Damn, she'd been naive to think it wouldn't all come out.

"Yes, of course." Max wouldn't shy away from anything, he would say it exactly how it is, which he did. "I'm still living in the marital home . . . that is until August."

Anthony was too polite to say anything but she knew by his pained expression that she was in for a stern talk from him when they were alone. He wouldn't be happy about her seeing a married man, which is exactly why she'd avoided saying anything. But now she'd realised her silence had been a mistake.

"Separately though," she quickly interjected before turning to Max, "we perhaps need to clarify your marriage is over, darling. I don't want anyone to think I'm the other woman."

He reached for her hand in a comforting way and raised it to his lips. "As if you could ever be the other woman."

She smiled lovingly back at him, grateful he'd confirmed their status in such a tender way and watched him skilfully deflect from anymore questions about their relationship.

"What about you, Anthony," Max asked, "have you got any kids?"

"No, I haven't. Not something that's ever been high on my agenda, I must say. My late wife was a career woman and it just didn't figure in our plans."

Max nodded as if completely engrossed in the conversation, but she was thankful to feel his hand as it rested on her knee. He'd know she'd feel awkward about how he still lived in the marital home and it coming out the way it did. But it was probably for the best, she was going to have to tell Anthony eventually anyway. She wouldn't be telling him though about her and Max's plans to join forces and become a dominant spa brand in the UK, and hopefully expanding eventually into Europe. The world would be their oyster, but she was doing nothing until they were married. Once they'd had the ceremony, she was going to concentrate on children and Max could oversee the business side of their lives, but only on a part-time basis. Anthony would still be a huge part and could take on the heaviest load. There was no way she was having this Fiona-the-cleaner anywhere in the equation. She had a plan already formulating in her mind. She was going to get rid of her sooner rather than later. Certainly before it became impossible to do so.

Chapter 12

Annabelle

"So what did you think of Fiona?" Annabelle called from the ensuite as she applied her La Mer night cream and checked in her magnifying mirror that it was still holding back the wrinkles. She'd left her touch of mascara on, the last thing she would ever do is be completely bare of make-up around Max. He was sat up in bed going through his emails as usual. Did the man ever not have a phone in his hand?

"She seemed nice enough. What did you say she does, cleans his house?"

"Yes. I'm sure he could do better than her. A cleaner, for God's sake. He seems quite taken with her, don't you think?"

"Well, he certainly was attentive, that's for sure. He might as well have eaten his meal with just a fork the amount of time he spent holding her hand."

"I thought that. I'm surprised to be honest," she patted a tiny amount of eye cream around her eye with her ring finger, "he can't be serious about her, surely?"

"He seemed to be. It doesn't matter to you anyway does it? He only works for you."

She came into the bedroom in her prettiest silk and lace basque. The beautifully enticing turquoise and black stitched panels created a sexy silhouette which should ensure it wouldn't be on for long. She pulled back the sheets on her side of the bed and climbed in, but Max was still engrossed.

"It's a bit more than that, but he's quite a wealthy chap in his own right, Daddy saw to that. I'd hate to see him rush into something with her that he'll regret. A couple of years with him and she could walk away with a hefty sum."

"Yeah, well she won't be the first or the last to do that. Not much you can do though, it's his life. It might just run its course anyway."

"You could be right," she agreed but was leaving nothing to chance. She needed to get rid of her before Anthony did something stupid and married her.

Max raised an eyebrow, "He seems devoted to you."

"He is. Remember, I've known him since I was a little girl."

"Tell me again about him," he put his phone on the bed-side table, "I know you have done before, but I never really took much notice. Now I've met him, I'm interested how he became such a prominent man in your life. In fact," he grinned sexily, "I need plenty of reassurance tonight that I haven't got anything I should be worried about."

"Definitely not," she slapped him playfully, "I've told you, there's nothing between us. Never has been."

"That doesn't convince me he doesn't want something between the two of you."

"That might be the case, but he knows the score. I love him dearly, but not like that."

"That's a relief then. So go on, tell me about how he came into your life."

"It's no amazing story. Daddy was best friends with his father, they started school together and despite my grand-father having money so Daddy didn't want for anything, Anthony's father had very little, and sadly he was injured in an industrial accident and couldn't work. So over the years, Daddy helped them out as best he could. The Gormans were proud people so he couldn't just give them money, so he had to be creative in lots of ways. He paid for Anthony to go into higher education which he wouldn't have been able to do. The family needed him to work to bring in some money. But Daddy insisted, and then when he had completed his degree in hospitality, he took Anthony on, starting at the bottom and it was up to him to work his way up. And he did exactly that and seemingly excelled at everything. And as soon as Daddy was diagnosed with a brain tumour, Anthony held the fort and continued to do so all the time he was in and out of hospital having treatment. We've always trusted Anthony implicitly; he has been a loyal servant to the whole of my family."

Max frowned, "Haven't you resented him over the years?"

"Not at all. He'd never let Daddy or me down, and the company would be nothing without him. He is Claybourne Leisure."

Max took a deep breath in. "So what do you think he'll be like when we start to formulate our partnership?"

"Not happy, that's for sure. He'll advise against it."

"And you're prepared for the fall-out?"

"Yes, because I trust you completely."

"Good because I've started to develop some tentative plans so your accountants can look them over. Any sort of merger would take months to formulate anyway so I thought it might be wise to start the ball rolling."

"No," she replied emphatically, "I've already said, I don't want to do anything until after we're married. We'll have much more clout that way." Did he think she was completely stupid?

He interrupted her with his persuasive lips. The lingering kiss left no uncertainty as to what his intentions were. "No more talking," he breathed moving his mouth down her neck.

Excitement gushed through her, knowing how much he

wanted her. And an even greater thrill was – there'd be no rushing home to clingy. They had the whole night together.

Chapter 13

Claire

The barometer on the wall in Pippa's garden indicated twenty-eight degrees, so the awning shading the outside terrace was welcome. Claire smiled at her new friend as they sipped their chilled chardonnay. "I can't believe you used to sing in a choir."

"Why not? People in wheelchairs can still sing, you know."

"Oh, I didn't mean that for a minute." She was gutted Pippa had misinterpreted her comment. It was more that she just didn't seem to be the type to spend her spare time singing.

"Don't be daft, I know you didn't. You'll have to get used to me, sometimes I engage my mouth before my head. I think it's because I've had to toughen up since the accident."

Claire smiled kindly, trying to imagine the ordeal of having to carry out everyday activities from a wheelchair, but Pippa saying she liked singing gave her an idea. "You don't fancy coming on a Wednesday to choir, do you? It's at the village hall and on one level so you should be able to get about easily enough."

"Aw, that's so kind of you to ask," Pippa took a sip of her drink, "I'd rather not commit though as I won't be here every Wednesday, and when my friend Liz comes, I don't want to leave her. And before you even think of it, Liz can't come either, she gets booed at karaoke."

That amused Claire. Who couldn't possibly do karaoke? "Yeah, right," she grinned, "I'd forgotten your friend was coming. Not to worry, it was just a thought. And I'm sure you and Liz will be busy anyway."

"I hope so." A wave of sadness passed over Pippa's eyes, "I'm worried about how she'll be if I'm honest. And selfishly, I'm really disappointed we didn't get to go on our trip to Oz, we were both looking forward to it so much. Liz is lovely. She's such a tonic, she accepts me exactly as I am, not Pippa in a wheelchair."

"Did she know you before your . . ."

"Oh yeah, I've known Liz since we were kids. It was a car accident, that's how I ended up like this," Pippa clarified, "bit of a bummer, but hey ho, life can be like that sometimes."

Claire could only imagine. "Is it definite you won't be able to walk again, or is there any hope?"

"There's always a tiny bit of hope as my spinal cord wasn't completely severed, but I'm not banking on it. I got a huge payout from the insurance companies," she screwed up her face, "but none of that compensates."

"No, I'm sure . . ." Claire's mobile rang. "Excuse me a minute," she reached for her iPhone and checked the caller ID. It was her mother.

"Mum, are you okay?"

"It's not your mum, it's Adam. I'm afraid your Mum's had a fall."

"A fall," she screeched, "is she okay?"

"Yes, she's fine, I'll put her on."

"Hello, love," her mum's voice sounded shaky, "I'm alright, don't get in a tizzy. No bones broken, only hurt pride."

"What on earth happened?"

"I must have spilled something on the floor and not noticed. I went to make a cup of tea and slipped and ended up on my bottom. But I'm perfectly alright," she reassured, "I panicked a bit at first but I think it was just the shock. Fortunately, Adam was around and heard me shouting. He helped me up, bless him."

"Thank God you're okay. I'll come straight home. Put Adam back on, would you?"

She waited.

"Hi"

"Adam, could you stay with Mum until I get back, I'm only round the corner so I'll be about ten minutes. And could you make her some tea . . ."

"Already done that before I rang you."

"Thank you. I'm leaving now. I'll be there shortly."

She cut the call and reached for her bag. "Mum's had a bit of a fall. She's there with the gardener, Adam. I'm going to have to dash."

"Oh dear, is she alright?"

"Yes, she seems fine, thank goodness, but I'd rather see for myself."

"Lucky he was around to help. He'll be her knight in shining armour from now on."

Claire widened her eyes, "And mine. Thank goodness he was there."

* * *

Claire ran the short distance home. As she let herself in the front door and made her way towards the back of the house, she heard Max's raised voice. "I specifically asked you not to come inside the house."

"I know you did," Adam replied, "but I heard your mother-in-law calling for help. What would you have me do, ignore her?"

She entered the kitchen. "Max," she glared at him, leaving him in no doubt how furious she was about the way he was speaking, "Where's Mum?"

"Gone to have a lie down, she's fine."

"Why are you talking to Adam like that?" she snapped, "it's thanks to him that Mum's okay." Adam was standing near the bi-fold doors looking acutely embarrassed. She softened her tone towards him, "I'm so pleased you were here, thank you for calling me, and for helping Mum."

He didn't say anything, just nodded before exiting through the patio door. She watched him walk away down the garden and her tummy clenched at the way Max had treated him.

"That was totally out of order," she spat at Max, "what the hell made you speak to him like that?"

"I told you, I don't want him in the house."

"He came to help Mum. You should be thanking him not ranting at him. You need to go and apologise now," she said firmly, "while I go and see Mum. I can't believe you were so awful."

She made her way down the hall to her mother's room furious at how horrible Max had been. For some reason, he really seemed to have a problem with Adam. He'd even got a local company in to repair the fence panel at an extortionate cost rather than have him do it.

She tapped on the bedroom door and opened it. Her heart constricted seeing her dear mum propped up with pillows. Her sad eyes opened a bit wider as she rushed towards her.

"Now then," she sat on the bed and wrapped her arms around her tightly, "are you okay?"

"I'm fine, love, you needn't have dashed back. I opened a bottle of lemonade earlier and I think I must have spilled some on the floor. I hadn't realised or I would have wiped it up. Anyway, I'm sure that's what caused me to slip."

"Poor you," she stroked her mum's head, "I wish I'd been here."

"Don't be silly, there's no harm done. I wouldn't have bothered you but Adam insisted. He's been so kind. What a lovely lad he is. And would you believe, seconds after we'd rung you, Max arrived home. It's odd for him to be here in an afternoon, isn't it?"

"Yes, it is. I've no idea why, I'll have to ask him. Can I get you some more tea or anything?"

"No more tea, love, I'm fine honestly. I'll have a little sleep and then get up and have a warm bath I think."

"That sounds nice. Shout me when you're ready and I can give you a hand. You might be a bit stiff." She got up from the bed and closed the blinds, "I'll go and start preparing something for dinner. And now Max is here, I'll send him to get Freddy from school for a change."

"That'll be nice, he'll love that. I think he misses his dad with him being in London all the time. And your dad used to do loads of stuff with him, so it must be hard. He needs to do boy things with another a male; I'm sure that's why he's trailing after Adam. Maybe you should have a word with Max while he's here about spending more time at home. Work isn't everything, you know."

"You're right, and I have tried to tell him. I will have another go, though. But you know Max, I think the word soon is his favourite at the moment."

"Yes, well, soon might be too late. Look at your dad, you just don't know what's round the corner."

Her tummy knotted. She wished her mother hadn't said that. The doom cloak wrapped itself around her once again.

And it seemed to be getting tighter by the minute.

Chapter 14

Claire

They were seated at the kitchen table for dinner. Their dining room with its cool and contemporary San Marino furniture, and ridiculously over-priced light fitting over the table that Max insisted on having, was mostly redundant as they had all their meals in the kitchen around the stylish but practical family table.

Claire served them each a portion of lasagne and placed a large salad bowl in the centre of the table along with a plate of home-made garlic bread.

Freddy pulled a face. "I don't want salad."

"Just try a little bit," Claire urged putting some on his plate.

"Wine, Julia?" Max asked her mum. There didn't appear to be any side effects from the fall, judging by the portion of salad and garlic bread she'd selected to accompany the lasagne.

"Oh, go on then, just a small one."

"Make sure it is," Claire warned, "I don't want you falling again."

"I'm quite likely going to fall again, love, I'm nothing like as steady as I was." She took a sip of her wine. "Fortunately though," she grinned, "I've enough flab on me to ensure I don't break any bones."

"You need to be careful though. I'm dreading you going home and being on your own. Thank goodness Adam was here today to help."

Max twitched uncomfortably in his seat. She was nowhere near forgiving him for the way he'd spoken to Adam earlier. "Which reminds me," she said, "did you apologise?"

"I haven't had time," he dismissed. "I looked for him when I went to get Freddy from school, but he must have left early."

"He hadn't left, Daddy," Freddy chipped in, "he was leaving when we came home from school, he waved to me."

"Did he? I never saw him."

Max was lying, he never missed anything. He'd have seen Adam leave, especially if his nine-year-old son had.

"Well, make sure you apologise when he comes tomorrow. I'm mortified at how you spoke to him."

Max glugged down a huge mouthful of wine. He'd be cross she'd spoken to him like that in front of her mum and Freddy.

"You know how I feel about him," his eyes glanced sideways at Freddy, as if to say, not in front of him, "I made myself clear in the beginning."

She was having none of it. "You were far too hasty chastising him, and I'd like you to say sorry. And give him a bottle of wine or something to show you're genuine. It's the least you can do," she turned to her mother, "don't you think, Mum?"

"Well, he was kind coming and helping me," her mum looked at Max, "maybe you should apologise. He didn't really deserve a telling off. He's never strayed near the house since he's been coming. He keeps himself to himself."

"Okay, okay," Max held up his hands, "I'll apologise."

"Why can't Adam come in the house?" Freddy asked innocently.

"He's the gardener," Max responded quickly, "he gets all

muddy and I don't want him bringing all that mess inside. It's better he stays outside."

Claire wasn't entirely happy with his feeble explanation but it would have to do. Freddy seemed to accept it, which was the main thing.

"Oh, I forgot to tell you," her mum said munching on a piece of garlic bread, "Maureen rang this morning. Her and Derek are coming to Sandbanks next week and want to take me out for dinner."

"That's lovely, Mum, you'll enjoy that. How nice of them."

"Yes. The only problem is, it's Wednesday evening and it's your choir."

"That doesn't matter, you're not here as a babysitter. I don't have to go to choir."

"I know, but you do enjoy it."

She looked directly at Max, "Maybe you can come home early on Wednesday?"

"Erm . . . yeah, I'm sure I'll be able to. I'll check."

She wasn't giving him a chance to get out of it. It didn't matter a jot if she didn't get to choir, but it was about time he understood he had responsibilities at home as well as work.

"Great. Sorted then, Mum. It'll be lovely for you to have a night out with them and I can still get to choir."

"Daddy," Freddy interrupted, "Will you listen to me reading my book tonight? It's all about the Red Arrows. I picked it 'cause we saw them at the air show."

Max was itching to get away, she could sense it if nobody else could. "I can't tonight, son, I've got too much work to do. We'll spend some time tomorrow night doing something nice. You choose what you'd like to do."

"Can we play football?" Freddy asked eagerly. He had no idea his father was a master at deflecting and he was getting the brush off yet again. Max loved Freddy dearly, but he loved work more.

"Sure we can. Now, you'll have to excuse me, I've got stacks of work to do in the office."

He got up from the table and came round to kiss her head. "See you later, darling, don't wait up, I'm likely to be a while."

He ruffled Freddy's hair. "Don't forget your homework after you've eaten. I want you passing all your exams so you can take over from me one day."

Claire stifled the urge to tell Max he didn't know his son at all if he thought he'd ever be tied to office work and negotiating deals. Freddy was too much of a free spirit to be doing anything like that.

Freddy waited until his father had left the kitchen. "Mummy, Adam's still coming tomorrow, isn't he?"

"As far as I know he is. Why?"

"He's making me a run for Floppy Ears."

"Is he? Have you asked him to do that?"

He looked sheepish. "I told him I wanted to let Floppy out a bit, but I was scared he got away. Adam said he'd make me a run but he needed to do it in his own time at his house. It's going to be ready tomorrow."

"Well, I'm sure if he said that, he'll bring it."

"Even though Daddy was mean to him?"

"Daddy wasn't really mean, sweetie, he was just worried about grandma's fall and snapped a bit. He's going to say sorry tomorrow."

"But what if he doesn't come?"

"I'm sure he will, it's just a misunderstanding."

She'd have to text Adam to make sure he did. Max needed to apologise to him at the very least. She had his mobile number somewhere that Max had jotted down when he first came and looked round.

"You go into the snug and do your spellings with Grandma for your test tomorrow and I'll clear the dinner dishes up."

"What about dessert?"

"I'll bring you some ice cream when you've done your spellings."

"And Grandma too?"

"Yes, of course, Grandma too."

"None for me, love," her mum chipped in, "I'm pretty full," she said getting up from the table.

"You have to have some, Grandma," Freddy insisted, "so you can try the chocolate sprinkles I told you about."

"Oh, alright then, maybe just a little."

As they both headed for the snug chattering together, Claire began rooting through all the receipts and rubbish in the kitchen drawer until she eventually located the piece of paper with Adam's number on it. She reached for her phone and sent a text.

Hi Adam, it's Claire Maric. Thank you again for today. My husband is sorry for being short tempered. I do hope you still come tomorrow. I'm sure he wants to apologise himself.

Within seconds of sending it, a text pinged straight back.

Of course X

The kiss at the end of his text made her prickle inside. *He probably puts one on all his texts. That's what people do.*

It must have been all the joking with Pippa about Lady Chatterley's lover that set off the little flutter of excitement inside her.

Chapter 15

Annabelle

Her driver approached the Ritz hotel in Piccadilly. Today was going to be special; finally she was organising her wedding.

"Thank you, Carl," Annabelle said, "I'll ring when I'm finished. I'll most probably be a couple of hours."

"Fine, ma'am, see you then."

She tended to use a company for journeys in central London rather than drive herself. It was easier in terms of parking and she most probably would be sampling some wines.

The car door was opened by a uniformed concierge. "Good morning, madam, welcome to the Ritz Hotel."

"Thank you," she smiled and made her way up the steps to the foyer. She loved the Ritz. She had fond memories of school holidays when she was home from boarding school and her father taking her there for afternoon tea. He always told her it was the best hotel in London. Even though she'd been there on numerous social occasions, she still got the same buzz of nostalgia when she entered the lobby.

An attractive young woman dressed smartly in an elegant suit as only a member of the Ritz staff would be, was waiting for her at the reception desk.

The girl recognised her, "Ms Claybourne?"

"That's right, and you must be Serena?"

"I am, yes," she held out her hand, "pleased to meet you in person finally."

Annabelle shook her hand. Serena was the Ritz's wedding co-ordinator. They'd had telephone conversations about her wedding preferences; today was all about formalising it.

"Is your fiancé joining us? I know you said on the phone you weren't sure?"

"I'm afraid he won't be, not today. He's tied up with business, but he's quite happy with me sorting things out."

Serena smiled, "It quite often happens that way. We'll be meeting again before the wedding, anyway, so do bring him along any time."

"Yes, I'll be sure to do that."

"I've taken the liberty of ordering us coffee if you'd like to follow me. We can go over what we've already discussed on the phone, and firm things up today. In an hour, I've got the wines ready for you to sample, and the desserts as you requested."

"How lovely, thank you."

Over coffee in the confines of Serena's office, they discussed the number of guests attending and perused various wedding menus. The stumbling block was the date. Annabelle was familiar with the Grade 2 William Kent House, but specifically wanted the Marie Antoinette suite. However, on the dates she would have preferred, it wasn't available.

"I really wanted the wedding before it gets too cold," she stressed, irritated she couldn't have what she wanted.

"I am sorry we can't accommodate you on the dates you've suggested. The Marie Antoinette suite is extremely popular and I'm sure you can appreciate, it's often booked up years in advance."

"Of course, I understand. It's just the room has such special memories for me of my late father, so I really must have it."

"Would you consider moving the date, maybe towards December? I'm thinking the Christmas decor will be its usual spectacle of elegance, so that would make it really special." She checked her iPad. "We have Saturday the 6th December available."

Would December be so bad? Max's divorce would well and truly be sorted by then, and an autumn wedding was cutting it a bit fine, particularly if clingy got difficult. Plus the Christmas décor was rather appealing.

"Do you know, I think you could be right. A Christmas wedding would be quite special."

"It would give you a little more time to plan. Do you mind me asking if you have your dress yet?"

"No, I haven't. That's next on my agenda," she smiled, "that and the honeymoon. Yes, I think the 6th December sounds perfect. We'll go with that."

"Wonderful. Would you like to check with your fiancé and then we'll confirm the booking?"

"No need," she laughed, "Max is quite happy leaving everything to me."

"If you're sure." The girl looked at her as if she were mad.

"Of course I'm sure. You sold me on a Christmas wedding. I can't miss out on the suite. Please book it before someone else does."

"Very well. How will you be paying the deposit?"

Annabelle's fingers were shaking as she handed over her credit card. She clasped her hands on her lap, loving the thrill of it all as Serena confirmed the booking on her iPad.

"I think it's fortuitous you haven't got your dress yet. You now have different options to consider with the wedding being a winter one. There are so many possibilities. I personally love a bit of white fur, it seems very Christmassy to me."

Annabelle smiled politely. The last thing she needed was

fashion advice. She spent her whole life buying designer clothes, she never wore anything without an expensive label attached to it.

"Now," Serena said, "shall we go and have a look around the Marie Antoinette suite, and then I can show you on the PC some examples of how we can prepare the room for you? I know you're familiar with the suite as you've attended events before, but I always think one sees it differently when it's for your own function."

"Absolutely." Annabelle reached for her handbag. "You said something about the wines, too?"

"I did. Jason, one of our sommeliers is available to discuss with you the wines you indicated you'd like. He has some samples for you to try."

"Thank you, I'd like that."

"And you said on the phone you wanted our signature beef wellington as a main course for your guests," she raised an eyebrow as if to ask if that was still the case. Annabelle nodded.

"That's a great choice. The chefs have prepared some other tasters for you that you might want to consider to accompany the beef, and some samples of desserts. They're ready for us now if you'd like that?"

"How helpful, yes, I'd love to."

"Right, we'll do that first, and then meet with Jason for the wines, if that's acceptable?"

"That sounds splendid."

She followed Serena, making small talk along the way. It was all coming together perfectly. Next, she would choose the most stunning dress, and then plan the honeymoon. Somewhere hot and exotic where the waiters wore tuxedos and little else. Oh what fun. It was all getting terribly exciting.

* * *

Carl the driver collected her and took her home. They had an account with the firm but she always tipped her drivers generously. According to her father, the currency of cash spoke a thousand words.

She was buzzing from her day's achievements as she took a seat on the outside terrace. It wasn't a part of the house she used often enough despite how beautiful the outlook from it was. It was south facing and the sun was particularly inviting. When her and Max were eventually living together, she anticipated many evenings sharing a bottle of wine, watching the sunset together and talking about their day. The terrace overlooked immaculate lawns tended by an expert gardener. Gardens weren't of any particular interest to her, but days like today, when excited at the plans she'd made, she liked to spoil herself in the forbidden pleasure of a cigarette. She'd stopped smoking years earlier for health reasons, but sometimes when she was on her own and there wasn't a chance of anyone seeing her, she'd indulge in one of the French cigarettes she favoured. Discipline was part of her life, so she never had more than one per day, and on some occasions, never had one at all. But today she thought she'd earned one.

She lit up. The light-headed pleasant feeling from the nicotine rush was still there, especially now she smoked infrequently. It only lasted a second before she exhaled and experienced the familiar warm, comfort of pleasantness as she watched the smoke curl into nothingness.

The trip to the Ritz had proven extremely productive. She was thrilled she'd finally got the wedding planned exactly as she wanted it. Not a lavish affair like her first marriage, this one would be a small, intimate gathering, with a fabulous honeymoon. It gave her a huge kick to think that by the end of the year, she'd be Annabelle Maric. Not that she'd use his name, for business reasons she would stick to Claybourne. She'd never changed it before when she was married to Mark but that had been lucky as he'd been dead and buried within eighteen months of them tying the knot. And she'd hated him with a passion, so wouldn't have been happy stuck with his name.

The Ritz had been the right choice. She'd sampled an array of delicacies for the wedding breakfast and selected the ones she liked. The sommelier had been a delight advising on several delicious sparkling wines for the toasts, and rich wines to go with the food. Her father had taught her plenty about the difference between a good wine and complete rubbish. And for her and Max's wedding, she'd only selected superior ones. Not that they had any inferior ones at the Ritz.

She drew on the cigarette for another head rush of dizziness and contemplated when she was going to tell Max she'd got everything sorted for their wedding. If she told him now, he'd probably kick off and chastise her. He had this stupid loyalty thing to clingy which irritated her to death, even though she acknowledged an inner admiration for him showing a degree of respect, which would bode well for their union. She couldn't have a man disrespecting her. That was the mistake her fool of a husband had made. Maybe it was best to tell Max after clingy's birthday, when he'd moved in permanently with her. He'd said previously how much he loved the tradition of the Ritz. That had confirmed her decision to select it for their wedding. He'd no doubt be pleased it was all organised and he didn't have to partake, he was a bloke after all.

Her iPhone vibrated. It was almost as if Max knew she was thinking about him. She hastily crushed the cigarette in an ashtray and wafted the air before answering, as if by doing so, he wouldn't find out. It was her guilty pleasure and she wanted to keep it that way.

"Hi, darling, how are you doing?"

Chapter 16

Annabelle

She returned to her office above the spa feeling relaxed from her head to toe frangipani massage. Her preferred time for a spa treatment was first thing in the morning before the paying guests arrived. No sense in encroaching on that and taking up a therapist. The massage, according to the brochure, would relax the body until you entered a state of inner peace and harmony, which was exactly what she needed hence having them regularly. It was essential she maintained a state of calmness. Anything other than calmness wasn't good for her – she'd learned that in the most appalling way. Fortunately, since Max had entered her life, her disposition was one of self-control, and now she'd finally got a date sorted for the wedding, she was happier than ever. Next on her list was getting her friends, Della and Anthony onboard. They were the most important people in her life. She had other friends and business associates who would get an invitation, but none mattered to her as much as those two. They'd been at her first marriage, which had crashed and burned, so she needed to convince them this union would be completely different.

She started her PC so she could sort out the stationery for the invitations. Her modest wedding was far more appealing than the big flash one she'd had first time round. As she started to peruse wedding stationery online, the ringing of her phone interrupted her.

"Hello you," she said lovingly to Max, "I wasn't expecting you this early."

"I've just got a quick window and wanted to catch you. I've got a persistent problem with one of the Jacuzzis so I've got a meeting with a new maintenance contractor to sort that out. I'm waiting for him to arrive. Anyway, the reason I'm ringing is, I can't meet tonight as we'd planned, something's come up."

Her tummy tensed, "What's come up?"

"Nothing to worry about. I wondered if there's any way you can come here to the office this afternoon?"

Max had a similar work set up to her. He had offices above the spa he owned. She knew exactly what he meant by her visiting him. She'd done so on other occasions and knew that the request to *come to his office* was a covert way of inviting her for a bout of frantic sex there. A wave of disappointment gushed through her, she so wanted to go for dinner with him as planned.

"I could do, I suppose," she agreed reluctantly. Inwardly she was twitchy about her weakness where he was concerned. "What exactly has come up, before I say a definite yes?"

"I have to look after Freddy, Claire has got something on."

Bloody clingy. She had the ability to spoil everything.

"But I thought her mother was staying, can't she look after him?"

"She normally does, but she's been invited out and Claire's got an appointment she has to attend, so I'll have to be home. I'm sorry, darling, it's just one of those things. I'll make it up to you, I promise. I'm planning something special for your birthday as we speak."

That lifted her spirits. All the emphasis seemed to have

been on clingy's fortieth, yet it was her birthday before that. It would be nice for her to be the focus for a change.

"Have you now. That's nice to hear, any clues?"

"If you come and see me this afternoon, you might be able to wheedle the odd clue out of me."

She couldn't refuse him. Putty in his hands, that's what she was. But soon he'd be with her the whole time anyway. *Keep calm* she reminded herself. "Okay, I'll come. But I'm warning you now, I'm bringing handcuffs and a whip with me so I can make sure you crack."

She heard his laugh, "You're scaring me already. Come about three thirty, my secretary's leaving then. I'll put you in the diary as a business meeting."

"Yeah, you do that. But remember, I'm chair and we'll be following *my* agenda."

"Sounds good to me, boss. I can't wait. See you then."

She placed her phone down on the desk and gave a wry smile. Even though she was no longer going to dinner with him that evening, at least she was still seeing him and the fact he was organising something special for her birthday gave her a boost. Anthony usually had something planned but she wasn't sure he had this year. Too much focus on Fiona-the-cleaner.

A quick glance down at her embossed desk diary reminded her she had an appointment with her boring therapist that afternoon. She still preferred the principle of a diary, even though it was an outdated way of keeping track of appointments. It must stem from her father when there was no such technology as an electronic calendar. She could still hear him telling her to check daily for the following day's activities, *so she didn't miss anything vital.*

George Grey's name glared back at her for three thirty. Even his name had the ability to irritate her. He was taking up far too much of her time when she had other more important stuff to do. Now she'd let the cat out of the bag about Max, he was like a terrier. She'd only told him as she hoped it would get her off seeing him as often. No such luck though. Now he was trying to guide her into opening up about her past with Max. As if she was ever going to do that. She couldn't afford Max getting cold feet which he might well do if he found out everything about her. It was far better to leave the past in the past. They were happy, and pretty soon he'd be leaving clingy and they'd begin their life together. Plenty of time then to discuss what had previously happened. Or she might never, she'd have to see.

She buzzed the PA her and Anthony shared. "Angela, could you ring and cancel my appointment with George Grey this afternoon please, and then find Yegor and tell him I need to see him if he can come up to my office?"

"Yes, sure."

"Thank you."

She walked over to the huge panoramic window and stared out at the impressive grounds. Her and Anthony's offices were right at the top of the building because of the spectacular views the rooms afforded. Both of the offices had a seating area by the window. A few floors below, the same view was shared by the guests in the leisure seating area so they too could relax on the comfy sofas and enjoy the spectacular views of the restful countryside.

The task ahead now was to get rid of Anthony's cleaner-come-bed-buddy somehow, and she'd need Yegor to help. He'd delivered on the two they'd sacked that were taking them to court for unfair dismissal. She hadn't bothered questioning Yegor on how he'd managed to make it all disappear, she was just relieved he had. Anthony delivered the news that they'd dropped the forthcoming court case, and she'd managed to look suitably surprised. But it would cost far more to get rid of Fiona-the-cleaner, she was sure, but it'd be worth it. She couldn't have Anthony even contemplating making a life with that woman. No, he was dedicated to her and the business and in the not too distant future, her and Max would need him to manage things for them when they were building their life together. She was hoping they could travel until she got pregnant. Max didn't know it yet, but she had no intention of having him work all the time while she stayed at home once they had children. That wasn't happening. They would share the parenting.

A tap on the door indicated Yegor had arrived.

"Come in," she said as he opened the door. "Have a seat."

He was quite good-looking in a mafia sort of way, but absolutely huge in an unattractive way. She didn't even know if he was married or anything. Not that she needed to. She doubted he was somehow, though.

"I've got something I'd like you to do for me, totally confidentially of course."

"Of course," he nodded.

"There's a woman I want you to check out for me. I only have her name and a Facebook page. I don't have an address but I'd like you to find one. She flicked through her phone and found Fiona-the-cleaner's Facebook page that Anthony had shown to her. She handed it to Yegor.

He looked at the image and raised an eyebrow. "And when I've found her address?"

"Check on what she does, where she goes, that sort of thing."

"And that's it?"

"For the time being, yes. There'll be more."

"Okay."

She slid an envelope towards him with a wad of notes in it, "In case you have any expenses." Whether he bribed people for information, she wasn't entirely sure, but it was probable he did. He always delivered so she never asked.

He stood up and reached for the envelope, placing it in the inside pocket of his jacket. He rarely asked questions. She preferred that. He nodded and made his way to the door closing it behind him.

Once she had Fiona-the-cleaner's address, and more information on her other than her fawning over Anthony, she'd send Yegor to pay her off to disappear.

The only question was, how much would it cost to make certain the little tramp never sees Anthony again?

Chapter 17

Claire

It was late afternoon in the garden and Claire reached for the jug of Pimm's she'd made and filled two glasses, "Here you go, Mum," she passed one with plenty of fruit, "just what the doctor ordered."

"Ohhh, that's lovely, darling, thank you," her mum smiled gratefully, "cheers." She took a sip of her drink, "That rabbit run is keeping Freddy occupied, it was nice of Adam to make it for him."

"Wasn't it? I keep forgetting to ask him if we owe him something for it."

"I doubt it, it's just a bit of chicken wire."

"Yes, I know, but he needs paying for the wood and his time." She glanced at her son. "Freddy," she called, "put Floppy Ears away now and come and cool off. It's too hot for the rabbit, he needs to be in the shade of his hutch."

Freddy gently picked the rabbit up and moved towards the hutch, stroking him and talking all the time; he was a sensitive soul that loved animals. Claire had often thought about having a dog but knew that would never happen. Max wouldn't allow it.

"Put that on for a while," she handed Freddy his cap and a glass of lemonade with strawberries, mint and cucumber in it.

"Is it proper Pimm's?"

"Yes, just diluted a little," she fibbed, winking at her mum. The bitter fruit would make it taste different from ordinary lemonade, "How I always do it."

"Can Adam have a drink with us?" her son asked eagerly.

"Erm . . . he could do," she glanced around the extensive gardens, "but I'm not sure where he is right now."

"I can go get him. He's in the shed."

Her young son sprinted off towards the bottom of the garden not giving her any chance to say no, while her mum fluffed her short hair up with her fingertips. "I would have done my hair if I'd have known Adam was joining us."

Claire rolled her eyes, "You dafty. Do you really think he'd be interested in either of us? He's only young."

"Not that young," her mum shook her head, "I bet you he's older than he looks."

"Shush, he's coming . . . look." Her little sweet boy was pulling Adam towards them, holding his hand. He'd be teased at school if they saw him even holding an adult's hand at his age. It thumped hard seeing Freddy clutching another man's hand other than his dad's and chatting away to him. If only Max would give him a bit more time.

"Afternoon," Adam smiled at them both and stood awkwardly by the table, "this young man says I *have* to come and get a drink."

"That's right," Claire said, "please have a seat." She poured him a glass of Pimm's knowing he walked each day to their house so alcohol wasn't a problem.

"How are you getting on, Adam?" her mum asked as he sat down, "there must be stacks for you to do. Will you get it all done do you think before you finish?"

"Afraid not. It's a mammoth job; it'll probably take a year or two to see the results. A garden as large as this needs constant work and you don't always see the benefits of your labour straight away."

"But you've made an enormous inroad in such a short time," Claire reassured, handing him a glass, "you're making a difference already. At least the gardens are beginning to look like gardens now and not a building site."

"Thank you," he smiled. He took a mouthful of his Pimm's, "That's refreshing."

"Good." Claire pulled a face, "I've got a confession to make . . . the drink's a bit of a bribe. I've a favour to ask you."

She watched as he took another sip of his drink. Her mum was right, he really was good-looking. She could deny to herself all she wanted that she didn't find him attractive, but she'd be lying. The excited fluttering when he was around was alien to her. She'd berated herself for being silly a couple of times when she covertly watched him from the house. She'd never ever thought about another man since she'd met Max.

He took another mouthful and licked his lips, "Okay, the bribe has worked, what can I do for you?"

"I'm wondering if you could help me put the gazebo up?" She glanced at her son making ridiculous noises with a straw and his drink, "Someone is having a birthday party tomorrow and I'm hoping we can have the food outside as the forecast is for sun all day."

"Sure, where do you keep it?"

"In the garage . . ." Freddy interrupted, "Hey, can you come, Adam . . . to my party?"

Adam's penetrating green eyes caught hers. He'd know exactly what she was thinking. Max wouldn't want him at his son's party, no way.

"I'm not sure I can make it buddy, I already have something on."

"Aww." Freddy's little face was a picture of disappointment, which hurt her.

"I bet you've got loads of mates coming though, you won't miss me. You'll be too busy."

Freddy soon forgot his disappointment, "Yeah, and we're having the goal posts out aren't we, Mummy?"

"Definitely. I daren't do any other with all of the boys being crazy about football."

"Sounds good," Adam said, "will the boys take on the girls?"

Freddy screwed his face up, "Not having girls."

Adam widened his eyes but he was suppressing a grin. "Ah, I see, so it's a boys only day, then?"

Her mum chipped in, "I've said he should have some girls . . . girls are nice. But he's not keen are you, Freddy?"

"No," he pulled another face, "I don't want girls."

Her mother grinned playfully, "Well you won't be like that in a few years, that's for sure."

"Can I help Adam put the gazebo up, Mummy?"

Claire looked enquiringly at Adam, "It's up to Adam. I don't want you getting in the way."

"Course you can, matey, no probs." He knocked back the last dregs of his drink, "Do you want me to help move any tables and chairs or anything once I've got it up?"

"If you're sure you don't mind. Max says he'll be late home tonight so I don't want to be having to move the stuff in the morning as the children are arriving at eleven."

"Don't mind at all," he said, "I'll get the gazebo up first then."

Freddy chipped in, "Can you come to my party for just a little while, it's on all day?"

"Adam's already said, sweetheart, he's busy tomorrow. You'll see him Monday and then you can tell him all about it."

"Tell you what, buddy, I've got a bit of work I can be doing in the garden. I'll call on Saturday and do that, then I can see you with your mates, how about that?"

"Yeah!" Freddy squealed.

Delighted as Claire was to see her son's smiling face, a

knot was forming in her tummy. She knew how Max would react to the gardener being part of their son's birthday party – and it wouldn't be pleasant.

* * *

Adam had spent the rest of the afternoon setting up the gazebo and garden ready for the birthday party the following day. It didn't appear he minded Freddy helping at all, in fact he'd been patient letting him join in which had given Claire time to make some sandwich fillings and quiches while her mother iced the cupcakes. She came out in the garden to see Adam and Freddy fixing a Happy Birthday banner to the changing huts at the side of the swimming pool.

"Here, you two," she called, "come and get a drink." Adam gave her a nod then stepped back, checking the banner was straight. He'd been brilliant setting it all up. She was furious with Max who had originally told her he was only working until lunchtime and coming home to help, then sent the usual text saying he'd been delayed. When he did eventually make it, if he dared to mention Adam in a negative way, he'd get a rocket from her.

Adam and Freddy approached the table.

Where's Grandma?" Freddy asked.

"She's on the phone. Here," she handed them both a glass of fruit juice.

"Cheers," Adam said swigging his down in one.

"Please, sit down. Would you like some cake?" she asked indicating to the slices of lemon drizzle cake she'd plated for him and Freddy.

"Sure," he said sitting down and taking the plate from her, "thank you." He took a bite, "Mmm, this is so good. You could open a tearoom and sell cakes."

She could feel the blush heating up her cheeks. "I don't

know about that. It's just a hobby. If I had to do them all the time, I'd soon lose interest."

"Well, I've never tasted any cake as good as this. Don't you think so, buddy?" he smiled at Freddy who was munching through his and gave him a muffled "yeah" back.

"You're too kind," she said, secretly loving his praise, "that's a nice thing to say. Anyway, it's my turn to be thanking you, I can't believe how much we've managed to achieve today with you and Freddy working outside."

"No probs, we liked doing it, didn't we, mate?"

"Yeah," Freddy said again. It seemed to be his favourite word around Adam.

"I've got a bit of a confession though," Claire cringed, "the cake is another bribe really. I'm hoping it helps my cause."

"There's more to do?" Adam widened his eyes playfully, "And here's me thinking we were all done."

"Well we are, or should I say, you are." She felt guilty asking him to do more. "You've done more than enough really,"

"Go on," he said pushing the last piece of the cake in his mouth, "what is it?"

"Would you be able to help blow up some balloons for me?" She quickly added, "If you've got time that is. No problem if you have to go home."

"Er . . . no, I can't say I do." He smiled as though she'd said something amusing. She was drawn to his green vibrant eyes, they lit up his whole face and she couldn't help staring at him until his voice dragged her out of her trance, "I can't think of anything better than blowing up balloons right now, as opposed to heading home."

She sensed there was a hidden meaning and couldn't resist probing further. "I've never even asked you where you live. Are you with your parents?"

"God, no. I live alone. But it isn't the most palatial of surroundings, so no, you're not holding me up. I'm happy to stay. And as blowing up balloons is my forte, lead me to them and I'll get started."

"Thanks Adam, you're so kind. Max should be here helping but it looks like he's delayed."

"He'll make tomorrow, won't he? You don't want to be on your own trying to manage all those excited boys. And having to referee the football could be a significant challenge," he grinned cheekily at her and turned to Freddy, "Can your mum referee the footie?"

"No," Freddy giggled, "she doesn't understand the rules."

"Er . . . listen here you two, I do understand the rules, thank you very much. But I won't have to be the referee as Daddy will be here so he can do it."

She felt a pang of guilt as Adam stiffened. There certainly was no love lost between him and her husband. He smiled, "That's good. Let me know if there's a problem and I can . . . maybe change my plans and come over and help."

"That's kind of you. Thank you." She knew he never really had plans. "Would you like another slice of cake?"

"Definitely." He exaggerated licking his lips, "I need sustenance for my lungs so I can blow up the balloons."

"Can I have another bit too, Mummy," Freddy copied Adam, "for my lungs."

She laughed cutting them both another slice. Adam took his from her and gave her a wink. It was just a small, friendly wink, but it somehow knocked her equilibrium right off its axis.

He really was attractive.

Chapter 18

Claire

She held her camera, videoing Max walking from the kitchen to the table she'd set up with the huge Manchester United football cake in his hands with ten candles on it. He led the Happy Birthday singing and the boys all joined in. Freddy waited patiently for them to finish. They all cheered as he blew out the candles in one go.

"Can we play footie now?"

"Course you can," she said, delighted that Freddy was having a nice day, "Daddy's going to organise you while I cut the cake and put some in the party bags."

Right on cue, Max interjected, "Yep, I've got some coloured tabards. But first of all we need to put you into teams." He produced a black bag containing some ping-pong balls and proceeded to let each of the boys select one from the two colours. The boys' faces were a delight as they each delved in and selected the colour indicating which team they were on.

Once they'd all gone outside with Max to play football, Claire was in and out of the garden bringing the left-over food into the kitchen while her mother covered and refrigerated it and loaded the dishwasher.

"I think we're all done here," her mum said, "shall I go and see how they're getting on?"

"Thanks, Mum, that'd be great. I'll be with you shortly."

Claire carefully wrapped portions of the cake and placed a piece in each party bag ready for the boys going home. The shouts she could hear from the boys outside indicated they were enjoying themselves. Freddy was thrilled to have his dad there and she knew it was necessary to somehow have the discussion again with Max about him neglecting Freddy and her. There was no question he was absent far too much lately. That could be the only possible reason she was attracted to Adam. She didn't want to be, and thankfully nobody knew, but she couldn't suppress the flutter of excitement each time she saw him. The urge to find out about his life, his likes and dislikes, was increasing each day. Freddy had told her he could play the guitar and sing, which had her yearning to hear him. There was something attractive about a man with a voice and she just knew he'd be good.

Max approaching the kitchen jolted her out of her stupid fantasising. "Football finished?" she asked.

"Yeah, they're just getting changed for the pool, your mum's supervising them. She's like a teacher with her instructions, but I must say, they do as she tells them."

"Oh, she'll have them sorted in no time," she smiled, knowing her mum. She'd not have any nonsense. "I'll come now." They'd agreed they both needed to be in the water with the boys just to be safe. There was only an hour or so to go and the parents would be arriving to collect them.

"Quick beer?" she asked taking one from the fridge and opening it for him.

"Cheers. Who'd have thought refereeing a football match with ten boys would be so hard. That Luke's a little sod. I could swing for him."

"Now, now, who's the adult here," she grinned, "they are only kids."

He took a swig of beer and wiped his mouth on the back of his hand, "I tell you, I need danger money with them, they're really competitive. It's only five-a-side, for God's

110

sake. The way they tackle and argue, you'd think it was a cup final."

She laughed out loud, "What are you like. They can't be that bad."

"They are. I'm telling you, half an hour of that and I'd more than had enough. Forty-five minutes was my max and I blew the whistle. I've just told them to get ready for the pool and to use the outside toilet before they get in. I don't want them peeing in the water."

"They're not babies, I think they're well past that."

"I doubt it. Everyone pees in water."

"Thank you for that image, I've got to swim in that pool."

She slipped her sun-dress off over her head to reveal her swimsuit. He widened his eyes appreciatively. "Very nice. Do we really have to go and supervise ten boys? I can think of much better things to do right now," he grinned suggestively, dropping his empty bottle in the recycling bin. "Do you think your mother would miss us?"

"I'm quite sure she would. How's she going to cope if you can't," she smiled sexily, "you'll have to save that thought until later." She wrapped a sarong around her waist. "Come on."

As they walked towards the pool, Max frowned, "Do you know why the bloody gardener's lurking around today? I don't expect him to work on a Saturday."

"Yeah," she fidgeted with her hair, "he did say he'd be around today, something about paying some time back with taking the other day off for an appointment." She'd quickly made up the excuse, knowing Max wouldn't be happy if he knew Freddy had asked Adam to his party. "I think that's all it is."

"I'll tell him to go home," he scowled, "I don't want him round the house on a weekend when I'm here. And I certainly don't want him around my son's party. I'll just go and have a word."

"Can't you just leave him? At least he's working, you should be pleased."

"Yeah, well I'm not."

"I could go and tell him, if you'd like?"

"What, looking like that? You must be joking. I don't want him seeing you in a swimsuit. You get in the pool before he sees you and I'll go speak to him."

A heavy feeling filled her gut. She really should have been firmer and explained things properly. Now Adam was going to get his marching orders, which wasn't fair. Especially as Freddy had wanted him to come and she'd not discouraged it. The thought of Adam being dismissed spoilt the day somehow.

Her mother had the boys sat patiently on the edge of the pool with their feet dangling in.

"Oh good, here's Mrs Maric," she said, "go ahead, you can all jump in now."

A couple of the boys slid in the water, but most jumped in, making a hefty splash. Her mood was lightened by Freddy's joyful face. Hopefully, after the party, he'd start to have a few more friends. She'd only decided to host the party as a way of including some of the boys from his new school. Freddy was a loner and she did so want him to be involved with more boys. Although she didn't agree with Max's assessment of him being a mummy's boy, she recognised he was a sensitive soul and rather young for his age, therefore would benefit from mixing more with his peers.

Max had put two basket ball nets in the pool, one at each end, so they could play water polo. She was pleased he'd made such an effort, it was rare these days. Maybe things were finally changing with him.

"Dad's on my team, Mummy, you're on Luke's," her son told her.

"Okay, but your dad's not allowed to try for the net. He's too tall. You boys have to do the scoring."

Max came back and slid into the pool. "Are we all ready?" he cried lifting the ball above his head ready to throw.

"Yeah," the boys screamed in unison.

Max threw it in the air and they were off.

What had he said to Adam? Claire knew he would have been dismissive, and somehow that hurt. She inwardly chastised herself. She really must stop worrying about the gardener, who'd be leaving them soon anyway. She needed to grow up, act her age and concentrate on her own family.

Almost forty and she was behaving like a teenager with a crush.

Chapter 19

Annabelle

She glared at Yegor over the desk, "You did what?"

"I trashed her car. That'll teach her to ask for more money."

She'd sent Yegor to Fiona-the-cleaner's house with a hefty sum to clear off for good. No explanation, just to leave. It wasn't too difficult to feign shock . . . she was shocked. "I can't believe you did that. I didn't ask you to."

"I know you didn't. But she needs to understand that we aren't messing about."

"And you really think trashing the car will do it?"

"Yep, I do. And when I go back again she'll know that's just the beginning if she doesn't take the offer."

"How did you do it?"

"Does it matter?"

"It does if she goes to the police."

"There's nothing to link me or you to her."

"Yes, but once we give her the money, there'll be a link."

"Yeah, well the car will be an incentive to keep her mouth shut. I might just throw in I know which university her son attends. She'll be scared shitless and clear off, then."

"Do you think any of it will work? I need her to go, Yegor," she said firmly.

"She will do."

She liked his confidence. Yegor always delivered.

"Okay. When are you going back?"

"In a day or so. I'll give her a couple of days' thinking time, then I'll have her eating out the palm of my hand."

"I hope you're right. I can't afford for her to tell Anthony."

"She won't. I've made sure of that."

She checked her watch in an obvious way to give him a nudge to go. "Right, I'd better be going, I have an appointment."

He nodded and left her office. She didn't want to think exactly what Yegor had said to Fiona, she didn't want to go there. It was the end result she was after. Fiona clearing off. And it didn't matter what it cost. She had to go.

* * *

Annabelle sat in George Grey's office waiting for him to begin. It was all pointless anyway, she'd got her life well and truly back on track and, as far as she was concerned, she didn't need to see him at all. And she certainly didn't want to be slipping away to see a therapist when her and Max lived together. She'd have to somehow end the sessions.

He leant forward to start the tape. "I'll begin today, if that's alright?"

"Yes, that's fine." He could talk for the whole session as far as she was concerned.

"I was concerned that I hadn't received your latest assessment from the psychiatrist, so I contacted Dr Stead's secretary to try and speed up getting the copy to me." He paused giving her time to understand where he was coming from. "I was surprised to hear you hadn't attended for your recent appointment, and seemingly, you were given a second appointment and you didn't attend for that either. Is there a reason as to why?"

She shuffled uncomfortably. He had the ability to make her feel like a naughty child not a thirty-six-year-old woman running a business.

"I didn't go as I don't feel I need to anymore. I've told you, I'm in a completely different place right now. I'm happy, my personal life is better than it's ever been, so I don't want to see Dr Stead to tell him all this. It's a complete waste of his time as well as mine. He'd be better dealing with people that need his help."

"You don't get to decide, Annabelle," he said firmly, using her name for emphasis, as if she was being disobedient. "The court stipulated you had to be under the care of Dr Stead and myself until we jointly see fit to discharge you. And I have to say, the way things are going, it looks very much as if you'll be continuing with us for a while yet."

"But it's ridiculous. Look, I'm happy right now. I'm going to be getting married at the end of the year. I want to concentrate on that not spend time in a stuffy office going over old ground. That's all finished with now, I've moved on. Surely that means your job is done?"

"The sessions aren't over until Dr Stead and I agree they are and even then, we might still need to see you periodically. And right now, stopping them isn't something I could consider. Just because you've met someone that makes you happy and are making plans, we haven't discussed anything about the impact when things go wrong, which they do, in all relationships. It's the coping strategies we need to look at. We cannot have a repeat of last time."

"There won't be a repeat," she said firmly, "I love Max and he loves me. We're going to have children together. I've got the wedding date booked and right now, I couldn't be happier. Each day is a joy, except when I have to come here and see you. You're like a lead weight hanging over my head and spoiling my happiness."

"I'm truly sorry you feel like that, as it isn't my intention."

He widened his eyes which emphasised his hideous birth-mark over one of them, "I will be able to add to my report about the improvements you're making, and that you continue to take your medication which keeps you on an even keel. But we haven't yet tested how you are going to cope when things don't go according to plan. Remember before, things spiralled quite quickly out of control. It could easily happen again."

"It won't. I keep telling you, I've moved on. I've never been happier in my life."

"You told me last time we met you hadn't shared your past with your future husband. Has that changed?"

"No. I don't think he needs to know. I don't want him to be thinking he's marrying a nutter, he's already got one of those."

Bugger. She'd let that cat out of the bag, now she'd have to tell him Max was married. She really didn't want to discuss clingy . . . that was all under control. But she'd said it now.

"Got one of those?" He purposely showed no surprise; nevertheless he would be now she'd said that. "Care to enlighten me?"

She took a deep breath in. "Max hasn't left the marital home yet. He and his wife still live in the same house but not together. He's leaving in a couple of weeks."

"I see. And how does that make you feel?"

Bloody hell, that sentence was a joke. They must be taught that at therapy school, every therapist in the world uses it.

"Well, I'm not exactly jumping up and down with excitement. But it is what it is. Very shortly he'll be with me and we have our future to look forward to, together."

"And you're planning this future based on withholding information about your mental health to the man you are intending spending it with?"

"I will tell him when the time is right. I'll tell him everything that happened. But not right now. And correct me if I'm wrong, but the court didn't say that in the future I needed to share my past with anyone."

"No, that's right, they didn't. But you seem agitated. As if you're not comfortable with your decision making. Or is it that you aren't happy that your future husband is still in the marital home?"

"I'm not happy about that, no. But it's only a question of a few weeks. He has a ten-year-old son and it's not easy dissolving a marriage when there are children involved."

"No, I'm sure you're right. Tell me, how do you feel about becoming a step-parent?"

She shrugged, "I've not thought much about it at all if I'm honest as his son will be living with his mother."

"But he'll still want to spend some time with his father, and I'm quite sure your future husband will want to see his son."

"Of course he will. Look, we'll work these things out once we move in together. I'm getting tired now, can we call it quits for today?"

"As I said in the beginning, these sessions are to help you and can be as long or as short as you wish. But they have to happen, you can't decide when to come or not. And I will need that psychiatric assessment. As soon as that is complete, I can finish my own quarterly report."

"And what's that likely to say? Shall you focus on the changes I've made and how happy I am right now?"

"Yes, most definitely. But I will be recommending our sessions continue. I think it's important, as you embark on your new life, that I still see you and how it's impacting." He stared sternly at her, "We cannot afford a repeat of what happened before. Don't you agree?"

"That seems such a long time ago," she sighed, "I'm a different person now, and all I'm focussing on is my marriage and any children we might have together. I really do not want to be going over old ground all the time."

"Okay," he stopped the tape, "we'll leave it there for now and pick this up after you've had your psychiatric assessment. So if you could have that, and then book in with me for our next session, that would be helpful."

She got out of her seat, eager to get away. Every single time she met with him, she ended up with a blinding headache. Wasn't therapy supposed to make the client feel better?

Chapter 20

Annabelle

Despite her protests, Max had taken the liberty of having some initial plans drawn up about their business merger. First thoughts, he called it. He wanted to organise a preliminary meeting with Anthony but she kept putting it off, determined nothing was going to happen until they were married. She made noises to pacify him but she'd been firm that she wouldn't be merging anything, not right now. He wasn't stupid, just persistent, she'd give him that. But that's what she loved about him, a charismatic entrepreneur which were qualities that were reminiscent of her own father.

Clingy's birthday wasn't that far away, and after that he'd be moving in with her. His wife invaded her mind much more than she wanted. Even though Max was leaving her, and they'd soon be a couple, she was always going to be in the background with that stupid son of theirs. That caused her the most angst. It didn't sit well at all. But the prospect of them being married and merging their companies was exciting. And having Max permanently with her and having his children was her ultimate goal. Business paled into insignificance compared to that.

Her mobile rang. It was Max.

"Hello, you," she injected as much love into her voice as she could. It wasn't difficult. She loved him beyond anything in her life.

"Hi, beautiful. I'm just about wrapped up here, how are you doing?"

"I'm all done too." She was up for an afternoon of love-making and couldn't wait. "Shall I meet you at the house in an hour?"

"Perfect."

"If you're there before me, open a bottle for us."

"Will do. And make sure you hurry up," he breathed sexily, "cause I'll be stripped off ready for you."

She grinned, loving how he wanted her as much as she did him. "Me too, if I'm there before you. See you soon."

She put her iPhone in her handbag just as the internal phone rang. "Hello."

"Hi, Annabelle, Dr Stead's secretary is on the line."

"Didn't you cancel my appointment like I asked?" she snapped, eager to get away. The bloody psychiatrist could do one.

"Yes, I did. She says Dr Stead has asked her to call and speak directly to you."

There was no time for a chat or an appointment, not when she had the chance to spend an afternoon with Max. Nothing was going to get in the way of that.

She took a deep breath in. "Okay, put her through."

"Hello, Annabelle Claybourne speaking."

"Hello, Ms Claybourne, it's Dr Stead's secretary. He's asked me to call to remind you of your appointment today."

Yeah, I bet. It'd be that stupid therapist George Grey giving him the heads-up she'd met Max.

"I'm afraid I can't make it today. If you could arrange another date with my secretary, then I'll make every effort to attend the next one."

"I'm sorry, but Dr Stead has asked that you prioritise seeing him today."

She sighed, and quickly thought up a lie. "I'm afraid I can't. I have a medical appointment which I do need to attend. It's rather urgent."

There was a pause, obviously the secretary was contemplating the implications of what she'd said.

"Oh, I see, I'll let Dr Stead know."

"Yes, please do. Now, I really must dash. I'll put you back to my secretary so you can rebook my appointment. Thank you."

Bloody George Grey notifying the psychiatrist. How dare he? Her dislike of him was increasing. It was almost as if he was keeping tabs on her. If it wasn't for the courts, she'd tell the two of them to get knotted. She'd never been better health-wise so she didn't need either of them poking around in her head and spoiling her future happiness. She grabbed her handbag. No need to dwell on that now though. Not when she had an afternoon with her future husband. Thirty minutes maximum and she'd be with him. Excitement kicked in.

* * *

Max had made love to her like a stallion. He had so much stamina. They hadn't even made it to the bedroom, as soon as she'd come into the house, true to his word, he'd been naked and lost no time in getting her clothes off.

Still panting from their exertion, she reached for the fur throw off the back of the settee and covered them both. She snuggled into his arms and kissed his cheek, "You've just reminded me why I want to spend the rest of my life with you."

"That good, eh?" he grinned obviously loving she'd appreciated his lovemaking.

"Yes, that good. I can't wait until you're here all the time."

"Me too," he kissed her brow. "Hey, I didn't realise you took a load of tablets?"

"Tablets?" she faked a puzzled voice. He must have used the downstairs closet where she kept all her medication.

"I used the toilet and was looking for some mouthwash in the cabinet and spotted them all." His frown said everything, "What the hell do you take all those for?"

"I don't, they're old," she said knowing that Max's whole ethos was fitness and health, "I must get my housekeeper to have a clear-out. They were prescribed for me . . . during a difficult patch in my marriage. I never actually took them for long anyway. You know doctors, they have a prescription ready before you take a seat. And by all accounts, they make a lot of money out of prescription drugs. They gave me all sorts at the time as I was feeling down. All I take now are tablets if I get a headache or stomach cramps."

"That's a relief. I understand if people have to take them for a specific condition, but I hate all these random tablets that promise to make you feel better. It's all a load of rubbish. Unfortunately so many people fall for it."

"I know. I try really hard to keep away from doctors now."

"Me too. Nothing but tests and trouble if you visit a medic. I'm glad you don't take all that crap, I'd be worried about you if you did."

"Yeah, I'd be worried too. It was good to have them when I needed them, but thankfully not anymore." She needed to get off the tablet conversation, "Do you fancy a shower with me?"

"Is the Pope Catholic?" he said flinging away the throw to expose his fit virile body.

She took his hand, loving their nakedness as they made their way up the huge spiral stairs to the master bedroom with the ensuite luxury power shower they could sit in and take pleasure in the multiple massage jets.

He was right. All that medication was crap. She shouldn't be taking it. He was all the medication she needed. From now on she wasn't going to take another single tablet.

She was going to bin the whole lot, first thing in the morning.

Chapter 21

Claire

Max had texted to say he would be late, so once again they'd eaten dinner without him.

"We'll miss you, won't we, Freddy?" Claire said after her mother had insisted over dinner she was ready to go home.

"Yeah, can't you stay a bit longer, Grandma?" her son pleaded.

"No, darling, I can't. I need to get back to my own home. Grandma wants to see her friends and go to all the clubs, like bridge and my swimming classes. And you need your house back, you can't have me here forever."

"But we like you being here with us, don't we, Mummy?"

Claire stood up to remove the plates from the table. "Yes, we love having Grandma here, but it's right she goes home now she's ready. We can visit."

"Who will look after me when you go to choir?"

"Daddy will."

"But he's never here."

"That's because Grandma's been here so he's been working. But he'll come home earlier on choir night."

"Can I come and stay with you, like before," he looked eagerly at his grandma.

"Yes, of course you can. How about at half-term you come for a couple of days, what do you think, Mummy?"

"As long as your grandma's well, then I don't see why not. Right, custard or ice cream with your apple pie?"

"Ice cream please!" her son said before his attention was diverted to the patio doors, "Hey look, Adam's coming."

Claire's heart rate accelerated. She moved towards the door, which was open slightly and widened it, "I didn't realise you were still working, it's late for you, isn't it?"

He smiled that lopsided grin of his she found quite charming, "Yeah, I wanted to do a bit extra as I can't come tomorrow. I have an appointment," he looked a bit sheepish, as if he needed permission to have some time off, "if that's okay?"

"Of course it is." She felt the need to offer him something after his long day, but wondered if he'd say no. He could well have a date or something. "Would you like some apple pie before you go?"

"Mummy makes the best apple pie in the world," Freddy said.

"Well, if it's the best in the world, how could I refuse?" His grin made her feel ridiculously girly, which in turn made her cheeks heat up. "I'll eat it here on the patio if that's okay?"

Now she was embarrassed for a different reason, irritated with Max yet again for saying Adam couldn't be in the house and to keep him away from Freddy. It completely backfired though when Freddy asked, "Can I have mine outside with Adam?"

He got down from the table and rushed towards the door capitalising on her silence as a yes. Her mum got up too, "It's such a lovely evening, why don't we all have our dessert and coffee outside?"

"Good idea, Mum, you go ahead, I'll see to it."

Claire took a tray with cups and a cafetiere outside and left her mother playing hostess while she dished up the apple pie and ice cream. She knew her baking was good, she'd had the perfect teacher, her mother, and she welcomed the praise from Adam as he scooped up a mouthful, "Mmmm, Freddy, you're dead right, this *is* the best apple pie in the world."

And now she was blushing again. How embarrassing.

"Ah, that's because I had an excellent teacher sitting right next to you," she said quickly, trying to deflect from any further praise.

Her mum was like a fluffed-up peacock loving the reference to her, "Well, you've far surpassed me with the delights you conjure up. I'm more a basic old-fashioned cook, unlike you. You can turn your hand to anything." She turned her attention to Adam, "Can you cook, Adam?"

"I get by. I used to like to dabble a bit," he hesitated, no chance of cooking where he'd been the last few years, "but since I've been here in Sandbanks, I make do with basic stuff and my desserts consist of yoghurt or chocolate, so tonight has been a real treat for me."

"So you live alone?" her mum asked, forgetting she'd been told he did.

"Yes."

"Can he take some home, Mummy, for later?" Freddy asked eagerly, clearly embarrassing Adam by the look on his face.

"Sure he can, sweetheart," she smiled reassuringly at Adam and her eyes were drawn to his mouth as he wiped it with a napkin. She liked his mouth, his full lips . . . and those enchanting green eyes, and his physique. Fantasising over him like a lovesick teenager was the cue she needed to clear the plates. But she couldn't resist watching from the window as Adam talked to her mum and Freddy. Her tummy dipped at the cosiness of it. She knew it should have been Max sat out there, but right now she was pleased it was Adam. She made sure the piece of pie she cut for him was a generous portion, wrapped it carefully in foil and sealed it in a plastic container.

She returned to the patio with a warm feeling she wasn't quite used to. "Here you go."

"Thanks very much," Adam said, "I'll devour this later."

She had to turn away when he licked his lips.

"Is it about time for this young man's homework?" her mum said and Claire was glad of the distraction. "I think he might benefit from an early night too, he can't stop yawning."

"It's 'cause I'm full up," Freddy scowled, "Mrs Rogers says when you get a full tummy, you get tired."

"That's right," Claire said, "Did she explain why?"

"Yeah. She said it's because we need more blood to digest the food we've eaten, so for a short while, there's less blood for the brain. That's why we yawn."

"Well done, sweetheart. But Grandma's right," Claire glanced at her watch, "it might be a good idea to crack on with your homework and have your bath right now as we are a bit late."

Adam shuffled in his chair, "I should be making a move, too. Thank you . . ."

"Don't dash off," her mum interrupted, "if you've nothing to rush home to. Stay and have another drink." She turned to Freddy, "Come on then, sweetheart, say goodbye to Adam."

"Bye," Freddy smiled, "will you come the day after tomorrow?"

"Yep," he said looking slightly amused that Freddy had remembered he wouldn't be there the following day. She ought to tell him Freddy had a memory like an elephant's.

"I'll see Adam off and I'll be in shortly," Claire said and watched him go inside with her mum. She pulled a face, "Sorry for Mum asking about your living arrangements, she can be a bit nosey."

"Not at all, it's no secret. I wasn't sure if she knew I'd just come out of prison, that's all. And I didn't want to say anything in front of Freddy," he tilted his head, "I'm sure he doesn't know?"

"No, he doesn't. Mum does. I don't want it to be a problem though. You don't have to feel you've got to hide it or anything." She injected some sympathy into her voice, "It must have been an awful time for you?"

"It was, but it is what it is, thankfully it's all behind me now. I'm keen to turn the page really."

"Yeah, I'm sure." His handsome face darkened slightly, so she quickly changed the subject, "You're doing a terrific job with the gardens, I was saying to Max we're lucky to have you."

"Thanks. I'm hoping your husband will give me a reference once the work's complete."

"Oh, I'm sure he will," she wasn't sure at all, but she'd do one if Max wouldn't. "Are you hoping to continue to do other houses in this area?"

"Not necessarily round here. I'll probably move on. It was good of my dad to sort this job out so I could start to rebuild my life, but I'm not sure around here's right for me."

"That's a shame as there are plenty of people requiring gardeners I would have thought. Once you got established, you'd never be short of work."

He winced, "I'm not sure they'd employ a convicted criminal to do their gardens."

"They might . . . we did."

"Yeah, but I'm guessing that's more down to you than your husband?"

"No, to be perfectly honest, it was more your father asking Max."

He nodded knowingly, "And I bet I'm right in thinking he wasn't that keen? I'm guessing you had a hand in it, to which I am truly grateful by the way. I certainly owe you one for giving me the opportunity."

"Nonsense, you don't owe me anything. You're doing a great job. Anyway, Freddy tells me you play guitar and can sing, is that right?"

He raised his eyebrows, "Has he now? I did used to be in a band in a previous life. Now I just sing for pleasure, just me and my guitar, with no audience. I like it, it's therapeutic."

"Me too. I love singing. I've started going to a local choir on a Wednesday night," she pondered for a second, "you should come. They're desperate for male singers to balance the females."

His eyes crinkled at the edges when he grinned, making him more attractive, if that was possible. "I'm not sure my voice is fit for a choir, to be honest."

"I'm not sure mine is either, but I still go. They are a really nice, jolly group, it's very relaxed. They go to the pub afterwards."

"Ah, it gets more promising by the minute," he said, "that sounds good. Do you go to the pub . . . with them?"

She shook her head, "No."

"Why?"

"Not sure really, I guess I don't know them that well, I'd feel a bit like the odd one out."

"You're a sociable person, you should go."

"Maybe you're right, I should really. I might this Wednesday, it's Mum's last week here so I haven't got to rush back."

"Good for you. Right, on that note," he rolled his eyes, "pardon the pun, I'd better be going." He picked up the apple pie container and carefully placed it in his rucksack. "Thank you again for this," he stood up, "Freddy wasn't wrong. You do make the best apple pie."

Yes, and you're going to devour it later.

Her mouth watered at the thought.

"Enjoy," she said.

"Oh, I will," he flung his rucksack over his shoulder, "don't forget I'm not here tomorrow."

"Yep, got it. Goodnight."

"Goodnight, Claire."

She watched him walk away. He'd used her Christian name, which gave her a warm tingly feeling deep within her. It was nice.

It reminded her that she hadn't tingled for a long, long time.

Chapter 22

Claire

She pulled up outside her mother's house in Southbourne, applied the handbrake and cut the ignition. "Here we are, Mum, home sweet home."

Her mum smiled lovingly at her as she took off her seatbelt, "Thank you, love, for bringing me. I'm glad the consultant said I can drive now, I won't have to be relying on you anymore to ferry me around."

"Oh, yes, I must check your car before I go to make sure it's okay. You go in, and I'll bring your suitcase."

Claire made her way towards the boot to retrieve the suitcase and watched as her mother steadily made her way down the drive. It was a relief to see her mobility was nearly normal and she was walking more confidently. She'd have never let her come home if that wasn't the case.

She reached for the case and put it on the pavement before closing the boot – intending to come back for the grocery shopping they'd done earlier. There was plenty of time to settle her mum in before she had to leave to pick Freddy up. As she turned to follow her mother down the drive, a feeling of déjà vu spread through her as she caught sight of a car parked further down the road. It was a Nissan Juke, virtually the same as the car her father used to drive, red in colour with a black roof. She cast an eye on the number plate which was different to her dad's car they'd sold after he died, but it unnerved her as it wasn't the first time she'd seen that particular car. The previous week she'd seen it near the school gates and a second time when she'd come out of choir practice. Now she was seeing it a third time near her mother's house, it felt almost creepy. If it wasn't so distinctive, she wouldn't have even noticed it.

She carried on into the house, wheeling the suitcase, "Just leave this here, Mum, I'll take it upstairs when I've brought the groceries in. Oh, good, you've got the kettle on. I'll be back in a second."

As she reached her car for the Waitrose bags of shopping, she glanced again at the Nissan to see if anyone was inside, but she couldn't tell due to the tinted windows. It puzzled her as to why she'd seen it three times in succession. She wished she had the nerve to go over and see if anyone was sat behind the wheel and if so, challenge them. But they'd think she was pretty odd peering inside their car. And if there was someone inside, what could she say, 'Excuse me, I've noticed you going to the same places I do, why is that?' They'd think she was completely crackers.

She grabbed the shopping bags and returned to the house. By the time she took her mother's suitcase upstairs to her bedroom to empty it, she checked again from the front window but the car had disappeared. She took a deep breath in and tried to dismiss it, but her anxiety levels were rising again as she made her way downstairs.

Her mother prepared a sandwich for them both and they chatted about mundane stuff over a coffee in the cosy lounge. It wasn't the house she'd grown up in, her parents had bought the house five years earlier when they decided to downsize which had turned out to be a blessing with her father's sudden death. She doubted she'd have got her mother to leave the family home had she still been there, because of the attachment and memories of her father.

"Now you're going to be okay, aren't you?" Claire asked for the twentieth time since the previous day. Her mother had been fiercely independent since her father's death so she knew she'd be perfectly alright.

"Of course I will. I've got Sue and Maureen coming round tonight. They're bringing homemade food so I don't have to prepare anything. Then I'll have an early night I think."

"Early night with Sue and Maureen," Claire scoffed, 'it's me you're talking to. Don't forget I know them both well."

"You could be right," her mother grinned, "but I am looking forward to it. I've missed them. And all the other stuff I do. I am grateful for all you've done, love, but I do need to get back to normal."

"I know you do. And I do know deep down you'll be fine, I'm just checking. Worry seems to be my middle name at the moment."

Her mother took a sip of her coffee, "Well that leads nicely on to something I wanted to mention to you," she smiled lovingly, "I've been a bit concerned as I don't think you've quite been yourself lately."

"In what way?"

"I don't know really, I've just sensed something isn't quite right. I've been loath to say anything before, what with the stroke and staying at your house."

"I'm fine, Mum, honestly. Nothing for you to worry about, anyway."

"Now then, you know better than anyone as a mum we never stop worrying. What is it?"

Claire shrugged. She really didn't want to burden her mum, but she'd hit the nail on the head. Something wasn't quite right.

"It all started a few weeks ago. I got an overwhelming

feeling something awful was going to happen. The day you came home from hospital, actually. It's never really gone away. I can only describe it as a sort of darkness, and I feel jittery, as if someone is going to knock on the door with some bad news."

Her mum moved from the armchair and sat down next to her on the settee. She took her hand. "I think we've had our share of bad luck with your dad and then my stroke, we're due a reprieve now, I reckon."

Claire tried to stifle the tears, she swallowed a couple of times, but once her dad was mentioned, they rolled down her cheeks and her mother took her into her arms and held her tightly. "Come on, love, you're alright, I'm here."

Claire sobbed, and while she did so, she felt her mum crying too. Maybe not quite as wretched as her blubbering though. She sobbed for her dad so cruelly taken, for her husband who seemed more interested in work than her, for her dear mother returning home as she was going to miss her, and the simmering attraction to Adam which she knew wasn't right.

In her mother's embrace, she felt almost like a child again, savouring the safe and secure feeling wrapped in the arms that had always loved her. She let it all out, not being able to stop even if she wanted to. Eventually her sobs subsided and her mother reached for the box of tissues. They each took a tissue and blew their noses simultaneously.

"What are we like," Claire sniffed, "I'm supposed to be getting you settled, and here we are, both blubbering away."

"We needed it," her mum reassured, "it's still raw for us. Your dad was a giant of a man, and so dominant in your life. I know you have Max and Freddy, but I also know you were the apple of your dad's eye and you must miss him."

"I do. I try not to dwell on it too much, but I really do miss him, Mum, and I know it must be ten times harder for you."

"It doesn't get any easier, that's for sure, especially when I was admitted to hospital after my stroke. It was the first time anything significant had happened since he died. I missed so much him sorting everything for me. That was your dad, wasn't it? He got stuff done while others were thinking about it."

"Yes, that was him. Everyone says it gets easier, I think it gets harder as time goes on."

"Me too, love. But one thing I do know is, he'd be ever so proud of us. I think we're coping marvellously in our own way, and I don't know what I'd have done without you these last few weeks, you've really taken care of me."

"Course I have. You're my mum and I love you. I'll always look after you the best I can."

"You're a good girl and I love you too, very much. Now don't get cross," she gently warned and Claire knew she wouldn't like what was coming, "but I need to just say this. I'm not sure you're getting enough support from Max. It's still early days since your dad died, and I can't help thinking he should be making more of an effort rather than spending all those endless hours at work. I know," she held up her hand, "before you say anything, it's business, he has to put the hours in, but they're crazy hours. Something isn't right Claire. Surely you can see that?"

"I do see it," she reluctantly agreed, "and I've tried everything. It's getting to the point I'm having more conversations with Adam than with Max. Even Freddy spends more time with Adam as Max is never there."

Her mother raised her eyebrows, "And you've explained to Max how you're feeling?"

"Yes. He just dismisses it. He's determined to expand the business so it's keeping him busy. I don't want to at all, I think it's big enough, but he's not taking what I want into consideration. He just bulldozes along, doing everything he wants to do."

"Have you any idea how long he's going to be working all these hours? Has he said?"

"No, just that he has to do them. It's not just that though, it's other stuff too. He's pressurising me into taking Freddy to do practice papers for the eleven plus, which I don't want to do, and Freddy certainly doesn't. He's not interested in going to the grammar school. I don't think he's bright enough anyway."

"Well I've never believed in the eleven plus anyway, but you did take the exam when you were that age. Maybe in fairness to Max, you should let Freddy take it. That way at least you've tried."

"But he wants him to do the practice papers. I don't think that's right."

"And you've told him that?"

"Of course I have. He just won't listen. If I'm honest, he's not listening to anything I say these days."

"Then you need to spell it out for him. Tell him again how you're feeling until he does take notice. Only you can do that."

"I've tried, Mum, honestly. I'm getting to the point I just can't be bothered anymore." She took a deep breath and carried on. "He's now on about booking a holiday for us all at Christmas. And he's inviting you too by all accounts. I know him, it's all to appease me, as if I'm some sort of child complaining and he has to dangle an incentive to shut me up."

"That sounds like something to look forward to?" Her mum raised her eyebrows, "He doesn't have to invite me, though. Maybe it would be better just the three of you on your own?"

"We'll have to see. It's nothing definite but that's the latest thing he's come up with to deflect from the hours he's working and what he sees as the grief I give him."

"You have every right to question him. I know, how about me having Freddy so you can get away for a short break together? That might do the two of you some good."

"Maybe. I can mention that to him." She sighed, "It's probably not all him in fairness. He does need the cut and thrust of business to thrive, he's always been the same. I just expected once the house was done he'd be doing less not more."

"I think you should talk to him about a little break away," her mum smiled kindly; "it's amazing what a change of scenery can do. At home we get tired with the humdrum of routine, so yes, maybe start looking for a short break somewhere."

"Yeah, maybe I will."

"Is it just the hours Max is working and those eleven plus papers, there's nothing else bothering you, is there?"

"Not really, although," she hesitated, was it worth telling her? "You know Dad's car we sold," her mum nodded, "well, I've spotted one exactly the same three times now, parked near me. It's almost as if I'm being followed."

"Being followed," her mum's eyes narrowed, "why would anyone be following you?"

"I don't know. It sounds daft now I'm saying it. But the car is unusual in red with a black roof."

"Yes, love, but there are plenty of them around."

"I know. But then there's the other thing, the fence being knocked down. Adam said he thought someone might have been watching the house. It unnerved me thinking someone might have binoculars and spying on us."

"And he also said it was probably teenagers."

"But there were cigarette butts."

"Yes, well, teenagers do smoke, you know. Listen, I'm sure it's just a coincidence that the red and black car has been in your vicinity. Either that or," she looked over her shoulder playfully to indicate someone was watching, "Max has paid someone to follow you. Maybe he thinks something is going on with you and dishy Adam."

Claire laughed out loud, "Don't be daft, Max knows I'd never do anything like that."

"Forget about it then. It's nothing, darling, I'm sure of it. Just an overactive imagination as you've got a lot on."

Her mum looked at her watch, "Now then, shall I put the kettle on for a quick one before you go for Freddy?"

"Yeah, that'd be nice. I'll just go and check your car while you're doing that and make sure it starts."

Claire went into the garage. Her mum's car fired up as soon as she turned the ignition so she let it run for a few minutes. It was reassuring her mum was okay, she'd miss her being around but it was nice for her to be back in her own home. She was going to watch carefully to see if Max was a bit more attentive now they'd got the house to themselves. She had to acknowledge maybe part of the reason Max was not rushing home each evening was because her mum was there.

"It's fine," Claire said placing the keys back in the kitchen drawer, "it'll need a decent run though."

"That's good, I thought it would be. I'll get it out in the next day or so, I could do with a trip to the garden centre."

"You're sure you'll be okay going on your own?"

"Yes, course I'm sure," her mum placed their teas on the kitchen table.

Claire took a seat and reached for a biscuit, "Don't forget, ring me if there is anything. I'll be cross if you don't."

"I will, but honestly love, I'll be perfectly okay. What are you doing the rest of the week, anyway?"

"Not much really, just choir on Wednesday."

"What about Pippa, are you seeing her?"

"Nothing definite. I did suggest we went out for lunch, but she doesn't seem keen."

"Do you think it's because of the wheelchair?"

"I don't think so. It sounds like she does all sorts, so I'm not sure why she won't meet outside of her home. She just seems happy enough with me going there."

"That is odd. She drives, doesn't she, you said?"

"Yes, she drives all over the place. She was going off to Australia so she's definitely not housebound by any means. Anyway, her friend will be here soon and she's staying for a month so I don't suppose I'll see so much of her."

"Oh, I'm sure you will. She'll want you to meet her friend I would think."

"Maybe, who knows, we'll have to see. Right, I think I'd better be making a move."

Her mum walked with her to the gate and she savoured another reassuring hug from her, "I'll text you later, thanks Mum. All my love."

She started the car and waved goodbye as she pulled away. The good cry and support from her mum had lifted her spirits. She passed the empty place where the red Nissan had been parked. Her mother was right. Who would possibly be watching her? A woman with a school-aged child, happily married to her husband.

One thing was certain, if anyone was watching her, they'd soon get fed up.

Chapter 23

Annabelle

She closed her office door behind her and placed her designer handbag on the desk. *How odd?* Coming through the spa foyer towards the lift to make her way up to the office, she'd spotted her therapist, George Grey. A minute later and she'd have missed him. What on earth was he doing there? She hadn't got him down as the spa type at all. She checked her watch. Surely he would be in his office about now, boring some other poor victim to death? He knew she'd seen him, that's why he ducked behind one of the ornate pillars and stayed hidden. Not that she'd have attempted to approach him. No way – she saw enough of him in his office.

She took a seat at her desk trying to work out why he was there. *Of all the spas in all the world* sprang to mind. Why her spa? Surely it wasn't right to be visiting a client's place of work, even if it was recreational. She picked up the internal phone and pressed for reception.

"Good morning, Sally, it's Annabelle. Can you check how long Mr George Grey is booked in for please?"

"Yes, just bear with me, the computer's slow this morning. It's lovely out isn't it. I hope it stays like this until the weekend, I've got a barbecue planned for Saturday."

"Fingers crossed for you then."

Get on with it, woman

"Ah, here we go. Er . . . I can't see anyone of that name booked in. Do you want me to check for next week?"

"What about as a day guest. Maybe he's just booked in for that?"

"Nope, I can't see anybody of that name."

It didn't add up. She'd definitely seen him lurking around when she'd arrived.

"Email me a list of all the men you have here today please would you?"

"Yes, of course."

"Thank you, Sally." She cut the call. George Grey was definitely in the spa this morning. She wouldn't have believed it if she hadn't seen it with her own eyes. The question was, what was he up to? Was he spying on her?

The second the email arrived, she checked the men that were registered. No George Grey, just as she'd been told. He must be using an alias. Maybe he was there with someone he shouldn't be?

A tap on the door made her look up from the PC.

"Morning," she gave Anthony a welcoming smile as he entered. He looked slightly dishevelled and must have cut himself shaving as he'd got an unsightly nick on the left side of his jaw. Most unlike him, Anthony was usually pristine. He looked tired. By now he'd realise the person he thought he was in love with, was not genuine. Fiona-the-cleaner would be long gone thanks to Yegor, who had delivered, as always.

She feigned concern, "Are you okay?"

He took a deep breath in. "Not really."

"What is it?" She quickly stood up and went round the desk to him. "What on earth's the matter, you look ill?" She took him by the arm and led him to the comfortable seating area in her office overlooking stunning views of the countryside.

"Can I get you something to drink?"

"No, I'm fine."

"Please tell me what's wrong," she probed.

"It's Fiona, she's gone."

"Gone? Gone where?"

"I don't know, she's just gone."

"What, gone because your relationship is over, or gone as in disappeared?"

"Gone as in disappeared."

She put her hand to her mouth, faking surprise. "And she's not explained why?"

"No." His expression oozed pain, "And that's the most puzzling thing, she's just upped and gone. She must have got a new phone as her number is dead, and everything has disappeared from social media."

"How awful," she reached for his hand, "it's bad enough she's gone but to not offer an explanation."

"I don't get it," he shook his head, "we were so good together. I never thought I'd find anyone after Catherine. But then Fiona came along and I fell in love with her. I can't believe she's just disappeared. Why would she do that?"

She injected some sympathy into her voice, "Maybe she just got cold feet with things rushing along?"

"She wouldn't have changed all her details though, would she? That smacks of someone wanting to disappear completely."

"I guess so. I'm so sorry, Anthony, you of all people don't deserve this. Is there anything I can do?"

"No, there's nothing anyone can do. I've just got to accept it. If only she'd have spoken to me. If things were moving along too fast, we could have slowed it down." He almost sobbed his last sentence, "I can't believe I'm not going to see her again. We were made for each other."

She took him in her arms and held him tightly. She hated what she'd done to cause him so much angst, but she couldn't have him marrying Fiona. She needed him for her and Max's plans to work when they merged their companies. The last thing she wanted was Anthony heading off into the sunset with some random woman. She wanted him close, where she'd always had him, courtesy of the generosity of her father. And she was determined Max was going to be more husband and father, rather than working every day managing their company. That job had Anthony's name on it.

"I know," she injected some positivity into her voice, "why don't we go out for some lunch rather than eating here today? It'd be nice to get away for a couple of hours at least."

His face looked pained, "I'm not sure I'd be very good company to be honest."

"Nonsense, it'll do us both good to have a little break. I'm not taking no for an answer. I'll get Angela to book us in at the Coach House at twelve. We won't be more than an hour or two, she can ring us if she needs either of us."

Anthony loved talking business, so that's what she intended to do for the next couple of hours. She'd also discreetly explain how in the long term he might be better off without Fiona. The most important thing was she'd formulated her plan, and Yegor had made it happen. And as a result of his success, he'd been the recipient of a more than generous payment.

To have Anthony on his own again was worth every single penny.

Chapter 24

Annabelle

She'd invited her friend Della to the spa for the day. They were sitting on the outside terrace enjoying the chance to catch-up. It was a beautiful day and the views over the lake were calm and restful. Annabelle was hoping Max might call her that afternoon so she'd have to leave. Much as she loved her friend, she'd much rather be with Max if she got the opportunity.

Della got up from the table, "Excuse me while I go to the ladies'. It's all this water I'm drinking," she did air quotes with her fingers, "to flush out the toxins."

Annabelle smiled, "Shall I get us another coffee or are you ready for something stronger?"

"Oh, I think something stronger, don't you?"

"Definitely. I'll get us a prosecco." She watched Della walk away. Of late she'd been seeing a lot of Max and she'd missed her dear friend. She loved spending time with Della and had a purpose for inviting her today. It was to discuss her wedding.

While they'd both enjoyed a therapeutic treatment courtesy of the therapists, it hadn't had the usual calming effect on her. Della felt totally refreshed she'd said, whereas Annabelle felt tired and edgy. But she knew exactly why. During the night she'd rolled over in her sleep and a noise woke her. It sounded like someone coughing to get her attention and when she lifted her eye mask, she got the shock of her life. George Grey, her therapist, was sat in her bedroom in a chair by the window watching her. He must have physically turned the chair towards the bed as it normally faced outwards to the view from the window.

He didn't have his usual therapist's hat on though, he was fidgety and seemed nervous. His voice was barely a whisper – clearly he knew it was totally inappropriate to be in her bedroom in the middle of the night. But what he'd said quietly was potentially life changing and accelerated her heart rate. He explained a way to get rid of clingy and her whining son once and for all. It would mean setting fire to their house at Sandbanks and they'd both die from smoke inhalation. He was clear he couldn't actually do anything himself, but knew a way to do it that was foolproof so it would look accidental. She didn't need any thinking time – his idea was perfect. She explained about Yegor and how she could rely on him to help. She wasn't confident Yegor would actually get involved in arson, but he'd know someone who would. Yegor had proven over the years he knew a man for everything and she never asked questions. And as far as she was concerned, she was content not knowing.

Even though she'd been working on her own plan to get rid of clingy, George Grey's idea was much better than hers. The end result excited her. There'd be no maintenance to pay in the future for her and the kid, and she'd have no hold on the spa businesses when they merged them. They could easily rebuild the burned down house in Sandbanks that Max loved so much. In fact, that was rather appealing. There was no way was she ever living in their house even if Max did manage to get it as part of the divorce which she very much doubted, but if it had all been demolished, she'd engage her own designer and it could be rebuilt to her and Max's specifications. It could be a weekend retreat for them both especially when their children arrived. The thought of getting rid of clingy gained momentum in her mind. Although much as it thrilled her, she was cautious. If the house was set on fire, it would have to be when Max was definitely not around. She'd be fearful he got injured, or worse still, died. There was no way she could contemplate a future without him in it – she'd rather be dead herself.

Della returned from the bathroom and took her seat. "Is this for me?" she asked picking up her prosecco, "Cheers."

"Cheers. Drink up, there's plenty more where that came from. I've told the chef we'll eat later when the madness has died down."

"Sounds good to me. I'm not that hungry to be honest."

"Me neither, we'll have something though even if it's a salad." Annabelle took a sip of her drink, "I might have to dash off a bit later on . . . after we've eaten," she tentatively added.

"Oh no. Why? I was looking forward to a good old catch up. Where have you got to go? What's more important than spending time with your oldest friend?"

"Nothing's more important," she pulled a face, "I'm just waiting for a call and if I get it, I'll have to go."

"That sounds mysterious . . . is it a bloke?"

Annabelle grinned, "Right first time!"

"I see." Della widened her eyes, "And judging by the look on your face, he's someone special, am I right?"

"Yes," she grinned eager to share her news, "I'm getting married again."

"What? I can't believe it. Who? When? Come on, you're not going anywhere till you spill the beans. I want everything, warts and all."

Annabelle grinned. "His name is Max Maric and he owns a spa also, Maric Leisure, don't know if you've heard of it?"

"Yeah, course I have. Isn't he a bit of a rival though?"

"He is. I've known him for ages from a distance, you know at events, that sort of thing. Anyway, one night I was out at a function and he bumped into me and spilled red wine all over my dress. As you can imagine it made an almighty mess. I was furious I can tell you. He was awkward and really apologetic, like over the top apologetic, and offered to drive me home to change. I would have normally called my driver but I was so pissed with him I thought, why not. So he took me home, I changed my dress, but we never made it back to the function."

"What, you had sex?"

"Yep, eventually we did. We talked a bit at first though, and he did offer to buy me a new dress, which I thought was sweet. But there was a real lustful attraction between us and it seemed the most natural thing to give in to it."

"Crikey, that's bloody quick, even for you."

"I know!" she laughed, "But do you know what, after the first frantic time, we steadied down and he is the most fantastic lover. You know the type, he knows how to press all the right buttons. And he has stacks of stamina, I've never been with anyone that can last like he can."

"Fantastic," Della cooed, "has he got a brother?"

"Well if he has, he's not told me. Anyway, he stayed the night, and it went from there. Just like those whirlwind romances you read about."

"But he wants to marry you," Della's face was incredulous which was understandable as it had all been quick, "and you've said yes?"

"Absolutely. I can't wait. It just feels right between us. I want to spend the rest of my life with him and, I'm glad you're sitting down," she paused purposely, "I'm going to have children with him."

"Holy shit. I can't believe I'm hearing this. Annabelle Claybourne, business woman of the year, is swapping that for a life of domesticity. You must have it bad."

"I have. Really bad if I'm honest. That's why I wanted to see you today. I'm not bothering with all that bridesmaid crap this time, but I do want you to be there with me, by my side. You as my friend, and I've got to ask Anthony to give me away. So he'll be my . . . wing man, and you my lady-in-waiting. Please say yes, I do so want you to be part of my day."

"Course I will," she replied enthusiastically, and then hesitated, "I didn't bring you any luck last time, though."

"That was different," Annabelle said, "it was all rushed and I wasn't really in love with Mark, it was more in lust."

"And this isn't the same? Sorry for asking, but I do worry about you."

"Don't. I'm the happiest I've ever been. Wait till you meet him, you'll soon see why."

"Oh, I can't wait. Have you any idea when you'll get married?"

"It's all sorted. 6th December."

"What, this year?" Della widened her eyes.

"Yep."

"Crikey, you don't waste any time."

"There's just one snag, though."

Della tilted her head, "Oh God, what?"

"He's still married. He's separated though so we have to wait for the divorce to come through."

"How recently separated?" she frowned, "I'd hate you to be some sort of rebound fling. You know what blokes are like, they can't stand being on their own."

"No," Annabelle dismissed confidently, "it's nothing like that. He loves me. His marriage was one of those that they fell into after college and married as it was expected."

"Any kids?"

"One, a boy."

"Really?" Her eyes narrowed, "I can't see you playing the stepmother somehow. I'd hate you to get stressed and poorly again."

"I won't. He'll be going to boarding school shortly anyway. And when he's home at school holidays, he'll see his mother, and on the days he does stuff with Max, I can do other things, like this with you. And remember, I'll have my own kids before long. Max wants a large family."

"Then I'm thrilled for you if this is what you want. Have you told him about . . . your past?"

"Yeah, course," she lied, "we don't have secrets."

"That's good then. Are you still seeing the psychiatrist and that boring therapist of yours?"

"God, yeah, but I'm hoping for not much longer. I've stopped my medication now and feel fine, so everything is good."

"Oh, Annabelle, that is great to hear. You've done amazingly well if you've been able to stop the medication. I'm really proud of you. And I can't wait to meet your Max. Is he terribly good looking?"

She grinned, "Just a bit. You'll see. I'll sort something out for us all to meet. Now tell me, how's things with you and Aaron. All still going okay?"

"Yeah, all good. He's hinting at moving in, but I'm not sure about that. I like him taking me out and away for weekends. If I let him move in though, that'll all stop. I'll be washing his socks and undies in no time."

Annabelle tutted, "You've never washed anyone's socks and undies in your life."

"Well, my housekeeper then. It's still the same. I don't want men bits messing up my tidy house."

"What are you like . . ." the vibration of her phone interrupted her. She glanced at the caller ID, it was Max. "Excuse me a second while I take this."

"Hi, darling."

"Hello, beautiful. How's it going with your friend?"

"Great, we're going for some lunch shortly. How are you doing, any chance of getting away later?"

"Every chance. I reckon in about a couple of hours, I can be at yours. That will give you time to have your lunch."

"That'd be perfect. Shall we say about three thirty?"

"Great. Will your friend not mind you dumping her for me?"

"Not at all," she grinned at Della who was hanging on to her every word, "I told her I might have to leave if you called. Della's self-sufficient. She'll just use the facilities until she's had enough. We had our treatments this morning."

"That's good then. Thank her from me."

"I will do. You'll get to meet her soon I hope. I can fix something up for us to go out to dinner with her and Aaron, her boyfriend."

"Sounds good. Not too soon though, I'm enjoying just us. Plenty of time later for others."

Her heartbeat went up a notch. "Yeah, you're right. Okay then, see you at the house around three thirty."

"Right, and don't whatever you do have dessert after lunch."

"And why not?" she knew where the conversation was going.

"Cause I'm going to give you dessert, and you'll enjoy that better."

She grinned, loving the way he made her feel. Any more of that talk and she'd ditch her friend right now.

"Sounds exciting. I can't wait. See you shortly, bye darling."

* * *

She was content lying next to him in her huge king bed, in the lovely state of being half asleep after their mammoth lovemaking session. She daren't move a muscle as she knew, if she shuffled an inch, he'd extract himself from her and leave to go home. Sadly, her contentment was short-lived,

"Annie," he whispered gently, "I've got to go." He pried her naked body away from him and swung himself out of the bed and headed for the ensuite. She hated him leaving her and she hated his clingy wife who was going to get to spend the whole night with him and wake up next to him in the morning.

He better not be having sex with her? Although it seemed that they were living more like friends under the same roof. Anyway, Max couldn't keep his hands off her so she knew he had more than enough sex with her to keep him satisfied. The thought that he might have sex with any other woman, ripped her insides to shreds. When he returned from the bathroom and pulled his trousers on, she couldn't resist asking, "What excuse do you use when you arrive home so late?"

"Claire's usually in bed," he shrugged, putting on his shirt.

Clingy's Christian name rolling off his tongue, thumped her hard. "So she doesn't wait up for you coming home?"

He started to do up his shirt buttons. "No, she'll either be reading or asleep."

"Doesn't she ever want sex?" she held her breath waiting for him to answer. She'd die if he said yes.

His face was puzzled, and he deflected from answering directly, "What's made you ask that?"

"I don't know. I guess I'm just wondering."

The bed dipped as he sat back down and leaned towards her. "You give me everything I need," he kissed her lovingly and stroked a stray curl of hair from her forehead, "what man could ever want any more than making love with you?"

She kissed him back, loving his tenderness. "I love you, Max Maric, hurry back."

"I will." He kissed her forehead, "Now you stay there and I'll let myself out." He made his way to the bedroom door and paused, "Hey, do you set the alarm after I've gone?"

"No, I don't tend to bother."

"You should you know . . . a woman on her own and all that."

"Yes, I know I should. Thanks for reminding me, officer," she smiled, "drive carefully. Chat tomorrow?"

"Yep, definitely. Sleep tight, beautiful."

It wasn't until she snuggled down to sleep that she realised he hadn't actually answered her question as to whether he still had sex with clingy. The very thought of them in the same bed made her seethe.

The sooner clingy and the brat were gone, the better.

Chapter 25

Claire

Freddy had come home from school lethargic and with a sniffle. He hadn't eaten his tea so she'd insisted he went to bed early. He fell asleep almost immediately which indicated he wasn't well. Max had rung and said he'd be hosting clients after work so would be staying at the flat. So yet again she was feeling down, which seemed to be an emerging pattern lately. She should be used to it by now but it continued to hurt. Despite her objections, Max still wasn't putting her and Freddy first. Work was his priority which narked her, particularly right now when she was feeling vulnerable. She still hadn't been able to shrug off the feeling of doom that increasingly was occurring and wrapping itself around her.

She was bored, sitting at the kitchen table scrolling endlessly through Facebook and Instagram until Adam caught her eye approaching the house. It was ridiculously stupid but her heart gave a little flutter. She opened the bi-fold door. "Hi, Adam, you're late tonight."

"Yeah, I started to put down some top soil and I wanted to get it finished. It took longer than I thought. Is Freddy okay? I've missed him coming to say hello."

"I think he's starting with a cold so I've encouraged him to go to bed. He didn't argue so I know he's off colour. He was fast asleep almost as soon as his head touched the pillow."

"I thought it was odd I hadn't seen him. Maybe he just needs to sleep it off, then?"

"Yeah, I think so. Have you got to dash off or can I tempt you with a drink?"

"If you've got beer, I can be tempted," he said with a smile.

"Yep, I have that." She nodded to the outside seating, "Pull up a chair and I'll bring you one."

She filled a glass of water from the all singing and dancing dispenser Max had insisted they had installed despite her protests that tap water was fine, and retrieved a Bud from the fridge. She took a glass doubting whether Adam was a glass sort of man. It was a hot and sticky evening so the slight breeze was welcoming. She took a chair opposite with the table dividing them.

"Cheers," he said taking the beer from her. She was right, he ignored the glass and took a swig from the bottle.

"I hope I'm not keeping you from someone," she said praying that she wasn't. He was becoming her light against Max who was increasingly becoming her darkness, "I know you said you live alone. I never asked if you have a girl-friend?"

"Nope, no girlfriend, there's just me."

An inexplicable sense of relief flooded through her.

"In that case, I've got some sausage rolls I made earlier; you must take some with you."

He grinned, "If not having a girlfriend gets me sausage rolls, I'm not going to tell you when I do get one."

She smiled at his playfulness; it made his handsome face even more so.

"I always make far too many, so there's plenty. Freddy loves them in his lunch box. Anyway, you deserve a re-ward, you're doing a great job with the gardens, even Max is pleased."

"Is he?" He took another mouthful of his beer, "He never says much, so it's hard to gauge."

"Don't take any notice of his silence, I'm sure you've realised by now he'd soon be saying if he wasn't happy."

"Yeah, I get that. Is he still at work?"

"I'm afraid so."

"He works long hours, doesn't he?"

"Yes, he does. The idea was to work from home for part of the week and commuting in when necessary. That was the plan anyway, but it hasn't quite worked out like that. It was easier when we lived in London, even though he worked long hours, we saw more of him then."

"It must be hard. It's a shame he can't work from home, this house certainly beats any office I've ever seen."

"Thank you, it is rather nice, isn't it? I don't mean to complain, it's just it can get a bit lonely, as I don't know many people here yet."

"Yeah, tell me about it. Loneliness sucks."

"Sorry, it must be hard for you, too. And here's me boring you with my problems." She quickly changed the subject, "Where did you used to live before . . ?"

"Bournemouth. We bought a house near the seafront."

"How lovely. Have you still got it?"

He shook his head, "It was sold when I went inside."

"Oh, that's a shame. Bournemouth is lovely and quite a prestigious area to live in."

"Yeah, I liked it."

She sipped her drink not wanting to pry, but at the same time, she was desperate to know more about the 'we'? Where was she now? Obviously, she hadn't waited for him.

"Another beer?" she asked.

"Nah, I'm fine. I really should be making tracks."

"You're sure?"

He pulled a face, "I don't like to encroach on your time."

"You're not. I'll only end up going to bed and flicking through the channels on TV until I get tired."

"Alright, then, you've persuaded me, another beer would be great, as long as I'm not drinking on my own."

"Okay," she grinned, "now you've insisted." She nipped into the kitchen and got herself a glass of wine and him another beer.

"So, what next after this job?" she asked, sitting back down.

"That's the million-dollar question. For the first time in my life, I don't know."

"Well, there's no rush, you have another few weeks here. Max might keep you on." Why was she even saying that, there was no way that would happen, "But then again, I don't suppose there would be enough for full-time work, that's the only thing."

"Don't worry, I won't be hanging around. I'd like to do something similar to what I was doing before I went inside. I had my own design and landscaping business. It was only small but quite lucrative. It's hard though once you've got a conviction – the very word jail means people look twice at you, which isn't good if you're trying to get work."

"No, I'm sure. Could you try and resurrect the old business?"

"Not something I'd want to do really. Too many old memories." His eyes glazed over, as if he was thinking back. The silence between them stretched, she wanted to interject and find out more, but it seemed a bit crass to question him. He surprised her though when he spoke again and expanded, "It was a particularly happy time in my life. I'd just got my first home, and my dream job. Life was good."

"What changed?"

"New neighbours moved in next door." He paused again, as if considering whether to say any more. But he took a deep breath in, "To put a name on it, Pete Craven and his three sons."

"What did they do?"

"Everything to get us to move. My partner went from a confident young woman, to a blithering wreck. They persecuted us from dawn till dusk. They had an Alsatian dog, and that alone was enough to send you crazy. Its constant barking was a nightmare. But it wasn't just that, it was other stuff. You name it, we got it. A mouse through the letter box, dog crap, pizza deliveries we hadn't ordered, garden rubbish over the fence . . ." he shrugged, "I could go on but we'd be here all night. The only time we got any peace was if we went away, our home became a prison."

"Why would they do those things?"

"I now know they wanted the house themselves so they could knock through and make theirs into one large one. So it was a well thought out plan to get rid of us."

"Did you consider selling just to be able to get away from it all?"

"Often. But there was the stubborn part of me that wouldn't be driven out of my own home. And I didn't realise at the time they wanted to buy it, they never actually said that. They just relentlessly persecuted us. But when it eventually went up for sale, they purchased it, that's how I now know that had been their motive all along."

"How terrible for you and your partner having to live like that."

"Yeah, it was pretty bad. She sold it when I went to prison. They would be the last people she'd have sold to after everything that happened, but they got a family member to buy it and then I guess they sold it onto them. Lucy, my partner, gave it away for a song by all accounts," his expression darkened, "just like our relationship."

Her heart ached for him. What a terrible time he must have had.

"I am sorry." She tilted her head questioningly, "I take it there was no way back for you both after you came out of prison?"

"No, she wasn't prepared to wait. The time inside changed everything. She's American and went back to live in Chicago. I could never have gone over there with her once I had a criminal conviction anyway. And all her family were there."

"That's so sad, especially if you loved each other."

"Yeah, I thought so too. But if you break the law, you pay the price."

She couldn't resist, "What happened?" but instantly regretted it. She was being too personal. "Forget I said that, sorry, it's none of my business."

"It's okay," he shrugged, "you can read about it online. I got into an altercation with Pete Craven and knocked him down. Nine times out of ten, a bloke would get up and hit you back twice as hard. But he never got back up again. He hit his head and it killed him."

She couldn't help the gasp of breath at his words.

"I know," he said, "it's not an easy thing to live with."

"Surely that was an accident though? You didn't intend to kill him."

"No, but try telling a jury that. I had threatened previously I'd kill him, which was only in retaliation for something, but that statement goes a long way to prove intent."

"But they were just threats? We all issue them in the heat of the moment and don't really mean them."

"That's true although I did sometimes wish him dead, I think we both did. But no, I didn't intend to kill him. It just got out of hand. I'd come home from work, Lucy was upset as she'd been sunbathing in the garden and they'd been leering at her over the fence, shouting obscenities. I saw red and went round to his garden and we argued. He said something about Lucy needing a good seeing to, and I lashed out and hit him. I can still hear the prosecutor now, 'You did strike him first, Mr Bishop.' And he was absolutely right, I did. My barrister wasn't that brilliant really. Anyway, the long and the short of it is, I went to jail, served my time for manslaughter and here I am ... minus a girlfriend, minus a house, and minus any real prospects."

"That's awful," she felt genuine sympathy. It seemed to her that the court had been harsh. "I feel so sorry for you. What a terrible shame the way things have turned out. You've paid the price for what you've done though, so you need to turn the page now. You're doing a fantastic job here, and when you've finished, we'll recommend you to friends," she pulled a face, "not that we have loads round here, but Max is in that secret society your dad's in."

"Thanks," he smiled, I'd appreciate that. You're a kind woman. Max is lucky to have you."

Heat rushed to her face. "Can you tell him that next time you see him?" It was all she could manage. She was ridiculously pleased with the compliment he'd paid her.

He stared at her, as if he wanted to say more, but when he did speak, he changed the subject completely. "Anyway, on a lighter note before I go, how would you feel if I made a little garden patch for Freddy to plant some bits? It's a great way for children to learn. I used to love growing stuff at his age. There's a lovely area down by the outbuildings that gets plenty of sun."

"What a lovely idea, thank you, that's really kind of you to think of that. Freddy will love it. Max gets cross as he isn't the most academic boy, but he's ever so happy and I'm not that bothered. I want him to do well of course, but I'm not worried if he doesn't get a business degree either. Whatever he wants to do is fine by me."

"Too right. I think he is a bright boy, he's just bright at other things. He knows a lot about the weather he's learning at school. He's very knowledgeable for a kid his age."

"Do you think so?"

"Yeah, definitely. I originally wanted to be a primary school teacher and did a year at teacher training college so I know a bit about children's learning and I can see Freddy's like a sponge and takes in all I tell him."

"That's so reassuring to hear. I keep telling him to let you get on but he does love being around you. Now I know why if you had training to be a teacher. Why didn't you finish the training?"

"I realised I'd be much happier outdoors than stuck in a stuffy classroom and did a Landscape Design degree instead. So, with my half a teacher's hat on, Freddy is fine and he'll do well whatever he decides to do, I'm sure of it."

"I can't tell you how pleased I am to hear you say that. Thank you."

"Right on that note, I'd better be off." He stood up.

"Let me just get you those sausage rolls," she blustered off into the kitchen and wrapped eight sausage rolls in some foil and placed them in a Tupperware container. She went back outside and handed it to him. As he took it from her, her eyes were drawn to his hands as he placed it in his rucksack. They were hard-working hands, large just like her father's. She swallowed a lump forming in her throat.

He must have sensed it. "You okay?"

A breath caught in her throat, "Yeah, I'm fine. I lost my father a few months ago, and just lately I've been struggling a bit. The more time that passes, the more it hurts."

They stood on the patio, a short space separating them, but she felt drawn to him. He stood still, not moving from his spot. She could tell he wasn't sure what to do – whether to go or stay a little longer. He broke the silence, "I'm going to miss all your food when I do have to go."

"It's not for a while yet, though." A powerful yearning to keep him there and not let him leave, overwhelmed her. She swallowed to hold back the threatening tears. "I'm really sorry about what you've been through."

He nodded, and then surprised her by stepping forward. It seemed the most natural thing in the world to lean into him. He wrapped his huge arms around her slight frame and held her, his chin resting on her head. He was just being friendly, she told herself, it was only an innocent hug.

But for those few short seconds, with their arms wrapped around each other, it felt like so much more. The urge to stay exactly as they were, was intense. Something significant had shifted between them. But her feelings weren't appropriate. She needed to stop herself before things got out of hand.

"Hey," she pulled away from him, "you better get off before I get even more maudlin." It took an almighty effort to appear casual when deep inside she felt bereft. All she really wanted was to go back into his huge arms and stay there.

Adam's face looked strained but only for a split second before he quickly composed himself and moved away towards the chair. He picked up his rucksack and flung it over his shoulder, "Thanks for tonight . . . and the food."

"You're welcome. See you tomorrow."

"Will do. Night Claire."

He walked away and she stood on the spot and watched him go. She wanted to call him back and beg him to stay and spend more time with her. But she was being stupid. She reminded herself she was married and not the type to indulge in a casual affair. Especially with all she and Max and had gone through when he met someone. No, Adam wasn't for her. He was too young anyway. He needed someone his own age.

That said, she couldn't help thinking what a fool his girlfriend was for letting him go.

Chapter 26

Claire

"Am I ready now?" her son asked coming into the kitchen wearing his wellington boots. It was the weekend and Freddy was eager to get out in the garden with his dad who'd been outside since the crack of dawn. Max had been restless during the night and at six a.m. as the light shone through the blinds, he got out of bed and said he was going to do some gardening which was really odd considering they employed Adam. What was the matter with him, she had no idea, but she knew one thing, Max was a sleeper and the occasions when he couldn't sleep, something was bothering him. A chat was on the cards later to find out exactly what. But that morning she was happy to have two whole days to look forward to with her husband, and Freddy had his dad's attention for once. It made her light-of-heart as opposed to the anguish she'd been experiencing lately.

She smiled lovingly at Freddy, "Yes, you'll do. We'll have to get you some new welly-bobs, I think your feet have grown." She squatted down to fasten the zip on his jacket as it was early and chilly, and he was still getting over his recent cold. "Okay, go find Daddy and see if you can help."

"I'm going to show him my garden that Adam's helped me with."

Adam had patiently helped Freddy to cultivate a little

patch around the corner which wouldn't interfere with the main garden and planted some lettuces, carrots and peas. She'd completely forgotten to tell Max about it. That was another thing starting to irritate her. Their normal everyday chats as a family weren't happening because Max was hardly there.

Freddy paused at the door, "Are you coming to look too?" he asked eagerly. He was such a lovely little boy, always wanting praise and approval.

"Yes, I'll come, just let me sort out the breakfast dishes and I'll put my boots on and come and see."

She watched her son run down the garden. It would be nice for him to spend some time with his daddy. Max was neglecting his parenting role, as well as that of a husband. There was no doubt he loved her, but of late she couldn't deny something was missing between them. She needed to speak to him again about it. Maybe that was part of the suffocating darkness she kept experiencing?

She'd loaded the dishwasher, wiped down the surfaces and was just disinfecting the sink when a movement caught her eye. Freddy was running towards the kitchen with tears running down his cheeks. She pulled the door open.

"What's happened?" She looked into the garden trying to see Max, "Where's Daddy?"

"He's . . . he's dug up my garden," he sobbed, "and all the lettuces and carrots are gone."

"Why?" she couldn't believe what she was hearing, "Did he say?"

"He said . . . it was in the way," he sniffed, "but then said he didn't realise it was mine."

"Oh dear, it sounds like a bit of an accident. Let's dry your eyes and we can go and try and rescue it. Daddy wouldn't have done it on purpose." She reached for a tissue, "Come on, blow your nose and I'll come out with you and we'll see what we can do."

He blew his nose, "But we'd planted some lettuces," he blubbered "they've gone, Daddy's put them in a bin bag."

"Well, we can fish them out. Come on give your nose another blow and let's get you a drink."

She reached for a glass and filled it with water.

He gulped his water and her heart went out to him. What the hell had Max done that for?

"Come on then," she held out her hand, "let's go."

They headed off for the bottom of the garden. She should have told Max about it, she'd completely forgotten. But he should have used his head and realised that it was Freddy's little garden. Honestly, sometimes he was so thoughtless. No doubt he'd seen it and thought Adam was doing something and he didn't like it so dug it up. He could be so petty at times. One more thing to add to the conversation that evening, at the rate she was going, she'd have a list.

* * *

Claire came back into the lounge after settling Freddy to bed. Fortunately, they'd salvaged his garden and Max had replanted the seeds, so all was well on that front. They'd had quite a nice day in the garden, and, after lunch, Max had thrilled Freddy by taking them both out to the ice-cream parlour down the high street where they'd eaten a huge knickerbocker glory each. That evening though, there was still plenty to discuss and she wasn't looking forward to their conversation. Confronting Max always made her anxious because of his reaction. He never ever accepted he was to blame for anything. Sorry wasn't a word in his vocabulary and her spirits had taken a nose-dive since her optimism first thing that morning.

She reached for the glass of red wine he had ready for her on the coffee table but moved towards the armchair. She didn't want to be next to him on the sofa when she tackled him.

"He gets later and later," she sighed taking her seat. "Honestly, it's a million questions every night. It's only stalling, he's getting older and wants to stay up."

"Yeah, well, I've told you," he said, barely glancing at her as he flicked through the TV channels with the remote, "he should be taking himself off to bed now at his age. He's not a child anymore, he's growing up. You do pander to him, that's half the problem."

"I don't pander to him, I give him time, which is what he needs. He'll be off on his own soon enough and not needing me."

"Is he still going on about that bloody garden?"

"Yes he is, and who can blame him? Can you stop flicking through the channels please," she snapped, "I'm trying to talk."

He put the TV on mute and the control down. His expression indicated he was irritated but she didn't care. She was irritated with him.

"I still can't believe you did that to his little garden patch. Even if you thought Adam had done it, why would you dig it up?"

"Because I don't want him doing stuff I've not asked for. He knows what I want and that's what he gets paid to do. Same as Hazel in London, she did the cleaning you wanted her to do. You didn't want her doing stuff you hadn't asked for."

"That's not the same."

"It's exactly the same."

"You can be so insufferable at times you know. Why are you so awful about Adam? He's a nice man when you get to know him."

"What's that supposed to mean? How well do you *know him?*"

"I mean he's had a hard time. It can't be easy rebuilding your life after what he's been through. I don't know him as such, I just feel sorry for him. And he's doing a great job, he works hard and I don't get why you're so against him."

"Because I don't want him doing stuff with Freddy, I told you that in the beginning. And it sounds to me like he's getting rather cosy here, we'll probably have to let him go."

"Let him go?" Her voice went up, "Why on earth would you do that when he's doing such a good job? The gardens are looking much better."

He shrugged, "I don't want him around, that's all."

"You're being stupid and you know it. It's only until the end of August and he'll be finished anyway."

"Yeah, and that can't come soon enough. Anyway, enough of that," he topped up his wine glass, "you know I mentioned before about a holiday so we'd have something to look forward to? I've been looking at Disney in Florida for a week or two, Freddy will love that. And like I said before, if you want to take your mother, we can do."

The last person he'd want to be on holiday with was her mother. But as always, he'd get his own way. That's why he was successful in business, he always had a bargaining tool in his back pocket. He knew how much her and Freddy would love Florida, and normally he'd never in a million years suggest taking her mother. But right now, he was deflecting away from what he truly wanted, which was to continue working the way he was doing and that would mean her and Freddy on their own most of the week.

"A holiday would be nice, but that doesn't address the situation right now and the hours you're working."

"I know it doesn't. But it'll give us something to look forward to as a family. You keep saying we never have any time together, well we will by having a holiday." His expression smacked of annoyance, "I thought you'd be pleased."

"That's half the trouble, you have no idea. It's not about

holidays, it's about you being here, you're spending far too much time in London and I'm tired of it."

"I told you," his tone altered to irritable, "it's because I'm in negotiations about expanding. We've been here before, this is what I do."

"Yes, but it's still hard on Freddy and me. I don't know why you can't be here some of the time. Surely not all of the work is face to face?"

"Most of it is. Honestly, I don't know what your problem is. I do all this so we can have the lifestyle we have."

"Yeah, but at what price? The pace you work at could make you ill, then what? Do we actually need to expand the company when you're doing okay with what you've got?"

"You can't stand still in business. If I can get this next deal sorted, it'll see us through to our retirement."

"Can you afford it? Or is it that you're going to borrow yet more money?"

"That's business. I'm in the process of persuading them it's a good deal, and then we're good to go."

"What," she frowned disparagingly, "so it's by no means sorted. You're doing all these extra hours for something that might not happen?"

"No, it is more or less sorted, well in principle anyway. I just need to get the finer details ironed out, that's what's taking the time. They need to deal with me directly, hence the evening meetings, there's so much to discuss. Anyway," he reached for the wine bottle again, "do you want a top up and I'll put a film on and we can relax?"

"No, I don't." She couldn't even be bothered to finish her wine and placed it down on the coffee table. It seemed pointless trying to talk to him, he never listened. "I think I'll have a soak in the bath and go to bed to read, I've got a bit of a headache coming on."

"Take some aspirin, then" he grinned suggestively, "so your headache's gone when I come up."

Was that all the man ever thought about? All the issues they had between them, and he wanted sex. Almost as if everything was okay if they did. And it had worked for many years, but right now, having sex with him was the last thing that was going to happen. She wasn't being punitive, she never rejected him, but somehow she couldn't face it. It troubled her as she made her way upstairs to the bathroom.

It was definitely a first. She'd never felt like it before.

Chapter 27

Annabelle

Max was having an early dinner at her house. She was smarting as he couldn't stay over and she desperately wanted him to. She wasn't sleeping well and right now she should be as for the first time in her life, she was happier than ever. It was the bloody therapist George Grey. Since the first time she spotted him sat in her bedroom watching her, he'd taken further liberties of visiting her in the night. The previous evening, she turned over half asleep, and he was sat in the armchair in her bedroom again, just watching her. It was frightening to wake up and see him there. She asked him what he thought he was doing in her bedroom and told him she could have him struck off but he didn't answer, which was most unusual. In her experience with him, he always had an answer for everything. He just glared at her in that boring old grey suit that matched his complexion. He even had his staid plain tie on, in the middle of the night. Didn't the man have down-time?

She wanted to know more about the plot to kill clingy and her son, but he wouldn't go into details about how, just that he was working on it. She told him she needed to speak to Yegor to get him on board and he reassured her he'd explain the plan as soon as he could. He needed to hurry up though, she didn't want to waste any time. Clingy had to go.

She's already been working on her own plan to get rid but that might lead back to her so George's plan was better. And if she could get Yegor involved, she wouldn't be implicated. It would cost plenty, but she had plenty. It would be a price worth paying, she was confident about that.

Max savoured the creamy beef bourguignon and wild rice the housekeeper had made that she'd heated up. Annabelle smiled lovingly at him as he devoured every mouthful. Normally she and a lover would be out and about in the finest places of London and maybe even in Europe, but with him, she was content just watching him eat and knowing they'd be making love afterwards. They rarely met without making love. And this evening, he'd made her heart beat a tiny bit faster as when he'd arrived, he'd brought a holdall with some clothes in which he said he would leave there, all ready for when he moved in permanently. She'd allocated him a dressing room in one of the spare bedrooms. Currently it looked completely bare, with just a pair of trousers and a couple of tee shirts, but now he'd made a start, over the next few weeks he'd be able to fill it. Each day they were getting closer to their life together.

She drained her glass and reached for the wine bottle to top it up.

"You're not holding back," he frowned, "what's up?"

"Nothing. I didn't realise I was being monitored," she snapped.

"You're not. It's just you don't usually drink loads, but the bottle has nearly gone and I'm on my first." He looked disappointed in the way she'd been short with him. It was unusual; she never spoke to him like that.

"Sorry, I shouldn't have snapped. I've had a lot on lately at work."

"Anything I can help with?"

"No, honestly, it's sorted now anyway."

"Long as you're sure because if there is anything bothering you, I want to know, especially if it's work related. I might be able to help."

"I know and I do appreciate your concern, but I'm fine."

He took another sip of his wine. "That's good then. While we're talking work, I had a meeting with my finance manager today."

"Did you?"

"Yes. I mentioned about our merger."

"Oh, Max, I wish you hadn't. It could easily get out and we said it's the last thing we wanted until we were sure we had a deal. I thought we'd agreed that."

"We did and Derek's extremely confidential. But he was of the same mind as me that drawing up all the plans were going to be a lengthy process so it might be useful to make a start."

She sighed heavily, he was grating on her when she'd already told him no. "We've gone over this dozens of times. I don't want any merger until we're married. It makes sense to wait until then."

"Yes, but that's going to take a while yet. Not only do I have to leave Claire, we've still got to get divorced. It all takes time."

"And whose fault's that? It's ridiculous this waiting until Claire's birthday. Why should we have to wait? You've said yourself the marriage is over. Why not make the break now?"

"You know why. I've organised her 40th party. Family are travelling from all over for it. I can't just walk away from that. It's only a few weeks away."

"Three. It's three weeks away. Three weeks we could be together."

"Look, we've been over this. I know it's hard on you," he squeezed her hand, "but I don't want to make the move until after her birthday. And my accountant made the point . . . I know this is a bit delicate, but merging our companies is another thing that will go in our favour. If we do it before the divorce, Claire will get much less. As it stands now, she'd be entitled to half."

"Yeah, well, as far as I can see, that's one of the reasons not to merge them yet. I understand you will have to provide for her and your son, but not at my expense. And I know my accountants will say exactly that. And surely you have your assets organised for an eventuality of your marriage breaking down? If you haven't, then I am surprised."

"Don't worry your pretty little head about stuff like that, I have things well sorted on that front."

"Max, please don't say stuff like *worry your pretty little head* – I find it patronising. Try to remember I'm a successful woman with a business acumen I've inherited from my father. I work hard along with Anthony to make sure my business thrives. I don't want to be talked to like an air-brained blonde bimbo."

"Annie, don't be like that," he caressed her cheek with the back of his fingers, "I am sorry. I didn't mean it like it came out, forgive me. I know what you've achieved and I'm proud of you for it. And I can't wait until we are working alongside each other. All I'm saying is, the whole process from start to finish is going to take time. I'm only suggesting initial steps, that's all."

"I know you are, and what I'm saying is, while I'm all for merging the businesses, I want our future to be about us first of all and the business to come second."

"I know, and I want that too."

"That's perfect then, we're on the same page." She leant forward and kissed him. "Can I get you some dessert?"

"Sounds good," he replied and she knew he was watching her walk towards the fridge. She'd purposely dressed provocatively in a sheer blouse with a dark bra underneath accentuating her ample breasts.

She was glad to have something to do while she broached the next subject. It was only going through the motions anyway, but she needed to play the part. She cut into the cheesecake and placed it on small plates. "And while we're on the subject of finances, we'll have to have prenups drawn up before we get married."

He didn't answer so she carried on. "You'll want to make sure your son is provided for."

She filled a jug with cream and brought it back to the table with the plates and placed it in front of him.

"Yeah, I guess so," he said. "Shall we just have a business meeting first of all between you, myself and a couple of finance legal beagles? More of a first thoughts meeting?"

She took a deep breath in, watching him pour cream over his portion and scoop some into his mouth. How many times did she have to tell him? Maybe though, not for much longer? If, as she hoped, clingy and his son would be burnt to cinders, then all of the discussions they were having were irrelevant. But right now, she had to go through the motions – she couldn't have any suspicion pointing towards her, least of all from him when the time came for the disposal of them both. She just needed to be patient and find out what George Grey's plan was. Killing clingy was almost like a light bulb going on. The sooner she got rid, the better. As Max wasn't staying over that evening she was going to remain awake and wait until George Grey visited her bedroom again. And when he got there, she was going to ask him if they could expedite things so that when Max eventually came to live with her, he'd come as a widower rather than a husband and father. Clingy and the kid would be history and she'd be his only family. Excitement surged through her.

"You're miles away, but I'm liking the sexy pensive look," Max said reaching towards her with the last spoonful of his cheesecake. She opened her mouth wide and took it in.

"You have such a sexy mouth," he breathed huskily.

She licked her lips, "All the better to eat you with. Come on, let's go to bed. I've fed and watered you, now it's my turn."

He stood up. "I'm all yours," he said and reached for her hand.

Chapter 28

Annabelle

"I'm worried about you, Anthony, you've lost weight, aren't you eating?" She was having coffee with Anthony in the seated window area of her office with the panoramic view.

"Course I'm eating, just not that much. I seem to be drinking a lot though."

"What is it? You aren't still fretting over Fiona, are you?"

"I am a bit, yes."

"You'll have to let go, you can't have her making you ill."

"I know that. I just don't get it though. We were happy together, I don't understand why she just left. I think there must be more to it. Something must have been wrong and she didn't tell me."

"You're probably right, but if she didn't tell you, she had her reason for that. You can't dwell on it. Maybe you just have to accept your feelings ran deeper. I think you need to move on and put her out of your mind. It's for the best."

"I've tried, believe you me, but all my thoughts come back to her. When I'm alone at night, I keep thinking about our time together, I can't believe she'd throw that away."

"Well unfortunately she has done just that," her voice conjured up fake sympathy, "I know it's hard, but maybe you need to turn the page and move on."

"Easier said than done. Don't laugh," he looked directly

into her eyes, "I've been thinking about hiring someone to find her."

Jesus Christ. Her tummy plummeted, "Hiring someone?"

"Yes, like a private investigator. Not that I have any experience of using one, I wouldn't have the first idea. But there are plenty of them around that find missing people."

"But Fiona isn't missing as such. She's moved on. Would it be wise to contact her when she clearly doesn't want that?"

"You're probably right but I have to do something." He let out a sigh, "I can't carry on like this, I've tried forgetting her, but it's so difficult. The problem is, I love her."

She couldn't have him finding Fiona which no doubt a private investigator would be able to do easily. It could all come out about paying her off to disappear. She needed to think, and quickly.

"I know someone who could help you . . . someone I've used before."

The creases on his brow became more pronounced, "What, you've used a private investigator before?"

"Don't look so shocked, yes I have."

"What on earth for, if you don't mind me asking?"

"To check up on Mark. And I got precisely what I paid for, discretion and efficiency."

Anthony didn't ask what exactly she'd been checking on her previous husband for, which was good. She didn't really want to elaborate further. She'd learned over the years to keep any untruths or fabrications to a bare minimum so there was less chance of being caught out.

A tiny bit of light crept into his eyes. "Can you get me his details while I'm still thinking about it? I hear what you say, but I do want to know why Fiona upped and left the way she did."

"Okay, if you're absolutely sure, I'll get them for you. They're at home, though. And it's not a he, it's a she."

He pulled a face, "A female investigator?"

"Yes, and she's very good. But do think carefully before you do anything rash, won't you?"

"I will do. Thank you, my darling," he leant forward and grasped her hand, "I don't know what I'd do without you."

"I don't know what I'd do without you either. I hate to see you hurting, you deserve better. Right," she checked her watch, "you'll have to excuse me, I've got a counselling session with Dr Dull-as-dishwater, I'm afraid."

"How's it going?"

"Same old, same old. He asks how I am, I tell him I'm fine. He asks if I'm taking my medication, I tell him yes. That's about it really."

"But the sessions are still of benefit, aren't they? You've come such a long way, so they must be doing some good?"

"I think that's more down to meeting Max although the sessions were good in the beginning. I've got a completely new life now and so much to look forward to. I've a wedding to plan, and then I'll be busy baby-making shortly," she smiled enjoying the thrill of excitement shooting through her veins which happened every time she thought of having a baby.

"I'm pleased for you, you deserve to be happy, and if Max makes you feel like that, then I'm happy too."

"And I want the same for you. There's someone out there for you too, I know it."

"I wish I had your confidence. I need to pursue this, Annabelle," his eyes looked pained, "I have to do that before I can move on. Get that number for me will you?"

"Yep, I'm onto it."

He got up and walked towards the door, his gait not as confident as usual. His normally upright frame was slightly hunched which caused a pang of sadness as she'd been the one responsible for it by paying Fiona to disappear. She waited until he'd closed the door behind him and picked up the internal phone to call reception.

"Could you find Yegor for me please and ask him to come to my office."

* * *

She spoke firmly to Yegor, "I want you to find a bent private investigator, and it has to be a female. Someone I can pay to do what I want. And when you've got one, give me the details. I need to give them to Anthony ASAP."

"For what?"

"Anthony wants to find Fiona. You'll remember Fiona, you trashed her car to get rid of her," she said sarcastically.

A man of little or no words, he nodded.

"The investigator needs to assure Anthony she'll find Fiona and then, a couple of days later, she needs to report she's found her and she doesn't want to be contacted. Anthony will think it's some sort of *women sticking together movement*. He's too much of a gentleman to question any further."

Yegor raised an eyebrow, "Private Investigators don't work like that. They find the person and supply the details. They don't get involved in any other rubbish."

"I don't care what usually happens, Yegor," she snapped, "just do as I ask. Tell whoever you get she'll be on a win win. I'll pay her for basically doing nothing, and Anthony will pay her for a non-existent service. She will need to tell him she's not prepared to hand Fiona's details over. Hopefully, he'll think it's some sort of female allegiance."

"Okay."

"So, she needs to tell Anthony she'll find Fiona, and then tell him a day or two later she's found her and she doesn't want to be traced. Do you think you can find someone to do that?"

"I guess so," he shrugged, "if not, have you got a plan B?"

"Yes. You'll have to pay someone to pretend to be an investigator. And you'll have to get some fake business cards done if we have to go with Plan B."

She reached in the desk drawer for the long white envelope. She wanted rid of Yegor. Her head was throbbing and she needed a drink. Of late she'd taken to carrying a small bottle of gin in her handbag which helped ease the tension that was occurring more frequently as each day passed. It was bloody George Grey, he was everywhere. That morning she'd been flicking through the channels for the news and there he was, large as life on television whispering to her they were close to getting rid of clingy. She just needed to wait for his instructions.

She handed Yegor the envelope, "Quick as you can, get whoever's details to me and tell her to wait for Anthony's call. Her job then is to reassure him she'll do exactly what he wants. I'm hoping he just speaks to her on the phone and gives her the information he has on Fiona, but if he does want to meet her in person, then she'll have to do that. Find someone who can pull it off convincingly. It's hardly a strategic undercover operation so anyone with an ounce of sense should be able to."

Yegor took the envelope from her.

"There's enough in there for you to pay this woman and yourself. But please, Yegor, use someone you can trust to carry this off. I can't have Anthony finding out about any of this."

"Will do. I'll get onto it now."

"Thank you."

He made his way towards the door.

"As soon as possible would be good and I'll pass the contact details on to him."

She waited until she was alone and reached in her handbag for the plain bottle of water which disguised her more recent prop. Since stopping all her tablets, she found herself becoming more reliant on alcohol. But she could easily justify the need. It was a mammoth thing stopping all the medication. Therefore if she needed a small crutch to see her through, then the odd tot of alcohol would be okay. Her intention was only to self-medicate for a few weeks. Once Max was with her permanently, she wouldn't need it quite so much. She knocked the gin back, enjoying the heat as it burned going down.

It took a third of the bottle before a sense of calm kicked in.

Chapter 29

Claire

She'd dropped Freddy at school and was driving along the A35 toward Bournemouth enjoying the beautiful melodic tone of Adele on the CD player; her destination was to her friend, Emma's house, to spend the day with her. They'd been through secondary school and college together and Claire had been eagerly looking forward to a face-to-face catch-up with her oldest and dearest friend until she checked her rear-view mirror and spotted a red Nissan with a black roof a couple of cars behind her. Her tummy plummeted. Not again. She'd convinced herself the other times she'd seen it in her vicinity had been chance and dismissed them, but not anymore. This was the fourth time she'd seen it – it was too much of a coincidence. But who could possibly be interested in her? And why?

There was a fifty miles per hour restriction in place and she kept a watchful eye as the journey progressed. Frustration was building as the two cars behind made it impossible to make out who was driving. And even though her tummy was doing somersaults, she convinced herself it would be wise to stop. That way she'd be able to watch if the car continued on, and more importantly, see who was driving as it passed her.

As the next lay-by came into view, she indicated at the last moment and turned off the road, glancing at the rear-view mirror. The Nissan didn't turn off, just kept going, any possible view of its driver obscured by a big truck.

Her head thumped almost as if it was her heart beating in it, and her tummy felt jittery. She reached for some water and eagerly glugged it down. It was getting creepy now. She'd have to tell Max.

She contemplated leaving the A35 at the next exit, turning round and going back home, but she feared the Nissan might still be around and hidden somewhere waiting for her. And Emma would have gone to a lot of trouble preparing lunch so she didn't want to let her down, especially with being so near. But her heart wasn't in it. Something was wrong and she was clueless what to do about it. Despite her anxiousness, she eased the car into gear and pulled away, continuing on her journey, deciding it would be better to spend a few hours at her friend's house and then if someone was lurking, they'd have a long wait.

Eventually she manoeuvred her car down the red bricked drive on the prestigious estate that from a glance boasted superior living, and spotted Emma waving in the bay window. A tear threatened at the familiar face eager to welcome her as she parked. They Face-timed regularly and spent a lot of time catching up, but it wasn't like seeing her in the flesh. And even though she felt absolutely crap following the Nissan car incident, she was determined to try and put it out of her mind and not to let it spoil the day with her dear friend. She reached for the flowers she'd bought off the back seat and got out of the car.

Emma rushed down the drive and threw her arms around her. "God I've missed you."

Claire clung on with one arm, savouring the familiar smell of Christian Dior perfume her friend always wore. "Me too," she said, stifling the lump in her throat. Much as she hated how emotional she'd become, she hadn't any control. Tears were becoming a daily occurrence.

Emma pulled away, "Hey, don't get all maudlin on me, come on in. There's a glass of fizz waiting inside with your name on it."

"Ooo, that sounds perfect," she said, "plenty of soda with it though, remember I've got to drive back."

"Not for a while though," Emma linked her arm and led her towards the back door of the spacious town house.

"It's so lovely to see you in the flesh, Em," Claire smiled, "it's been far too long. I have missed you."

"It has. I wish I'd never taken on more hours at work, I like the money but it gives me less time for socialising." They made their way into the spacious kitchen area, "Anyway, because I'm off this week, I've pushed the boat out. For lunch I've made us baked fillet of plaice with a mushroom stuffing, courtesy of the wonderful Delia."

"That sounds amazing, but you shouldn't have gone to such a lot of trouble, especially on your week off, we could have gone out. These are for you by the way," she said placing the flowers down on one of the kitchen units.

"Aww, thank you, they're lovely, I'll get a vase. Yeah, we could have gone out, but it's nicer in the house, we can gossip more. Here, let me take your jacket, and you make yourself comfy. I'll put the flowers in some water and then we'll have our drinks."

Emma joined her on the sofa and they sipped their drinks. There was a lot to catch up on, Emma's increased responsibilities at work as a HR advisor, the new high-flying boss setting her totally impossible targets, her daughter and the dilemma about which secondary school to send her to – on and on their chat went. However long they spent apart, within minutes of meeting again, the conversation seemed to take up where they left off. And she loved hearing about Emma's life, she was bubbly and effervescent, just the tonic she needed. It was comforting to savour the familiarity of her friend that she seemed to have known forever.

She glanced around the homely kitchen as Emma dished up their lunch. It had a calming effect on her and she told herself to put the Nissan car out of her mind for now; she could worry about it later.

"Ready when you are," Emma said and they took their seats at the elegant dining table that seemed almost too grand for a kitchen. Emma had served her a portion of fish and had placed asparagus, and dauphinoise potatoes in tureens on the table, and a delicious smelling boat of cheese sauce. "Help yourself," Emma said, clearly pleased with her efforts.

Claire filled her plate, "This looks fabulous, Em, you are good going to this much trouble."

"You haven't tasted it yet," Emma grinned, "but go ahead and then tell me how your mum's doing. What a shock, a stroke at her age."

The food was delicious. Claire savoured the taste of something that she hadn't cooked. It made such a change. "I know," she said pausing from her meal, "who'd have thought. But she's doing great, you know Mum, you couldn't hold her down for long. She's gone home now and you'd hardly know, thank goodness, just a slight limp that's all. This is gorgeous by the way, I love it," she smiled gratefully.

"It's not bad, is it, even if I say so myself. Are you sure you only want water, I feel bad having wine when you're not drinking?"

"No honestly, I'm fine, you enjoy."

Emma sipped her wine. "Great your mum's okay. I sent her a couple of little cards, you know those ones with an inspirational verse inside, to spur her on."

"Yes, she said you had. You are thoughtful."

"She was good to me when we were growing up, far more like a mum than my own. I'm going to try and get to see her. We must fix up a lunch."

"Yeah, that'll be nice, she'd love that."

"We'll do it then. Help yourself to more if you want it."

Claire reached for some more asparagus. Her appetite wasn't great but she wanted to make an effort after Emma's hard work.

"Anyway," Emma said, "you look like you've lost a bit of weight, is it the house move or have you been cutting down on the carbs? I notice you haven't hardly had any potatoes?"

"No," Claire shook her head, "not cutting down on anything. I think first Dad's accident and then poor Mum so soon afterwards has put me off eating, to be honest."

"Well you be careful, you're wasting away."

"Hardly," she grinned, "but you're right, I do need to eat a bit more."

"You need to eat plenty of your fabulous cakes. Are you still making them?"

"Of course. You know me, any stress and I hit that mixing bowl. Fortunately, I've got a new gardener who appreciates them. He lives alone so I tend to feed him up."

"Oh, he'll love that."

"Yeah, he devours them. I should have brought you some. I was that excited coming to see you, I never thought."

"Hey, don't be daft. You don't need to bring anything, and the flowers are lovely. Right, tell me more about what's going on in Sandbanks. You said last time we Face-timed you'd met a new friend."

"Yeah, Pippa, she's lovely. It's strange how it happened really. I got a flier through the door about a missing dog, which we didn't find, but the gardener found a dog collar which had its name and address on so I took it back. Pippa answered the door," Claire sipped some water, "in a wheelchair, and was quite upset as I guess the collar pointed towards the dog being dead. Anyway, she lives alone so I couldn't leave her. I went in for a drink and I've been a few times since. She's such a nice person. Not one bit down in the dumps about what life has thrown at her."

"What happened to her, why's she in a wheelchair?"

"A car accident. Honestly Em, she's fantastic how she doesn't let it get her down. She still works and everything."

"What sort of work?"

"Admin type of stuff."

"Good for her. I'd just want to die if that happened to me. I can't imagine living my life in a wheelchair."

"Me neither. She's one of these coping types though that just gets on with it."

"I'm glad you've made a friend, that's nice for you with Max working long hours. Mind you, he's got offices at home now, hasn't he?"

"Yeah," Claire pulled a face, "but can you believe he's working more now than ever in London."

Emma widened her eyes, "That's one heck of a commute and I'm sensing you're not happy about it?"

"I'm not. It's causing a lot of tension between us. I've asked him to spend more time at home, but he's actually doing the opposite and taken to staying over at the flat. We hardly see him."

"He's always been like that though so you're used to it. Or are you worried something else is going on?" Emma's expression was full of concern, "after the last time."

"No, it's not that. It's probably just me really. It's hard to describe and I feel daft saying it out loud, but just lately I've had this feeling of doom hanging over me. I can't shake it off however hard I try."

"Bloody hell, that's not like you. How long have you been feeling like this?"

"A few weeks now."

"Have you told Max?"

"Not about these weird feelings I'm having, no."

"Maybe you should. Or perhaps visit your GP?"

"No, I don't fancy that, she'll think I'm depressed or something and prescribe tablets." She put her knife and fork together, "that was such a lovely meal, thank you."

"You're welcome, pleased you liked it. Anyway, carry on, you were saying about feeling a bit doom and gloom."

"Yeah, I think to be honest, it's a combination of the move, and Max working long hours. And then of course Dad and now Mum. It's been a pretty hectic time really."

"It has, and only you could pull through it all. You're always there for everyone else and I'm worried about you now you've said that."

"Aww, don't be. I didn't mean to worry you. I'm fine, honestly. I wish I hadn't said anything. There are so many poorly people out there with horrible things going on in their lives, and I'm moaning about nothing."

"Yeah, but we all do it, that's life. I know, how about next time you come, you stay over and we can hit the tiles. Me and you just like we used to, or I could persuade Amy to join us?" Emma gave a cheeky grin. They both knew Amy well. It was sure to be quite a night if she was involved.

"That sounds lovely, I reckon a good night out with the girls is just what I need."

"Then leave it with me and I'll get it sorted."

"Not until after my birthday though. You and Ben are still coming, aren't you?"

"Course we are. Wild horses wouldn't keep us away. I can't wait to see your face when you open my present."

"That sounds intriguing. Give me a clue."

"No clue, you'll have to wait. It's not that long anyway."

"I know. I'm still fighting the fact I'm shortly going to be forty. The gardener I was telling you about, he's only young. Looking at him, I realise how old I am."

"How old is he?"

"Thirty-four. And a really fit thirty-four at that."

Emma's eyes went wide, "I can't imagine anything better than feasting on a fit thirty-four- year-old on a daily basis. There must be a god up there somewhere."

Claire laughed, loving the company of her oldest and

dearest friend. Her mood felt much lighter just being with her.

"I have to say, he is rather nice. Between you and me, I seem to be quite drawn to him."

"Define drawn?" Emma asked.

"Erm . . . it's hard to say really, it's just that I like being with him, you know, chatting and all that."

Emma frowned. "You like being with him . . . what, in a serious like being with him sort of way, or more he's a good laugh?"

"Both."

"Hey, you need to be careful. You can't have any sort of temptation coming your way when you're trying to sort things out with Max."

"Oh, God no, I only meant I find him attractive, not that I'd ever do anything about it. And let's be clear, he won't see me that way."

"Yeah, keep telling yourself that. What man wouldn't find you attractive?"

"Give over, Em, it's nothing like that, honestly. It's just that I find myself chatting more to him than Max at the moment. And Freddy sees more of him too. He's great with him. But it's no more than that, I promise. Anyway, quickly changing the subject," she smiled, "it's done me the power of good being here today. Thank you. You've made me realise I need to get a grip on all my dismal thoughts."

"That's good then. But don't be so harsh on yourself. We all get down at sometime in our life. And you have had a lot to contend with lately."

"Yeah, and thankfully the doom and gloom isn't there all the time. Just sometimes I get a feeling that there's something bad around the corner and it's biding its time."

Emma tilted her head, "Maybe you should tell Max?"

"Nah, he's too busy," she dismissed, "and he'd only tell me to snap out of it. Which I am going to do now I've spoken to you, Dr Simpson," she smiled, "so thank you for listening to me rabbiting on."

"Don't be daft. I'm glad you told me. You've had loads on, Claire, and maybe you do need a bit more from Max right now. It might be worth at least having the conversation. You know what men are like, he'll be oblivious to anything being wrong with you. Long as they get their food and sex, they're happy. Most are pretty clueless about the emotional stuff. You have to point the obvious out to them."

"We'll have to see." She couldn't keep the sarcasm out of her voice, "I just need to get his attention somehow."

"Go out the two of you. You'll have his undivided attention then. Like a date night. It might clear the air a bit if he knows you're suffering with anxiety. I'm sure he'll want to help. Max is pretty decent like that. In fact, he'll be surprised I bet, and maybe more attentive."

"Yeah, that's a good idea, we haven't been out together for ages. And I have been nagging a bit at him lately."

"Sorted then. Do it now, while you're thinking about it. Book a table somewhere and then tell him so he can't back out."

She loved her friend for her kindness and putting things into perspective. But she'd said enough. The last thing she'd been expecting when she set off that morning was to pour her heart out. But now that she had, she felt better. At least she had a solution, or the beginning of one. She needed to tell Max exactly how she was feeling with the anxiety and the feeling of darkness hanging over her. Emma was right.

"Right, enough about my woes." Claire reached in her bag for her iPhone, "I've got a picture of the dress I've bought for my party. See what you think."

Chapter 30

Claire

They took a seat in the lounge at the Kingsway restaurant. She'd done exactly what she'd told Emma she would. She'd booked the table and told Max they were going. For once he didn't protest. It was nice getting dressed up for a change. Max looked even more appealing than he did going to the office. His jacket and chino's looked cool, and when he removed his jacket, the beautiful white linen shirt showed off his dark skin colour.

"Your shirt looks nice."

"It does, doesn't it? I picked it up in that shop I like in Knightsbridge."

"Yeah, you said."

"I think it's fair to say it had an expensive price tag attached to it, but I thought I was worth it," he smiled playfully.

The maître d' interrupted, telling them their table was ready in the restaurant which prevented her asking exactly how much. Not that it mattered. The truth was, Max was a walking clothes horse and was always buying himself new stuff. He prided himself on looking smart.

Their intimate table had a beautiful aspect overlooking the sea. Max would have tipped the waiter handsomely for it. Typical him, he'd always want the best seat in the house.

They'd ordered their meal while they had an aperitif in the lounge and as soon as they took their seats, their starters arrived. Max had pâté, she'd gone for soup. The waiter approached with the wine Max had ordered and he did the obligatory tasting. Once they were alone, she started the conversation about Freddy, determined she was going to speak about their relationship. But she wanted to tread steadily rather than go in all guns blazing.

"Freddy loved us coming out so he could have Mum to himself," she said, "she'll not put him to bed at his normal time. She never does."

"That's grandparents for you. Mine used to do as they liked too, which used to infuriate my mother and her rule book."

Max's upbringing had been quite strict opposed to her parents who were laid back. But she wasn't spending an evening talking about his parents. Not when she had something important she wanted to say. She opted for initial light conversation and then hoped to get to the main issue which was the two of them.

"Can you believe Freddy's already ten? It was a great party we gave him, wasn't it?"

"It sure was."

"Hopefully, now he's had the boys round, he'll make more friends. I'll invite a couple of them for tea one night I think. It's been hard for him starting a new school; he misses his friends in London. He doesn't say much but he is nervous about school some mornings. He stalls you know, and sometimes tells me he's got belly ache.

"I've told you, he needs to toughen up," he was concentrating on spreading his pâté on the thin crispy toast, 'it's no good moping in the corner of the playground, he needs to push himself forward. I know you don't like me saying it, but you do keep him tied to you. He needs to be gaining a bit of independence."

"I am trying but he's sensitive."

"And that's what kids pick up on." A smug expression passed across his face which she always hated. "Look, all I'm saying is, maybe stop fussing round him quite so much. I used to walk to school at his age yet you're either ferrying him in the car or walking him there. I don't see why he can't go on his own."

"Because there are far more idiots around now focussing their sights on young children than when you were his age. He's definitely not walking to school on his own. I'm not comfortable about him having to get the bus to secondary school when the time comes."

"Yeah, well, he's going to look bloody stupid with you taking him each day while his mates are on the bus." He took a bite of his toast, "That reminds me, have you contacted the woman about the eleven plus papers?"

"No, not yet."

"Why? I keep asking you. He'll need to work on them to have any chance of passing. Even you know he's not the brightest tool in the box."

"Don't talk like that about him." She paused from speaking while the waiter removed their starter plates. "Freddy tries hard even if he's not as academically bright as some children. That's why I'm in two minds about getting involved in extra tuition. I don't want him to feel pressurised to pass the exam. I think maybe just take it and if he doesn't pass, then he can go the comprehensive. I went to a comprehensive and it didn't do me any harm."

"Yeah, and I went to a grammar school and I've achieved all I have because of it. My father made me work hard at his age."

"Yes, I know he did and that was right for you. Freddy isn't an academic, he's a softer boy. He may go into the arts or something like that."

"Over my dead body," Max screwed up his face disparagingly, "he's not going into *the arts* – he'll be taking over from me one day, that's what he's destined for. I haven't done all this for nothing. And believe you me, he'll need his wits about him in the cut and thrust of the business world." He raised his eyebrows at her, "I mean it, Claire, I want him to do those practice papers. I don't want him going to the comprehensive."

She took a deep breath in and sat back as the waiter arrived with the main courses. There was little point in arguing with him especially as he was well ahead of her in the wine consumption and she could see the wine waiter out of the corner of her eye hovering to keep him topped up. Anyway, Freddy wasn't the purpose of the dinner out really. She'd deal with that later. She wanted to mention the anxiety she was experiencing and tell him about the Nissan car that she suspected was following her.

"It's nice to be out together, it seems ages since we've done anything like this."

"It is, but it's been a busy time lately."

"I know. That's what I wanted to talk to you about, well that and me really."

He had the grace to pause from his food, "Are you alright, what's the matter?"

"Nothing serious," she reassured, concerned it hadn't come out quite how she'd intended, "I've just been feeling down a bit lately and worrying all the time. It's hard to explain," she struggled as she didn't want to sound totally stupid, "it's as if something awful is going to happen."

He scowled, "Like what?"

"I don't know," she hesitated, trying to find the right words, "it's like a sick feeling, as if I'm going to get some bad news."

He resumed eating, "It's not all this worrying about me and the hours I'm working is it? Because if it is, you need to stop it. I promise you it will come to an end in a couple of months and we'll be back to normal."

"You keep saying that, but that's not helping right now particularly as I'm feeling a bit wobbly. Freddy and I are on our own and just lately, it's really making sort of, I don't know ... questioning why we are putting ourselves through all of this."

"Look, I know it's hard right now, that's why I suggested a holiday, a sort of light at the end of the tunnel to look forward to when all this extra workload's over. And don't forget I've got your party planned, so I am trying to do the best I can for you."

"I know you are, it's just that I miss you. I miss us. It's a really difficult time for me right now what with Dad, the house move, then Mum and all this extra work you're doing."

"Yeah," he took a mouthful of wine, "well that might get even more difficult after your birthday."

"Why's that?"

"You know I told you about expanding the business?"

"Yes. It sounded like you had to cross the T's and dot the I's."

"Yep, it was. But it's a bit more than that now. I'm actually working on a merger with another established company, which may require me spending more time in London."

"Tell me you're joking," she said in a warning tone.

"No, I'm not. It's real. I'm hoping to merge with another leisure company."

"Whatever for? Surely you have enough on with ours. Why do you need to even expand anyway?"

"I've told you," a hint of irritability was evident in his voice, "you have to in business, you can't stand still."

"What if I don't want you to expand? The business takes up far too much of your time as it is."

"Too late, I'm already working on the merger. It'll mean I need to be hands-on initially, so I'll be in London during the week and then try and get home at weekends. But you know the leisure industry, weekends are our busiest time."

"I can't believe I'm even hearing this, Max. You promised me that doing all the house up was so you could be at home more and work from here. What's the point of it all if you're now saying you're going to be in London? We might as well up sticks and go back there to live."

"Don't be so dramatic," he snapped, "we've made our forever home here; it's just going to be another couple of years before I can do what I originally planned. They'll fly by. We'll get Freddy into the grammar school, I'll get the merger up and running and then I'll make a move towards working from home."

She put her knife and fork down with force. Her appetite had completely disappeared. She couldn't eat another bite.

"Look, I know you're upset," he said, "but it'll work out, you'll see. Just give me a few months until I've signed on the dotted line, and then we're sorted."

"Don't talk to me like I'm a fool. Another leisure complex, how the hell will that mean we're sorted? There'll be twice the work, for God's sake."

"Yeah, well, I've thought of that. I'm going to be taking on a manager to oversee some of it."

"A manager," her voice went up, "as if you'd consider a manager. Half your trouble is you can't let go. You'd never relinquish your hold."

"That's because I never trust people. But this man is proven. Anthony, he's been running the company I'm merging with since it was set up. He's perfect."

She couldn't even be bothered to answer. Her hopes for sorting things out were in tatters. As always he bulldozed himself along, knocking anyone down that got in his way. Even her protests counted for nothing. He did exactly as he wanted, regardless. Did he even care about her anxiety?

Max took a sip of his wine, "Anyway, going back to our holiday," he looked mighty pleased with himself, "I've booked it, we fly on the 19th December."

"You've booked it? Did you speak to Mum?"

"No. But you said you wanted her to come so I've included her."

"Even though she hasn't confirmed she can come?" She glared at him, "You should have checked with her."

"Christ, Claire, I'm sure she's not going to turn down a free all expenses paid holiday on the strength it might clash with her bridge league."

"Do you know, you can be horrible at times? It's a courtesy thing. You bulldoze along expecting everyone to do exactly what you want. You never stop and consider other people's feelings."

He sighed, "I do, and that's why I've booked the holiday. You keep saying we never have any time together, well we will by having a holiday, all of us. I don't know what you're moaning about actually, you should be pleased."

"That's half the trouble, you have no idea. It's not about holidays. It's about you being here, not only for your son, but for me as well. You should be making sure I'm alright instead of spending half your life in London. I'm sick of it."

The whole evening had been pointless. Nothing had gone how she wanted it to. He hadn't shown any concern for how anxious she was right now. He'd been over powering with his business hat on.

She sighed heavily to make her point and the silence lengthened between them. Their evening out had been so promising. She hoped he'd reassure her that he'd cut down on his hours, not tell her he was going to be doing more. She'd wanted assurance, but he'd only added to her feeling of doom. And she'd not even got round to mentioning the Nissan car.

"Do you want dessert?" he asked in an overly bright voice as if it was a normal evening and he'd not dropped the bombshell into their conversation.

She looked down at her plate of half eaten food, "No. You have one if you want."

He glanced at the bottle of wine. "I might just have some cheese and biscuits to go with the wine that's left."

Typical. Her insides were in turmoil and he was thinking of his belly. He had no idea of the angst he'd caused by saying he was going to be working more.

Or did he?

Maybe he wasn't that bothered?

She gulped down the last of her wine and placed the empty glass on the table. She stared at the crystal glass, coated with the remnants of red wine. It reminded her of blood.

The dark foreboding feeling reared its ugly head again.

Something dreadful was about to happen – she was sure of it.

She had to get away. "Excuse me while I use the ladies'."

Chapter 31

Annabelle

Dr Stead, her psychiatrist, was at the forefront of her mind as she leisurely drove to his offices for her late morning appointment. She was early, so in no rush. Her nerves had been on edge all morning forcing her to leave the house as it felt oppressive. It wasn't that she was eager to see the psychiatrist, it was more she'd cancelled the last two appointments so she daren't again.

Mornings were usually her favourite time of the day, but of late she'd been feeling sluggish for a few hours first thing. It was all bloody George Grey's fault. Although initially she'd been pleased to have him calling at the house with his suggestions, now he was becoming a pain as he kept checking to see if she was okay. He was everywhere. Not content with visiting her at night in her bedroom, now he was speaking to her through the television at the end of the news. She ceased watching it, but he was industrious and found another way to speak to her by interrupting the local radio programmes to whisper stuff to her.

As she approached a junction and stopped, she reached across to the glove compartment for some mints to disguise the vast amount of booze she'd consumed the previous evening which might still be evident on her breath. Max hadn't been able to stay, so she'd spent most of the evening alone and drowning her sorrows. And as well as drinking far too much wine, she'd exceeded her one cigarette per day allowance.

She yawned. No wonder she was tired, George Grey was visiting much more frequently, and for longer each night, always when Max wasn't there. In the early hours of that specific morning, he'd explained he had the plan to get rid of clingy and the kid finalised. And most important of all, he had what he called a professional arsonist to do it. *Could you even have a professional arsonist?* It sounded quite bizarre to her, but she was happy to go along with it for now. However, there was part of her that would prefer to use Yegor, which she still might do rather than some random man. Yegor was reliable and never let her down, but she wasn't going to tell George Grey that. Not yet, anyway.

The professional arsonist he talked about, or maybe there was more than one bloke, she wasn't quite certain, was going to secure the house when clingy and the kid were asleep, especially the bedroom doors so there was no way out. He was going to use candles to set fire to drapes, which seemingly was a common cause of a house fire. The smoke detectors were going to be disarmed. He was going to be inside the house wearing breathing apparatus to make sure nothing was left to chance. Clingy and the kid were going to die of smoke inhalation, he was going to position them in the beds as if they'd slept through it, and then release the barred doors.

Although it sounded a bit like a TV movie, George Grey was extremely convincing, which added to her excitement and anticipation to finally have clingy and the kid out of the way. She'd had to reiterate again she didn't want any of it taking place until after the party and not until she'd given the okay. Max had to be well away from the marital home and living with her before anything happened.

George Grey had agreed to that but he had stressed a

particular proviso. They had to make sure there was no suspicion pointing to either of them which meant it was vital they maintained a client therapist relationship. He'd repeated that his office was bugged and there was covert CCTV watching everything they were doing. They couldn't let their guard down, he'd stressed, so they had to do their counselling sessions completely normally and not refer to anything they discussed privately. He said the only safe place now was her house.

His final advice had been that Dr Stead the psychiatrist she was seeing may also have secret cameras in his office and it definitely would be bugged. She had to appear confident, answer his questions positively and never falter or he'd easily pick up on it. She mustn't let him trick her. She needed to be on her guard at all times. He was trained to read minds.

* * *

She gazed around Dr Stead's office. He'd been impolite taking a phone call when it was her appointment time. It was supposed to be protected time and she'd always hated rudeness. Even though he'd notified her when she sat down he was waiting for an urgent call, it wasn't right. But every cloud and all that . . . at least it eroded the time she spent answering his questions. She'd politely asked if he wanted her to leave the room, but he'd said not. It sounded to her like a load of mumbo jumbo he was just saying yes and no to, so it clearly wasn't anything confidential. Unless it was some sort of code, she wasn't entirely sure. But she needed to do well and get out of there as fast as she could without arousing any suspicion about her mental health. Not that there was anything wrong with her.

She'd taken time with her appearance that morning which would go in her favour as the previous times she'd seen

Dr Stead, he'd been quite charming. Today she'd dressed in a particularly expensive turquoise suit teamed with huge killer heels. She'd switched them in the car as they were too high to drive in. Even her make-up had been carefully applied for maximum effect. In her experience, men behaved differently around an attractive woman, and Dr Stead might be a highly trained doctor, but he was still a bloke. And nobody could ever deny she wasn't beautiful. Her father said often enough her looks were her greatest asset. The only person she knew who hadn't been impressed by her was dull George Grey but she deduced he most probably was gay. What other reason could there be?

Dr Stead cut his call and dialled a number on the desk phone. "Elaine, could you reschedule my appointments for the rest of the day. I'll carry on with Ms Claybourne but after that I need to leave for the hospital. Thank you."

"Sorry about that," he gave his, I'm a friendly doctor smile, "I'm afraid it was urgent. Right, we'll make a start, shall we?"

The sooner they got started the sooner she was out of there. She concluded he must have to go see an inpatient nutter if he was dashing off to a hospital. She smiled back encouragingly.

He cleared his throat. "I'm pleased you've attended today as I do need to complete a quarterly assessment. I know you've cancelled," he looked down at his notes, "the last two appointments."

"Yes, I'm sorry about that, I've had some urgent business issues I've been dealing with and typically those appointments clashed with yours."

"I see." He didn't *see*, she could tell. But he seemed distracted somehow, as if the phone call had sidetracked him.

"How have you been getting on since I last met with you," he glanced again at his notes, he'd have so many patients, she'd just be a number, "in March?"

"Really well, thank you."

"Any changes in your behaviour?"

"No, everything is normal."

"You're still taking your medication?"

"Yes," she lied. She didn't need that load of crap anymore. She had Max, he was all the medication she needed.

"You're experiencing normal interactions with colleagues, friends and family?"

"Yes, all good."

"Socialising normally?"

She nodded.

"No episodes of anxiety, anger or confusion?"

"No, none at all."

He took a breath in. "So for all intents and purposes, the medication is keeping you on an even keel. It's doing its job, which is all positive."

"Yes, it certainly seems to be. I feel well."

"That is encouraging." He glanced down again at his notes, further proof he wasn't his usual self. He normally was much more alert. If felt almost as if he wanted rid so he could get to wherever he was needed, which suited her perfectly.

"Your therapist says you are now in a new relationship."

"Yes, that's right. I'm planning to get married."

"I see. And that's all going well?"

"Yes, very well."

"And what about your sessions with the therapist, are they still helpful?"

"Oh, yes, very," she lied again. "I've been working through certain issues especially about my childhood."

"That's encouraging. As I've mentioned before to you, episodes of psychosis can occur during teenage years, although as we've discussed previously, you seem to be a bit of an anomaly with regards to some of the symptoms. It appears you had an idyllic childhood."

"Well, it wasn't perfect by any means, and there were some issues between my father and me. He was extremely driven and pushed me. That's what George Grey and I have had discussions about."

"Good. It's worth recapping though, in light of this new relationship that you do recognise the signs of your condition and you must seek help if you start to become unwell. It is hard to recognise in yourself symptoms, particularly delusions, as a person with a diagnosis of schizophrenia and psychosis would not necessarily have the insight into that happening. But if, for example, you start to experience problems concentrating, or changes in your behaviour such as becoming easily upset, anxious, confused, suspicious or angry, then you need to see your GP for an urgent referral to me so I can assess your condition and make adjustments to your medication."

"Yes, and of course I would, but I'm absolutely fine I can assure you."

"Which is encouraging. I sincerely hope with the treatment plan we have in place that you don't regress. I know following the assessments after the accident, you were experiencing hallucinations. I recall you thought your husband was monitoring your every move and having you followed. It reached its peak when the accident occurred and you explained in court someone had taken over your body and was responsible for your actions."

"Yes, but there was some ambiguity about that."

"Exactly and that's what helped with the assessments and subsequent findings. It's important that we continue with our regular monitoring as things can quickly escalate. You've come a long way in managing your condition. As I've said before, with schizophrenia, patients interpret reality abnormally and they may experience delusions and hallucinations which impair daily functioning and can be disabling. That's why we need to continue exactly as we are currently, as you appear mentally well. So for now I'm not recommending any changes to your treatment plan and I'll be writing my report accordingly." He closed the folder in front of him and leaned back in his chair. "Do you have any questions?"

"No, none at all. I'm pleased everything is going as it should."

"Yes, you must be. You've made excellent progress and I hope that continues. But don't forget, even the smallest change that doesn't feel quite right, you do need to report it. I can then make an assessment which may be something as simple as adjusting your medication. We want to make sure nothing escalates and becomes unmanageable."

"Quite," she said, itching to be out of there.

"If that's all, I'll say good day to you then," Dr Stead nodded.

She reached for her handbag and stood up.

"I'll liaise with your therapist, prepare my report and you'll be sent an appointment for our next session through the post. Until then, good luck with your upcoming wedding."

"Thank you, that's very kind."

She made her way to the door, inwardly smiling. *You did good, girl.*

Dr Stead didn't appear to be at all concerned she'd started a relationship – he didn't give a toss. It was George Grey over egging the pudding by suggesting otherwise. If the truth be told, it was him that was kicking off.

Maybe he does find me attractive after all?

Chapter 32

Annabelle

Although the elite bridal boutique in Marylebone was brimming with incredible couture gowns, Annabelle stepped out of the changing room in an exclusive wedding gown by the coveted international designer she favoured. It would need a few adjustments, but it showed off her figure to perfection.

"Oh my God, Annabelle, you look amazing. It's stunning," her friend Della squealed enthusiastically. Were they tears in her eyes?

The assistant fussed around fluffing the train of the dress as Annabelle stood on the pedestal and gazed at herself in the full-length mirror.

"I like how it accentuates my waist, don't you?" she squeezed in her tiny waist and ran her fingers over her hips. She'd studied wedding dresses numerous times online until she had an idea which she'd like. This particular one with an astronomical price tag attached to it appeared perfect, but she thought she'd try a couple of others on to make sure it was definitely the one.

"Oh it absolutely does that. I love how it shows off your cleavage, it's so pretty and feminine. And you're right, ivory suits you."

"Yeah, I much prefer it to white."

"Are you planning to wear your hair up?" the assistant asked.

"Yes, I thought so."

"Good because the shoulder detail is so delicate, it would be a shame for your hair, lovely as it is, to cover that."

"No, I'll definitely wear it up. I've already got a headdress, well I say headdress, it's more a tiara type jewelled offering that was my late mother's."

"How nice. Have you got it with you?"

"I haven't I'm afraid. I should have done really."

"No worries, you can bring it with you next time once you've decided on which dress you're having."

"Yes, I will. Now, I'll go and put the next one on. You okay, Della?"

"Course I'm okay." She raised her glass of bubbly the shop had provided, "take your time," she smiled, "we've got all day. And make sure you drink yours too."

"I will. I'll have it when I get the dress off before I try the next one. See you in a mo."

* * *

They sat in the trendy low-lit Blind Pig cocktail bar in Soho above the Michelin star-winning restaurant they were booked to have lunch in. Annabelle had ordered them her favourite gin, mead and honey cocktails prior to their lunch and quickly downed her first one and beckoned to the waiter for more.

"Hey, steady on," Della grinned, "with all the bubbly in the shop, I need to slow down a bit."

"You're fine," Annabelle dismissed, "we'll be eating in a bit."

"Thank God for that. I can't believe you asked that assistant in the shop to open a second bottle."

"Why not? I'm spending a small fortune in there, the least she can do is cough up with a drink."

"Yeah, but it's not like you. You don't normally drink so much in the daytime. I don't think I've ever seen you knocking it back like this."

"I just wanted to have a nice day as it's special choosing my dress and having you with me. And we've got a driver so we can have as much as we want." The waiter arrived with their cocktails and Annabelle thanked him.

"Well no more," Della said firmly, "not until we've eaten otherwise you'll be wheeling me out of here."

"Righto light weight," Annabelle said knocking back a huge slurp of her cocktail.

Della sipped hers gently, "The dress you've gone for is absolutely stunning. Funny how you went for the first one you chose."

"Yes, I just knew that was the one. I'd always gone back to it again and again online. I did love the third one though, but I'm pleased with the one I've got."

"Are you definitely going for the 6th December?" Della asked, "it doesn't give you long to get everything sorted."

"Yes, it's going ahead on the sixth. I've got most things done anyway. The sooner the better as far as I'm concerned."

"What about the divorce, will that all be done in time? Won't Max's wife will be kicking off with a hot-shot lawyer anytime soon?"

She couldn't possibly let on about the plan to extinguish clingy permanently, and by the time of the wedding, she'd be long gone and pushing up daisies.

"It sounds like it'll be amicable. Max has it all covered, I don't envisage any problems and he certainly doesn't."

"That's good then. I hope you're right. I'd be a bit cautious though, you know a woman scorned and all that."

"Oh, it's nothing like that. Like I said before, they live separate lives anyway. He's only living there with his wife for a couple more weeks."

"So why not leave now?"

Annabelle sighed, hating having to explain it. "It all gets a bit complicated. He's organised a huge bash for her fortieth. Family are coming from abroad. He feels a heel telling her he wants a divorce before then."

Della's face said it all. It was obvious she wasn't convinced. She'd have to fabricate more.

"The other thing is, her mother has been seriously ill so his wife has been caring for her at their home."

"Is she better now?"

"Think she's terminal by the sound of things," she lied, "she's gone back home now though."

"God, that must be hard. You have to admire him then for not being cruel. I just feel for you after all that business with Mark."

She smiled lovingly at Della, "You are a good friend, but I'm fine, honestly. I'm going to be with him shortly, we're going to have a fabulous wedding, and I'm going to have his children. I couldn't be happier. If it means waiting a couple more months, then so be it. It just shows me what a great man he is and how lucky I am to have him."

"No, he's lucky to have you. And you deserve to be happy after . . . after all that business with Mark. I can't wait to meet him."

"Me neither, you're going to love him, I know you will."

"What's going to happen to his son?" Della sipped her cocktail, "Have you met him yet?"

"No. Max is waiting until he leaves the family home. I'd have liked to have met him sooner, but I have to respect his decision. If he thinks it's better that way, who am I to argue. It's his son."

"Yeah, it's hard when kids are involved, and he'll know his son better than anyone. I guess they'll have joint custody so his lad will be spending time with you both?"

Annabelle didn't want to think about the kid. She'd previously checked out boarding schools for him but they wouldn't need them now. He'd be dead and buried with clingy before long. But for now, she needed to play the part so there wasn't a scrap of suspicion on her part. That's what George Grey had told her at his last visit. They were close now so she had to behave normally.

"Probably, but I think he's one of those special needs children, he doesn't sound all there to me."

"What, like learning difficulties, or physically disabled?"

"No, not disabled, he just sounds a bit slow. We may have to get him into some sort of special school so he's mixing with peers that are similar."

"Gosh, sounds like a lot to take on. Does Max know about, you know, all that business previously?"

She didn't want to talk about all that. She had enough with George-the-dull with his therapist's hat on. She much preferred the informality of him creeping into her bedroom and discussing the plans to get rid of clingy. Excitement surged through her when he visited her bedroom in the night. She loved the thought of extinguishing clingy and the kid.

"Yeah we discuss everything. That's all in the past now so everything is hunky-dory. My complete focus now is the wedding. And I'm so glad I've got you to help me."

"Yeah, I still worry about bringing you bad luck, though. Your last marriage crashed and burned."

"That was different. I should never have married Mark. And we are doing things completely different. You're not even my bridesmaid this time."

"I'm glad you weren't offended by that. I really didn't want to go through it all again."

"No, and it isn't a problem. But I do need your help. I can't do everything on my own."

"Now you're being modest. You could build a hotel complex on your own if you wanted to. I've never met anyone as driven as you."

Annabelle laughed, her friend knew her well. "Yes, that's my father's genes for you. But right now, I'm only interested in my future with Max. Everything else is secondary."

"Oh God, you have got it bad. I'll remind you of this when you're stuck at home with two kids running around and your designer dresses are hanging in the wardrobe – a thing of the past."

"I can't imagine anything better. Come on, let's go eat. All this wedding talk has made me hungry."

Chapter 33

Claire

Her anger was simmering away as she drove to the village hall where choir practice was held each week. Max had arrived home later than the time he'd said, which irritated her, but she'd bitten her tongue and not chastised him as that was all she seemed to be doing lately. These days she was never sure if he'd eaten or not, so she'd left his dinner on low and fed Freddy and herself earlier. As she was putting on her jacket and grabbing the car keys, he casually dropped in that he was going to Paris for a couple of days the following week, supposedly on business. Seemingly, it was all part of the upcoming merger and with the possibility of expanding further. Fury didn't come close to how she was feeling. The hours he was putting in currently in London were bad enough, but the thought of him making regular trips to Paris didn't sit well at all.

Although she wasn't one bit interested in him pursuing any business opportunities outside of the UK, she suggested asking her mum to come and look after Freddy and she could accompany him. A few days together might be good for them, as her mother had prompted, and even though Max would be tied up during the day and she'd only get to see him in the hotel in the evening, she thought it might be good for them both to spend some time together. But as expected, he was having none of it and came up with vague reasons and lame excuses as to why it wasn't a good idea. An enormous sense of sadness kicked in, she was beginning to accept that her and Max were drifting apart and had to conclude maybe that was the reason she was anxious and expecting something awful to happen. Perhaps her and Max were the awful?

She pulled up outside the village hall, grateful to have a couple of hours where she could sing and forget about Max. It was such a delight to hear the singing in the relatively plush hall with high beamed rafters which enhanced the keyboard playing and voices.

Sheila, one of the older ladies, was sitting inside the doorway, collecting the money for the choir session. She greeted her with a welcoming smile. "Hi, Claire, how are you?"

"Fine thank you, Sheila, are you?"

"Yes, all good."

"Great. I've invited someone to come tonight," Claire looked around the hall at those that had already arrived, "I'm not entirely sure he will though. I can't see him."

"It's a man, is it?" Sheila didn't wait for an acknowledgment, "Brilliant, we need a few more of those. Graham's still not well, he says it will be a couple more weeks until he's back at full pelt."

"We'll let him off, then. Surgery is a big thing. He'll be back soon enough."

Claire felt a movement behind her. Her instinct told her it was Adam before she saw him, almost like a sixth sense that he was there. She turned around to see the man she'd spent all day hoping would come. And he looked pretty good out of his usual shorts and a tee shirt. He hadn't pushed the boat out with anything smart, it was only jeans and a shirt, but he looked pretty damn good from where she was standing. She had to take a deep breath to inwardly stifle her increased heart rate.

"Ah, you're here, so pleased you made it. Sheila, this is Adam I was just telling you about."

"Welcome, Adam, so pleased to have you join us. I was just saying to Claire we could do with more men."

"I'm glad to be here, although I must confess, my singing is rather contemporary. I'm more of a band and a guitar type of singer."

"Then you'll be fine here. It's all about participation, it doesn't matter if you haven't got the greatest voice," she smiled sheepishly, realising what she'd implied, "although I'm sure yours will be wonderful."

"What can I say," he grinned, "I'll try my best."

"Would you like a coffee before we start?" Claire asked, trying to suffocate the excitement that had surged through her that he was actually there.

"Yeah a coffee would be good."

She shouldn't be thrilled, but she was. They walked towards the tea and coffee stand and she loved the feeling of how tall he was next to her. It made her feel petite and stupidly desirable in a feminine sort of way. "I'll introduce you to Melvin who plays keyboard and directs us."

As she fiddled with the filter coffee machine, she had to suppress an acute feeling of awkwardness. Almost as if seeing him at the house was okay, but out at choir, she was doing something wrong.

"I'm so pleased you came," she stifled her discomfort and handed him a coffee, "they really are lovely people. I look forward to coming each week, and last week I went with them for a quick drink to the pub next door."

"What?" he widened his eyes playfully, "are you telling me that you actually succumbed? How late home were you, exactly?" he teased.

"Ohhh, I don't know, maybe ten thirty," she grinned, "we know how to party at choir. It was nice for a change, I must say."

He took a sip of his coffee, "Don't you get out much with Max?"

"No, we don't now we've moved from London. Not that I miss all the stuff we used to attend. Most of the people at those functions weren't what I'd call genuine. I prefer people like these at the choir. Don't tell Max though, he sees them very much like the little people in life. It's a side of him I don't particularly like, I have to say."

"Do you think we could join them for drink afterwards or will two late nights be stretching it?"

"I think I can push the boat out again, why not." She certainly wasn't in a rush to get home for Max, the errant husband. "Come on, let's get you introduced to everyone."

* * *

Choir practice had been fun and Adam seemed to have enjoyed himself. They'd sung a few of her favourites, such as Bridge Over Troubled Waters, Don't Leave Me This Way and A Hard Day's Night. She couldn't see Adam as he was stood well behind her, but she'd caught up with him walking towards the pub and his spirits had been high. He'd enjoyed it. She felt exactly the same way after singing.

They sat at the end of the table at the pub with some of the others. Adam had insisted on going to the bar for their drinks.

"So," she fixed her gaze on Adam sat opposite her, and spoke in a way to include the others, "can we tempt you to come back next week?"

"Sure, I'm up for it. I enjoyed it actually. I like the idea it's a rock choir rather than a more traditional one."

"Claire mentioned you used to sing in a band?" Paul, one of the choir members asked.

"I did, but that was a long, long time ago. Nowadays I just sing for pleasure strumming my guitar. I find it relaxing."

"I bet. But I'm glad you've joined us, you do have a good voice."

Adam nodded, "Cheers mate," he lifted his pint, "and that's before you've had a drink."

He turned to Claire. "Have you been attending long?"

"No, only a few months, but I find myself looking forward to it each week. Singing somehow has the ability to lift my spirits."

He paused for a few seconds while those closest carried on conversations with each other.

"So your spirits need lifting do they?" His green eyes stared intensely into hers.

"Not lifting as such. I don't know why I said that." She took a gulp of wine to suppress the wave of emotion rippling below the surface.

"I get it," he took a sip of his pint and wiped his mouth with his hand, "it's life. Not all days are good and I always find that loneliness creeps up on you when you least expect it."

She found his ability to understand comforting, particularly when he must be struggling too. He'd lost his liberty, his girlfriend, his home, and his livelihood. Yet here he was empathising with her.

"I am sorry. You've had a terrible time, too. I shouldn't be moaning about my troubles."

"Hey, no probs. And you aren't moaning, I asked the question. I hope things improve for you though and Max manages to cut down a bit on work, if that's what you want."

"I want that more than anything. Right now he's got some sort of deal he's working on but says once he's got that tied up, then he'll make more time."

"Your expression tells me you don't think he will?"

"To be honest, I'm worried that by the time he does, it might be too late. Don't get me wrong, I love Max, and I know he loves me, but he seems to love work more. He's always been driven, but of late, it seems more so."

"Must be hard, then. I must say, if you were my wife, I'd definitely make time for you. I'm amazed he even lets you out of bed."

She could feel her face heating up. *Where the hell had that come from?*

He had the grace to look embarrassed. "I shouldn't have said that, it's the beer. Sorry."

"It's okay, I'm taking it as a compliment. I'm flattered someone as young as you would say that about me, especially as my fortieth birthday is looming."

"What's age?" he shrugged, "You look pretty fit to me . . . and hot."

"Crikey, now I am embarrassed. It's a long time since I've been called hot."

The way he looked at her made her burn up all the more. "Anyway, there isn't that much of an age difference between us. I'm thirty-four."

"You seem much younger somehow. But maybe that's because I suddenly feel old." She took another sip of her wine. "Hey, enough of this, I'm getting all maudlin now and it's been a lovely night."

He gulped down the last of his drink, "I'm going to grab another pint, can I get you another wine?" he nodded to her empty glass.

"No, best not, I've got to drive. I can give you a lift home if you like?" She realised he might want to stay drinking in the pub, or maybe even not want her to know where he lived, "Or you might want to hang about here?"

"No, I'd love a lift. Do you want me to come now, or am I alright for another?"

"Yes," she glanced at her watch. It would do Max good if he had to wait around for her for a change, "that's fine, it's only nine thirty."

"I can't drink on my own though. Can I get you a soft drink?"

"Oh, go on then, I'll have a lime and soda please."

As he made his way to the bar, she was ridiculously happy that she was going to be spending a little more time with him. And he thought she was hot? She glanced across to look at him slouched on the bar with his jeans hung down his waist and his bulging pecs – a perfect specimen of what she'd call hot.

She placed her hands on her face to cool down her burning cheeks. She felt giddy and sensed her heart was racing a tiny bit faster yet again. It must be the wine. One more of those and she might be telling him exactly how hot she found him.

Thank God for soft drinks.

Chapter 34

Claire

"I want to go to Thorndike Academy with Jake," Freddy said firmly, changing from his school uniform in the bedroom.

She'd put off long enough having the discussion with him about school options as she knew what he would want despite Max's insistence.

"I know you do, sweetheart, and you probably will go there." She hung his blazer and trousers in the wardrobe, "But you need to do the test to see if you can get in the William Grange grammar school. Jake will probably be taking the test as well."

"No, he isn't. He's going to Thorndike, his brother's there. I want to go with him."

"Well, Daddy and I would like you to at least try the test. We can get you some help to do some practice eleven plus papers. Then when it comes to doing it, it won't be as difficult."

He screwed his face up. "But I don't want to take the test to go to that school!"

He had a point. In his little mind, why would you take a test, if you weren't going to go to the school?

"I'll have to talk to Daddy and tell him how you feel. He wants you to go there very much as it's the school he went to when he was your age."

His little face was sullen. He knew his daddy would insist about school. She'd need to have a discussion with Max even though she dreaded it. He'd only get cross.

"Let's forget about it now, shall we. How about we go and take Adam some coffee and cake. I think I saw him earlier at those huge conifer trees."

"Yeah, let's."

"Okay, get your cap as it's hot and we'll go find him. I'll just make some coffee for him and put it in a thermos mug to keep it warm."

"Can I take some Coke to have?"

"Course you can. I'll pack you cake as well, how about that?"

"Yeah," he squealed enthusiastically.

They made their way down the garden. Freddy was armed with his Manchester United sticker book which she hadn't been able to prise away from him.

Freddy was too busy talking to see Adam initially, but her radar was on and she spotted him, stood on a ladder chopping down the conifers. As she approached her tummy gave the usual flutter. She could tell herself all she wanted that she wasn't attracted to him, but it was a lie. Every day she looked for him arriving and managed to find some excuse to engage him and today was no exception, even though she'd got her son in tow. It was almost as if she needed someone there as she didn't quite trust herself.

"There he is," Freddy pointed. "Adam!" he called.

Adam stopped what he was doing and gave them an almighty grin. Why the hell wasn't he a boring old gardener like Pippa's? Her tummy wouldn't flip then.

"We've brought you some cake," Freddy shouted.

She smiled awkwardly. Thank goodness he wouldn't have any idea how her heart-rate accelerated around him. "And coffee," she said, "although it might be a bit hot for that."

"I'd drink coffee if I was in the desert," he answered coming down the ladder. He was just like her, she loved hot black coffee. Another thing they had in common.

She looked round for somewhere to sit and opted for a low wall. Adam dragged his ladders up to it and used a rung to perch his bottom on. She handed him the mug and focussed on his hands as he removed the lid and took a mouthful.

"Just what I needed." He wiped his mouth with the back of his hand. Stupidly she found it sexy.

Freddy brought her out of her spell. "Mummy's brought us some chocolate cake."

"Has she? That's my favourite."

"Mine too," Freddy replied gleefully. It was funny how he gelled so well with Adam. He really seemed to like him despite hardly knowing him.

She handed Adam a piece of cake wrapped in a serviette and gave Freddy one too.

"Aren't you having any?" Adam asked taking a huge bite.

"No, I'm fine."

She opened the can of Coke and handed it to Freddy. "I ate earlier and unlike you, I'm not doing any physical work so anything high in calories lingers."

"I doubt that," his eyes focussed on her body, "you have a great figure."

Now she was mortified. Thankfully, Freddy broke the moment, "I've brought my Man U stickers for you to see."

"Great," Adam replied taking another bite of his cake. But he was still watching her. Things were starting to shift between them and she wasn't sure how to react.

"Haven't you got a drink?" he asked, knowing full well she hadn't. "Here," he handed her his mug, "have some of this."

She took it from him feeling even more off balance. Drinking out of the cup he'd had his mouth round second's earlier, seemed far too intimate. *He's only being friendly,* she told herself. But a warmth spread through her as she took a sip from the very place his lips had been and passed it back.

"You're doing a fabulous job with the trees," she said to cover up her awkwardness. Max had said he wanted them left for privacy but cut right back. They seemed much tidier.

"Yeah, they needed doing. I'm just going to clear this lot up now. Trimming and pruning is the best bit of gardening, clearing up the worst."

"Oh dear, is there anything I can do to help?"

"Absolutely not. It's how I earn my money." He glugged the last of his coffee and handed the mug back to her. "Stopping for coffee and cake helps though, now I have renewed energy." She liked the way his eyes twinkled.

"Can I help you, Adam?" her son asked.

"No, sweetie, you can't," she cut in, "it's dangerous with the hedge trimmer. Adam has to do that on his own."

"I can finish the rest of that tomorrow, he can help me with clearing the leaves if he wants to." Adam looked at Freddy, "It's messy work though, buddy."

Freddy's eyes lit up. "Can I, Mummy? I want to help."

She gave Adam a look as if to say, I'd rather he didn't, but if he noticed, he didn't acknowledge it.

"It would be nice for me to have some company," Adam said, "and do him good in the fresh air, I'm sure."

He was right, but she was fearful of Max. Not that he was around and unlikely to be home much before seven. And because he wasn't around much, he had no idea the amount of time Freddy was spending with Adam, which was a relief.

"Okay then, I've got some bits to do in the house. But not for long, you still have spellings to learn tonight, and to practice your poem for choral speaking."

"A poem?" Adam asked, "I love poems. What's it called?"

"The Owl And The Pussy-Cat."

"I know that, we can do it together while we clear up the leaves, and your spellings if you want to."

Freddy gave an agreeable nod, obviously liking the thought of doing his spellings with someone other than his mother for a change.

"Can you remember what the spellings are?" Adam asked her.

"Not off the top of my head, I can't. But honestly, don't worry, I can help him with those."

"No need. Can you text me them and we'll learn them while we do our men's work, eh buddy?"

That tickled Freddy. "Yeah, while we do our men's work."

She raised her hands in defeat. "Okay, I'll go back to the house and text you the poem and spellings."

"No need to send the poem, I know it," Adam said, "I did it at school."

"What and you can still remember it?" she asked.

"Easily," he winked, "I never forget anything."

His wink unsettled her more than she wanted to admit. To cover up her embarrassment, she stood up and made her way towards the house and a warmth flooded through her as she listened to the gentle way she heard Adam speaking to Freddy, "Right then, matey, we'd best crack on. Pass some of those bags over there and we'll bag up the leaves, and while we're doing that, start the poem and show me what you can remember."

"The owl and the pussy-cat went to sea, in a beautiful pea-green boat," her son's voice drifted off in the distance but she hadn't missed the joy in his tone, having a male pay him some attention.

If only his own dad would.

Back inside the house after she'd texted Adam the spellings, she unloaded the dishwasher and prepared the vegetables for dinner. When she'd finished, Freddy still wasn't back, so she dialled Max's number and wandered down the hallway, half expecting to get his voicemail, but he picked up straight away. "Hi, love."

"Oh, hi. I was going to leave a message. Just wanted to know what time you're back tonight?"

"Er, maybe about seven thirty."

"That's good. I'll do dinner for then. I wanted to give you the heads up, too, Freddy wants to go to Thorndike Academy with his friend, Jake."

"Does he now? Well I hope you told him he's not going there. He's going to William Grange."

"I did but he's not really keen. I thought we could have a chat with him tonight over dinner. Maybe we ought to take into account what he wants?"

"He's ten years old, Claire, I think we are best placed to decide what's best for him at the moment, don't you?"

"Yes, but if he really doesn't want to go, I don't think it's right to push him."

"On this occasion, you're wrong. We should be pushing him. When he's eighteen, he can make his own decisions, but right now, we decide for him. That's our job."

Typical dogmatic Max. As if he'd allow Freddy to make decisions at eighteen. By then he'll be picking the university he wanted him to attend. She wished she hadn't rung. She'd only done so to pave the way for the comprehensive school but it had been a complete waste of time. Now she was dreading dinner.

"Okay, we'll see you tonight when you get home."

Her eyes were drawn towards the dining room door which was slightly ajar. She never left it like that. It was always closed off.

"Have you contacted the woman about the eleven plus practice papers?"

"No," she said making her way into the dining room, "I didn't see the point if he doesn't want to go."

The wedding photograph of her and Max had been moved. It wasn't in its usual position.

He gave an irritated sigh. "We'll talk about it later. Get me the woman's number and I'll ring her myself."

"Okay. Hey, just quickly before you go, did you move our photo in the dining room?"

"What?"

"The wedding photo of us. Have you been looking at it?"

"No, I haven't touched it. Look, someone's come in, I'm going to have to get off. I'll talk to you later. Bye."

"Bye." She cut the call.

Someone had moved the photo. And if it wasn't Max, it must be Freddy, although that seemed most unlikely. She'd have to ask him.

Still puzzled, she made her way into the kitchen area and was instantly distracted by Adam heading towards the house pushing a delighted Freddy in the wheelbarrow. He was running with him and Freddy was shrieking with laughter. It was such a joyful sight to see her son having fun. His grandad used to do so much with him and he missed that. And she desperately missed her dad too. Witnessing Freddy and Adam together, reminded her just how much.

She opened the bi-fold doors, "How dirty are you, young man!" she grinned.

Adam brought the barrow to a standstill. "Dirty?" he scowled playfully at Freddy as he climbed out, "did your mum just call us dirty? How dare she when we've been working hard. I vote we need to punish her for that outrageous remark."

Freddy jumped up and down, loving the fun. "Yeah, we need to punish her."

Claire held her arms up in the air joining in with the laughter. "Okay, I surrender. Please don't punish me. I have ice creams in the freezer as a peace-offering."

Adam widened his eyes at Freddy, "Mmmm, well, if she's

offering ice-creams, I reckon we should let her off. What do you think?"

"I think we should let her off, too."

"Oh thank you," she smiled, loving the delight on her little boy's face, "quickly come and wash your hands while I'll get you one each."

"Sit here, Adam, next to me," Freddy gleefully said from the table as Adam left the sink area.

"I might have mine outside in the fresh air, buddy," Adam said knowing full well Max would not be happy at him being in the house.

"You're okay, Adam," she reassured handing them both an ice cream, "sit here. It's fine, honestly." She knew Max wouldn't be back for hours.

"If you're sure," he said and took his seat next to Freddy. "Aren't you having one?"

"I don't generally eat ice creams."

"Aww, well you have to. That's the deal, isn't it, matey? Mum's got to have one, too."

"That's the deal, Mummy," Freddy repeated copying Adam word for word.

"Okay, okay." She made her way to the freezer and selected one and sat down with them both at the kitchen table and began to eat her own ice cream.

It gave her a warm glow seeing her son was having a nice time, and she had an inner joy too. It was only a little playful interaction, but it reminded her she rarely had fun anymore. She couldn't remember the last time she'd been light of heart as all she seemed to do lately was worry. And even though she was currently enjoying herself eating ice cream with Freddy and Adam, her tummy was twisting thinking Freddy was going to be in trouble later on that evening with his father if he protested about the grammar school. And she knew categorically she'd be in even more trouble if Max found out they'd spent the afternoon with Adam in the house eating ice-creams.

Freddy interrupted her anxious thoughts, "Shall I do the poem for Mummy now, Adam?"

"You better, then you can show her how you know your spellings too."

Chapter 35

Annabelle

Eating at Simone's was always a joy with Anthony for company. She finished her dessert and waited while he finished his selection of cheeses and biscuits. It was Friday evening and Max was home in Sandbanks with clingy. But they'd had a fabulous afternoon of lovemaking together so she was extremely happy and sated. That was until she noticed George Grey sitting at an adjacent table. Although she was onboard with the plan to go ahead to get rid of clingy and her brat, which was within touching distance now, she didn't like he was invading every aspect of her life. How could he even afford Simone's? And who was the awful woman he was with? She looked equally as grey as he did in her beige chain store dress. Not that he looked anything remarkable, he was in the suit he wore most often for their therapy sessions. He only seemed to have two from what she'd observed, and no more than three ties.

She didn't attempt to acknowledge him. The further she got away from him the better. He unnerved her sat so close.

"Annabelle," Anthony said, "you seem miles away."

"Sorry. Shall we have our coffees in the lounge?" she asked, "I need to use the ladies'." She retrieved her bag and stood up.

Anthony, always the gentleman, stood also. "Good idea, I'll get it sorted and meet you in there. The usual?"

"That would be lovely, thank you." She walked in front of Anthony as they left the restaurant. George Grey didn't try to acknowledge her. Too busy with his eyes on the woman sat opposite him. But he'd visit later, he always did the nights Max wasn't there.

Who'd fancy him with the hideous birthmark, for God's sake?

"I'm pleased you look a little brighter," she said to Anthony as they sipped their liqueur coffees seated on the Chesterfield sofa in the salubrious lounge. "I've been worried about you since Fiona." Over dinner they'd discussed business issues. She'd been itching to mention Fiona but didn't want to attach any importance to her so had left it until the end of the evening.

"I'm fine, my darling, don't worry about me. I've given myself a stern talking to. I'll not be rushing headlong into another romance in the future, that's for sure. The investigator was right, no point in pursuing someone who doesn't want to be pursued."

"I quite agree. But it's still hurtful what she did to you. Do you know if the investigator found where she was living?"

"Yes, she did, but said there was information that she couldn't share and would only say there was no going back. So whether she spoke directly to her, or saw her maybe with another man, I don't know. To be honest, I didn't ask. It satisfied me in my mind it wasn't meant to be. And I've left it at that."

Halleluiah. She leaned across and squeezed his hand. "I'm so sorry it didn't work out. You are such a lovely man. I'm sure there'll be someone out there that deserves your love. Look at me, I'd have never dreamt I'd be head over heels like I am."

"I'm pleased you're happy, Annabelle, I truly am. But I'd

be failing in my duty as . . . what can I call myself, maybe a surrogate father." She knew what was coming and wanted to deflect from it.

She smiled, "We'll go for surrogate brother I think. That suits you better."

"I'll not argue with that," he smiled lovingly, "but I do need to speak out, in my surrogate role of course, about you rushing along with Max Maric. I know you don't want to hear it, but I'm worried about him and his influence on you."

"Don't be. I love him, and he loves me, I can assure you of that."

"Yes, that might well be. But I can't help worrying that much as he loves you, he may also love Claybourne Hall. Let's be frank, it would be quite a coup if the two companies merged, and you're not telling me it hasn't come up in conversation between the two of you?"

She took a deep breath in. Maybe now might be the appropriate time to pave the way.

"I'd be lying if I denied that. But I promise you, Anthony, I wouldn't do anything to jeopardise all the hard work Daddy and you have put in to build it up. I'm not about to merge us with Max Maric's company. He might see that as an opportunity, but that's not on my agenda."

"Well, I have to say that's quite a relief."

"Good. And you know me, I don't do anything without running it by you. You are Claybourne Leisure. You're the brains behind all the innovation. So you can rest assured, if there was anything in the future, and I'm putting the emphasis on if . . . *if* there was anything to consider, you'd be the first to know."

He patted her hand, "Thank you, my darling, you don't know how delighted I am to hear that. I don't want anyone encroaching on all the hard work over the years that your father put in, and since his death what we've achieved."

"You have my word, so you can relax now. And that brings me on to something else I would like to ask you."

"Go ahead."

"When I married Mark, as you know we tied the knot in Edinburgh, but this time, when I marry Max, I'm doing it here in London. And I want you to give me away."

He looked hesitant. "That's a tough ask, Annabelle. You know how I feel about you. And I need to be totally honest, I'm not entirely convinced Max Maric is right for you. It all seems to be happening rather quickly. When exactly are you thinking of getting married?"

"December 6th."

"What, this year?"

"Yes, of course this year."

"But December isn't that far away."

"I know that silly, that's what we both want. Why wait?"

"Has he moved out of the marital home yet?"

"Partly. They live separately anyway, I've told you. He's moving in with me next week on the nineteenth."

He screwed his face up. "Yes, but why's he not with you now?"

"It's a long story which I don't want to go into right now. I love him, Anthony, so much, and I'm going to be his wife and have his children. Nothing is going to change that. The wedding is all booked, and I so want you to be a part of it. And when children do come along, I want you to be part of their life, just as you're part of mine. You're going to be their godfather, I hope. But for now, I would like very much for you to give me away on my wedding day. I haven't got anyone else. Please say you will?"

He smiled lovingly at her. "How can I ever resist you? I've only ever wanted your happiness. And while I secretly have always hoped from us being this high," he gestured with his hand, "it would be me, I have to accept defeat," he said graciously, "so, yes, I'll be proud to give you away. But I will say this, that man will have a lot to answer for if he doesn't take care of you. I promised your father I would always look out for you, and I'll honour that."

Thank God she'd got rid of Fiona-the-cleaner. She had Anthony back where she wanted him to be. Right next to her, looking out for her welfare.

"You don't know how pleased I am to hear you say that." She leaned across and kissed his cheek, "Thank you, you're a good man. Daddy would be proud of you. Now then, shall we have a brandy for the road?"

"Yes, of course we can, if you'd like one."

"Why not?"

If she'd like one – she couldn't seem to get by these days without the crutch of alcohol. But that'd be only temporary, with coming off her medication. She knew she was experiencing withdrawal symptoms as she felt heady most days, and had experienced on more than one occasion a feeling that she was on the outside looking in, but she reassured herself that would pass and if she needed a little extra to drink for now, then so be it. It wouldn't do any harm.

Anthony beckoned a waiter and ordered them a Rémy Martin cognac each.

Now she could relax.

Everything was in place. It was almost clingy's birthday and after that, Max would be with her for the rest of their lives. And now she had Anthony onboard for her wedding, everything was sorted. All that was left was for George Grey to facilitate his thugs to burn her nemesis, and once her and the brat were well and truly gone, she'd get her happy-ever-after.

And she so deserved it.

Chapter 36

Annabelle

It was her birthday, ten days before clingy's. She was with Max in Paris and she couldn't be happier. Two days and two nights in which they'd go to bed together and wake up together. They were going to do the touristy stuff such as a cruise down the Seine, and a visit to the Palace of Versailles and the Louvre museum, all of which she'd visited before but wasn't going to tell him. His thoughtfulness thrilled her and she wasn't going to spoil it. She was a proven actress and could um and ah as good as the rest of them.

At the back of her mind the special party Max had planned for clingy gnawed away at her, even though shortly after it, she was going to crash and burn – gone from their lives forever. The anticipation accelerated her excitement that everything was going according to plan. And she had a plan B if George Grey and his thugs didn't deliver . . . she had Yegor. He definitely would. So one way or another, clingy would be history after the following week.

The flight to Paris had only been short, but it was comforting to have the man she loved at her side. Her mood was so much better of late, her life was good. The only blot on the horizon was bloody George Grey spying on her. He'd been nosing around her house when she hadn't been there. Stuff had been moved around and she suspected he'd used her facilities in the bathroom.

She made the decision that as soon as Max was living with her, she was going to ditch the sessions with the therapist. It would be better in terms of the arson attack. She needed to put some distance between them and she didn't want Max to find out she'd been seeing him. If he harassed her to continue with the sessions, which he most probably would, she'd get Yegor to warn him off.

Right now, she couldn't be happier. Her life was mapped out, and her future sorted. She just needed him to get clingy's 40th birthday party out of the way, and Max would be with her all the time. The thought of the party and how he would no doubt be perceived as the perfect husband caused a tightness in her belly which she had to try and shrug off. The closer it got to the date, the more the waves of anxiety kicked in. She knew categorically Max was going to leave his wife, that's why she'd made all the preparations for the wedding, but she was really impatient and jittery. She'd waited long enough for him now.

"I'm hungry, shall we stop and grab something," Max suggested as they walked along the Champs-Élysées, browsing in the luxury shop windows.

"You're always hungry." She checked her watch, "It's only been a few hours since breakfast at the airport."

"I know, but my stomach can't remember that. It's saying feed me."

"And you had that awful soggy sandwich on the flight. I reckon you've got one of those tapeworms the way you consume food. I don't know how you manage to stay so lean, I really don't."

"Hard bloody slog on the cross trainer, that's how, and the older I get, the more I have to work at it. Anyway you didn't eat your snack on the plane so you must be hungry."

"I rarely eat on a flight, and the breakfast was huge. I never normally eat like that, so I'll definitely have to skip lunch in favour of dinner tonight."

"Well, can we feed this hungry man, otherwise I'll be useless in bed this afternoon."

"Oh, well we can't have that. We better get you some sustenance."

He laughed and gave her a gentle kiss. "A woman after my own heart."

"You bet," she smiled tenderly at him, already looking forward to their afternoon of lovemaking.

* * *

They were sitting at an intimate table in the secluded lounge area of the hotel restaurant they were staying at, sipping aperitifs prior to dinner. Max had said he wanted to eat at the hotel that night and crash straight into bed. The following night, he'd booked dinner at the top of the Eiffel Tower but he reckoned it was too tacky for her birthday evening. She didn't mind where they ate, the thrill for her was having him all to herself.

She marvelled that he was perusing the menu after all he'd eaten that day. He was insatiable, and not only on the food front. Her body was acutely aware how they'd spent the afternoon and hopefully there would be more of that after dinner.

"You order for me, something light though, I don't know . . . maybe a salad for starters and a fish dish. You choose."

She watched his handsome features diligently going through each dish and taking his time choosing the wines. She knew from experience Max's penchant for fine wine.

"You do love a good wine, don't you?"

"I most definitely do. Life's too short to drink cheap wine, don't you think?"

"Yeah, my father used to say exactly that and taught me to appreciate fine wines. But you take selecting a wine to a different level. You must know the list off by heart the amount of time you're taking."

"It can't be rushed," he raised his eyebrows jokingly, "food is only as good as the wine that accompanies it. Someone said that . . . I can't remember who though."

"Rubbish, that's you saying it. I've never heard that before." She finished the last of her drink. It was hitting the spot, she was beginning to feel more relaxed.

"Do you have a wine cellar at home?"

Blast, why had she asked that? She rarely asked him things about his home life. Not because she didn't want to know, it was just too painful to hear him talk about it. Yegor had provided her all the information she needed on his home front so she knew the answer anyway.

"Yes, it was one of the first things I sorted when I rebuilt the house."

"I know you're going to be sad leaving it, I hope we can get something equally as nice together to bring our family up in."

"Yeah, we'll have to see."

"What about your flat in London? You'll need to put that on the market as well."

"I guess so, yes."

"So initially we'll live in mine until we decide what to do?"

"That's what we said, didn't we?" He finished the last of his drink. "They're a bit slow don't you think?"

"What's the rush? Have another cocktail if you want."

"Nah, I'm alright, just ready to eat now. I'll give it another few minutes," he said making it obvious by the movement of his head to anyone who was looking he was ready to go through to the restaurant.

She wanted to get back to the *us* conversation.

"When do you think realistically we'll be all sorted with the merger so you can step back from work?"

He took a deep breath, "I was going to talk to you about business tomorrow night. I thought we'd have tonight just about you with it being your birthday. But now you've brought it up, I'd like to move sooner rather than later. I just need your accountants and shareholders to look over the plans I've had drawn up. I think we should steam ahead with that and then, once I leave Claire, we'll be all sorted. I really don't see the point in hanging around indefinitely." He took her hand, "You know how much I love you, you don't ever doubt that do you?"

"Of course I don't doubt it. But as I've already said, I'd rather wait until we're together permanently before we move towards any sort of amalgamation."

"Yeah, I do know that, you've told me often enough," she heard the disappointment in his voice, "I want to make a start, that's all. I'm not asking you to sign on the dotted line, it's more that these things take such a lot of time to process. And us being together has nothing to do with business, that's going to happen anyway. We'd still be together if there wasn't a business. I don't think either of us would last long apart, do you?"

The way he looked intensely at her won her over. She just couldn't resist the man.

He broke their gaze, "Oh, before I forget, I got you a little keep-sake. He reached into his jacket pocket and handed her something that was small and flat and gift-wrapped. He'd already given her the beautiful earrings she was wearing. He had impeccable taste, she couldn't have chosen better herself and they must have cost a pretty penny from the exclusive jewellers in Mayfair.

"For me? What is it?"

"Open it and see. I had it commissioned especially for you."

It was only a small thing, beautifully wrapped. She'd secretly hoped for a ring earlier that morning and tried not to show her sadness when she'd opened the earring gift from him. He quickly sensed her disappointment despite her trying not to show it and hurriedly explained he wanted to finalise their engagement once he'd made the break from clingy. She had no choice in accepting that. It made sense and demonstrated what an honourable man he was which would bode well for the future. But one thing she was sure about, once he had left the marital home and moved in with her, she was going to have one almighty diamond ring. She'd waited long enough.

She opened the pretty paper to reveal an envelope. In it was a beautiful card with a printed verse on it in the most delicate calligraphy writing.

Dearest Annie, if being loved by someone gives you strength and loving someone gives you courage – then I'm a powerful man thanks to you X

She was moved almost to tears. Nobody had ever been so kind and loving. It was the least valuable gift she'd ever been given, yet it was the most special.

She loved him for his sensitivity and his purpose. He knew the depth of their love, it had been just the two of them since they'd first got together. She had never met anyone she wanted as much as him. He was her soul mate and her future.

"It's the most beautiful gift I've ever been given. I'll treasure it. Thank you, darling."

She placed it carefully back in the envelope. "Okay, okay, you win, I'll have the merger agreement looked over, seeing as though it's not that long until you leave Claire anyway. We might as well get the ball rolling, but I'm warning you, Anthony's going to be devastated."

"It's got nothing to do with him," he dismissed, "don't tell him until you have to. It's your business, the one your father built up. And I'll be taking care of it, and you as well. You don't need Anthony."

"Yes, but he'll still have a senior job, I'm not having him tossed aside, Max, not for anything. He's like family to me and I want his job secure."

"It will be. I don't want him privy to our decision making though. That's private between you and I?"

"Yes, I know. But don't leave him out in the cold whatever we decide to do. I'm not having that."

"I won't, I promise. Now enough about work, tonight's about your birthday. You said you had something else to discuss tonight?"

"Yes, that's right. I wondered if you wanted me to organise our honeymoon and surprise you? I already have an idea."

"Steady on," he caught the eye of a waiter and raised his hand indicating two more cocktails. "We might as well have another drink the rate these are going. Sorry, were where we?"

"Our honeymoon."

"Oh yeah." He pulled a bit of a painful face, "I've got a divorce to get through first. Maybe it's a bit too soon to be thinking about a honeymoon?" He must have seen her dejected impression as he added, "A lovely idea though, when we can."

Men were so stupid. The whole wedding was sorted thanks to her tenacity. She'd tell him when he left clingy, though. He was going to be a widower shortly after that anyway.

"I know," she agreed, to pacify him, "I'm thinking out loud that's all. What do you think? I'd like to do something as a wedding present to you and I've got an idea you're sure to love."

"Not somewhere you've been with anyone else I hope?"

"Don't be silly. As if I'd do that. And you should know by now, there's never been anyone else." She glanced at him, "I mean it Max. Nobody has ever made me feel like you do. I love you beyond anyone or anything before you. You know that, surely?"

He was stopped from answering as the waiter placed their drinks down.

"Thank you," Max said, "we're ready to go through when you are."

"Okay, sir, give me a moment."

He waited until they were on their own and lifted her hand to his lips. "You are amazing, do you know that. After that declaration of love, I can't imagine anything better than spending a couple of weeks away with you. A honeymoon is certainly something to look forward to." He raised his glass, "Here's to us, beautiful, and our future together."

She clinked her glass with his and stared into the dark eyes of the man she loved. He was everything she wanted, and the best bit was, he felt exactly the same about her.

"Excuse me," the maitre d' interrupted, "your table's ready, sir if you'd like to follow me."

Max stood and beckoned her to go forward and she did so with a heart that was bursting. A bright future was ahead for them both, together. They'd be formidable as a team in life and in business. After the last horrendous business with her ex, it was something she was fearful would never happen.

But right now it was happening.

And she was one lucky lady.

Life was just a smidge away from perfect.

Chapter 37

Claire

They sat indoors at Pippa's, overlooking a drenched garden. The rain had been relentless that morning so Claire had driven round instead of her usual walk. She hadn't seen her friend for a while and had been delighted to receive a text inviting her for a visit.

She took a sip of her coffee. "I'm so pleased you asked me to come round, I didn't expect it as I thought your friend Liz would be here by now."

"Yeah, she should be but she's not been brilliant since her final chemo. I'm expecting her at the weekend all being well."

"Oh, that'll be great for you both. Here, I brought you this," she handed over a small envelope.

"What is it?" Pippa asked.

"Open it and you'll see."

Pippa opened the envelope and read the gold embossed card. "What a beautiful invitation. And how kind of you to invite me to your birthday party, you didn't have to."

"I know I didn't, but I'd love it if you did come. I want you to meet my husband and son. I talk about you to them so it'll be nice to put a face to a name. And I've put a plus one so I'm hoping your friend Liz can come as well. I'd love to meet her. And before you say anything, everything is outside in a marquee, and I have a toilet near the pool which you can use as it's big enough to get your wheelchair in."

"That really is thoughtful of you. Can I leave it open . . . I don't want to mess you about or anything, I just need to find out how Liz is when she gets here. I don't want to be dragging her out if she's not up to it. The reason for her coming is rest and recuperation."

"That's absolutely fine, just text me on the day and let me know if you're able to come. And don't worry if you can't, I do understand. But if not, I must get you round one day to meet everyone."

"That'd be lovely, I'll see what I can do for your party. Have you got many coming?"

"I think off the top of my head there's about fifty. I've not really had much to do with it to be honest, Max has organised it all."

"Has he? What a fabulous husband."

"Mmmmm, I wouldn't call him that exactly, especially not lately."

"Why, he's not been naughty, has he?"

"No," Claire quickly dismissed, "nothing like that." She was puzzled as to why Pippa would immediately come to that conclusion. "It's more he's working endless hours and neglecting his duties as a husband and father. Not that he sees it quite that way."

"Oh dear. Well it sounds like he's in debt to you, so a nice party should score him some brownie points, or should I say scout points?"

"Maybe, but if I'm totally honest, I'm not terribly keen on having a load of fuss. I can't stop it now of course as all the invites have gone out, but I'd rather have just gone away somewhere."

"Yeah, I get that."

"I mean, who wants to be celebrating reaching forty?"

Pippa laughed, "That's just a number though, you look nothing like forty."

"And you are a good friend to have. Believe you me, these days I'm feeling very much like forty."

"Why, because your husband's neglecting you?"

"Erm . . . I don't know really. It's just lately I haven't been feeling too brilliant. Nothing I can put my finger on. Just a bit tired and out of sorts."

"Maybe just hormonal or something, do you think? Or . . . any chance you could be pregnant?"

"Good God no, not a chance," Claire smiled wryly, "you'd need your husband around for that to happen and mine definitely isn't." It sounded desperate, saying it out loud, but it was the truth. It had been a while since they'd made love.

"Would you like more children? Forgive me if I'm prying, just tell me to shut up."

"No, you're not," Claire answered even though it did seem personal. "More children would have been nice, but it hasn't worked out that way. And now it's getting a bit late in the day for nappies and bottles."

"It's never too late for that, I wouldn't have thought." Pippa looked a bit dreamy, maybe she wanted children?

Claire's skin suddenly felt prickly, as if someone had walked across her grave. "Hey," she leaned back, "has anyone ever told you, you have the ability to draw information out of people. I seem to end up telling you all my woes when I'm here."

"You don't at all," Pippa said, "and I like listening about your life. It sounds so nice."

"Well, it's not perfect by any means, and I've had a few kicks lately that have knocked me down, but I'm fine really. So . . . swiftly moving on, are children something you'd like in the future?"

"Gosh, that's a biggie. I'd have to meet someone first and believe you me, that isn't easy at the best of times. Being in a wheelchair really isn't conducive to forming intimate relationships."

"Aw, I'm sorry, really I am. That was insensitive of me."

"Don't be daft. It's not beyond the realms of possibility. But the whole wheelchair thing is a massive problem. I'm sure it would be different if you were in a relationship when such an accident occurred, you know, in sickness and health and all that, but to meet someone from a starting point of being wheelchair bound, well that takes a special someone to take that on."

"Yes, I'm sure. But you're really attractive and such a lovely person, you deserve a husband and children. I'm sure you'd make a marvellous mum."

"That's so sweet, bless you for saying that. You're doing wonders for my self-esteem," she grinned. "Tell me, how are things going with that hot gardener of yours? Is he still as hot?"

"Definitely. He actually came to my choir group last week."

Pippa widened her eyes playfully, "Is that what they call it nowadays, choir practice."

"You are funny," Claire said shaking her head, "it's nothing like that. Between you and I, Adam has been in prison. It's a long story, but basically he killed someone in a fight. He's only just come out and this is his first job. He's lonely, so I invited him as he sings and plays the guitar."

"And he told you all this at . . ." she put some emphasis into her voice, "choir practice?"

"No, I knew that when he started with us, but we did go for a quick drink afterwards . . . with the rest of the group," she quickly added. "It sounds like he's had a torrid time by all accounts. I quite feel sorry for him."

"You need to be careful then," Pippa warned, "a neglected housewife and a red-hot gardener – it all sounds like a recipe for an affair if ever there was one."

"No, definitely not. I'd never cheat on Max. I couldn't live with myself if I did."

"What about Max," Pippa tilted her head, "do you think he'd ever cheat on you?"

The question added to Claire's discomfort. They were hardly old friends, she barely knew her and there was no way was she going to share details of her marriage and Max's brief affair. She couldn't have Pippa meeting Max for the first time and knowing that.

"No, he wouldn't," she dismissed emphatically. "Right, on that note," she had an overwhelming urge to leave and stood up, "I'd better be making a move if that's okay, Waitrose beckons." Pippa had hit a nerve that she'd considered, but she'd pushed it to the back of her mind not wanting to go there. But was it possible Max was cheating on her? It would certainly explain a lot.

Please no. She couldn't go through all that again. The previous time nearly destroyed her.

As Pippa went to retrieve her jacket, Claire glanced around the kitchen dining area. There weren't any intimate things around such as ornaments, photographs and books which you'd usually find in a house. But that was most probably because Pippa only used the house for a few days each week so most likely didn't want to transport all her personal items. She glanced down at the party invitation which Pippa had placed on the console table next to another solitary card which looked quite beautiful and personal. The slight noise of the wheelchair returning prohibited Claire reading further. The last thing she wanted was to appear nosy.

They made their way to the front door casually chatting about her party with Pippa assuring her she'd let her know if her and Liz could make it. Claire had an intuitive feeling that she wouldn't attend, and inexplicably, even though she'd extended the invitation, she was hoping she wouldn't. Her questioning that Max might be cheating, didn't sit at all well.

Claire kept her goodbye light and friendly. As she got

into her car and pulled down the drive, her friend was waving her off from the bay window and she waved back. Pippa would have no idea that her innocent questioning had somehow shifted their friendship. Whether it was the delicacy of the probing that made her feel uneasy, or how close to home it was, she wasn't sure.

All she knew was, now it had been said, it couldn't be unsaid.

Chapter 38

Annabelle

She was sitting with George Grey in his plush office. She glanced at the clock. Two minutes past three. She had fifty-eight minutes to come up with some fill-in rubbish. They both knew they'd moved on from the therapist and client relationship although he wasn't going to mention the night time visits, he'd stressed they must maintain a professional relationship at the office. And he'd emphasised about the covert cameras and tapes so she had to perform well and not raise any suspicion, just as she'd done at the psychiatrist's, Dr Stead.

Totally professional and behaving normally, he switched on the tape. He'd still have a job to do when it was all over and clingy and the brat were history. If anything did come out in the future with a police investigation, everything was all above board. He was her therapist and nothing more. She was more than happy to leave the planning of disposing of clingy to night time discussions in her room. He was quite right. They had to keep their meetings completely separate.

He began speaking to the tape as he always did, giving her name and the date before his voice turned to therapist mode. She got it. She just needed to play the game.

"I'm pleased to see you today, Annabelle. You've cancelled two of our last sessions." It seemed more of a statement than a question so she didn't bother answering.

He continued, "I've had a telephone conversation with Dr Stead. We discussed your upcoming marriage and the fact you've made your fiancé aware of your diagnosis, which will bode well for the future should things start spiralling out of control again. We both agree the fact you've made him aware of the situation, is good, but what I did want to discuss today was that he fully understands the consequence should you become ill again."

"Yes, he fully understands."

"Understands what, Annabelle? What exactly have you told him?"

She took a deep breath in, ready with another pack of lies she'd worked on during the drive to his office. "Everything you suggested last time. Naturally, he was a little concerned but I have to say, he's been very supportive."

"Concerned?" His brows creased together as only an enquiring therapist could. "Was he shocked?"

"A little, yes. Or maybe surprised is a better word."

"Tell me, during your . . ." he overdid the puzzled face, "how many months have you been together?"

"We've known each other years, but began our relationship four months ago." Even to herself it sounded a paltry amount of time, but she knew categorically that Max was the man she wanted to spend the rest of her life with.

He carried on along the same track, "So, during these four months, has he ever seen you get stressed or maybe lose your temper?"

"We all get stressed, but on the whole I'd say not. We don't really have a cross word. We both have the same goals in life and are completely compatible. I don't get angry like I did with my first husband."

"That's reassuring. But in everyday life, we all suffer with stress, or for want of a better expression, we all come under pressure. My concern is how you are going to handle that when such a situation arises, and more importantly, how your fiancé will react. We've worked together on coping strategies but we do need to be mindful that another incident could have huge consequences."

"Yes, of course. But as I've said many times since the episode with my late husband, I am now better. I'm a completely different person. That almost seems like it was somebody else. I'm on a new pathway in my life right now. Nothing like that will happen again with Max and I, I can assure you."

"But you do understand my apprehension regarding the speed in which you've progressed in your relationship. I'm reassured you have explained it all to your fiancé, but I'm somewhat sceptical about him not being unduly worried. No disrespect intended, but I think any man would be that enters into a relationship with a woman with a history such as yours."

"Yes, but he's relieved I have you helping me to move on as well as being thankful the courts were lenient. He knows I was ill at the time and is sympathetic about that. I've reassured him that I'm on medication to control everything. Dr Stead said as long as I keep taking it, he sees no reason for me to ever go back to that dark and dismal place."

"Has Dr Stead suggested that your fiancé accompanies you to any sessions with him?"

"No. He didn't seem to think that was necessary."

"I see. Then we must trust his professional opinion even if he and I differ. The main thing is, we are both responsible for your continued integration into society. You've been doing well with the bespoke programme, and we want to make sure that continues. But your life is going to change dramatically when you get married. Part of my role is overseeing your sustained positive mental health, but also I feel I have a responsibility to ensure that a man who has become central in your life, is aware of the potential chance at some stage of a reoccurrence of a negative episode which could put him in danger."

"Fine," she said firmly, "I'll discuss it in greater depth with him then."

"That's my advice. While I can't force you to bring your fiancé with you to one of our sessions, I am suggesting that he does accompany you. One session most probably would be all we'd need together."

"Right, well, I'll think about it. But before I do anything, is my medical history confidential? If I choose not to tell . . . elaborate further about my diagnosis, nobody else gets to know but you and Dr Stead, do they?"

She glared at George Grey knowing the answer but wanted to remind him of his place. He might have access to her bedroom and other aspects of her life, but he wasn't controlling her relationship with Max.

His face remained deadpan. "Of course your medical history is confidential. But we find ourselves in uncharted waters here. And as you've said yourself, you've explained everything that has happened to your fiancé, therefore," he peered over his glasses at her, "I'm finding it difficult to comprehend why you would object to him gaining more information. Information which could protect him and give him a greater awareness of how to support you if in the future you find your mood . . . fluctuating."

She needed to remain calm. Best to fake tiredness and get out of there.

"Look . . . with respect, I've spoken to Dr Stead and he's happy with me and my medication. And I've done as you previously suggested and explained everything that has happened to my fiancé. I'm feeling rather tired today and have a splitting headache. If you wouldn't mind, I'd like to cut today's session short."

"Of course. Just one thing that has occurred to me. You say you've explained everything. How clear have you been?"

"I don't know what you mean?"

"Have you told your fiancé there was an accident and

your husband died?" he paused giving her time to digest what he was saying . . . "or have you explained it was you that killed him?"

Chapter 39

Claire

It was her fortieth birthday. How the hell had that happened? As she carefully examined her foundation that boasted a flawless much younger skin, she studied every crease and wrinkle in the mirror. She still looked okay for her age, but not as perky as she once did. And there were days when she had to pluck out the odd grey hair from the top of her head. She smiled to accentuate her cheeks so she could apply the blusher in the right place.

"You need to get a move on, love," Max said poking his head round the bedroom door. He looked the magnificent specimen of a man in his immaculately pressed trousers and pale blue shirt, "Your mother's already holding court in the marquee, the other's will be starting to arrive shortly."

"Okay, I'm coming."

The door burst open and Freddy came in looking so grown up in his new shirt and trousers. "Come on, Mummy, hurry up."

She stood up, "I'm ready. Gosh, how handsome do you look?"

"Do I have to wear my glasses?" He'd only just been prescribed them and she sensed his discomfort since a boy at school had been teasing him.

"Yes, you must. You want to see properly what's going on. And they suit you."

"I don't like them."

"It just takes a while getting used to them. I think you look grown up. Come on, let's go join everyone."

"Don't forget my surprise at eight o'clock will you?"

How could she. He'd been talking about it non-stop for days. Not telling her exactly what it was, but saying he had something special for her. She had no idea what it was, but Max and her mum seemed to know so maybe they'd had a hand in it.

She headed for the marquee in the garden Max had organised. She wasn't even bothered about a party but he'd insisted. The one lovely thing though about having the party was her brother Philip and his wife Kelly had come over from Canada for a visit and were staying at her mum's. It was a delight to see them both with their daughter who had just entered her teenage years and looked every inch as if a family party was her worst nightmare.

Max handed her a glass of fizz, "Just a quick family toast before everyone gets here." He wrapped his arm around her, "To my beautiful wife, happy fortieth, love, here's to many more birthdays to come." He kissed her gently and relief surged through her. It was like the old Max. She was determined to have a good time with all her family.

"To Claire," they all said in unison and clinked glasses.

She smiled at her brother next to his wife. "I'm so pleased you're here, Philip, even if it is only a flying visit."

"Yeah I know, but Max was telling me you'll be in Florida at Christmas. I'm wondering how you feel about having a family of gate-crashers?"

"Really?" her spirits lifted, "that'd be brilliant, especially with Mum being with us too. Are you likely to come or just thinking about it?"

Her brother turned to his wife, "I think we're pretty much decided, aren't we, love?"

Claire couldn't contain her joy. It would be fantastic to all be together for Christmas. Especially as it would be the first Christmas without their dad. She took a sip of her bubbly, feeling happier than she'd felt in a while. Maybe everyone had been right, bereavement does take its toll, but you do come out the other end.

The first guests started arriving and pretty soon the marquee was full. Max had hired a DJ and asked him to keep the music low at the beginning of the night, but to ramp it up after everyone had eaten.

Claire was overwhelmed by all the gifts and placed each one in the house to open later. Freddy approached her clutching a present wrapped haphazardly, as if he'd done it himself. "This is for you, Mummy."

She frowned, "Another present? You and Daddy gave me my lovely gifts this morning. I didn't realise there was more."

"This one's from me and Adam."

"Adam?" Crikey, she hadn't expected a gift from him. Thank goodness Max wasn't around.

"Open it," he said eagerly, "I helped make it."

"Did you now? Let's have a look then." She tore the paper off to reveal a small bird box shaped like a Swiss cottage, with a blue roof and yellow sides. It had a circular opening at the front big enough for a tiny bird like a blue tit.

"Oh, how beautiful is this."

"We made it together in the shed. Adam showed me how to do it. I chose the colours and painted it. We can put it on a fence or hang it on a wall. Adam said that some birds come back each year."

"Oh, they definitely will, I'm sure. What a lovely gift, that is so thoughtful of Adam . . . of you both. Thank you, sweetheart, I'll treasure it and will love watching the birds go in and out of it." She kissed his head, "I'm being thoroughly spoilt today with all these gifts, what a lovely birthday I'm having."

"Don't forget my surprise as well at eight o'clock. That's part of your gift too."

"No, I won't. I'm looking forward to it."

"Dad says I've got to wait until everyone has eaten."

"Did he? Better do that then." Honestly, Max was so insensitive. Why didn't he just let him get on with it?

"Right, it looks like the buffet is going to be served. Come on, we'll go and get you some food shall we?"

A warmth flooded through her at the thought of Adam's gift. She looked around at all the faces enjoying the party, wishing he was there amongst them. No matter how she tried, she couldn't suppress a secret desire to see him there. She chastised herself, she was getting ridiculous about him. His time working for them was coming to an end and maybe that was for the best. She was married to Max and shouldn't be fantasising about another man.

"Ladies and gentlemen, can I have your attention please," she smiled at Max with the microphone in his hand. "I'd like you to welcome Freddy, who has a special surprise for his mum. Are you ready, son?" Freddy nodded eagerly and Max gave him the microphone. Everyone clapped. She was bursting with pride. He might not be the most academically able child, but he was gentle and kind, and had a huge heart. One thing she was certain of in her current world full of anxiety and doubt, Freddy was her stable and a credit to her and Max. They both loved him so much.

The DJ put some music on very low in the background. She recognised it as a particular favourite of hers. But the biggest surprise was when Freddy opened his mouth and started to sing. She hadn't expected that at all. The lyrics were so poignant. They were about a love between a male and female, but were just as applicable to a son loving his mother. Love was the theme which was relevant to them all.

Her heart was ready to burst watching him sing his little heart out. Max had his arm around her, no doubt as proud as she was of their precious son. It took all her willpower not to cry. This was her life, Max and Freddy, surrounded by family and friends. She vowed to herself that she'd no longer allow the darkness to creep in and take hold. She had everything she wanted in life with her family.

As Freddy continued with another verse, she caught sight of her mother who'd given in to her tears. Freddy's voice was still sweet, a child's voice that hadn't yet broken. His little face was a picture with all the applause when he finally finished singing. He left the area next to the DJ and came towards her and she wrapped her arms around him and held him tight.

"Out of all my gifts, that will always be the best. I didn't even know you knew that song."

"I've heard you play it so I knew you'd like it."

"I do, but I love it more now. You are such a good boy. Thank you, darling, you've made me very proud."

"Can I have some more trifle, then?"

She laughed, "Course you can. It'll be in the kitchen. I'll come with you as I'll need to do something with my make-up. I was trying not to cry but I couldn't help some tears escaping."

He pulled a face, "Crying? That's weird."

They walked into the kitchen. "There you are look, Grandma's in the place she loves best," she smiled at her mum, "any trifle left for the singer? I think he's earned seconds, don't you?"

"Absolutely. You were brilliant, sweetheart, you made us all proud. Did you learn the song at school?"

"No, Adam taught me it. I told him Mummy liked it so when we did the leaves, he kept singing it with me so I got it right. I wish he was here to see me sing it."

"I saw Uncle Philip recording it," Claire said, "we'll ask him to send us a copy and then you can show Adam how well you did."

"Yeah," Freddy looked pleased that his big moment was captured. "Adam said I had to ask you if it's okay for him to teach me how to play the guitar. He said he'd show me if you said yes."

She was already nervous about Max's reaction when he found out about the bird box gift, he'd not be happy, that was for sure. She wondered how much Max knew about Adam helping with the singing. Had Freddy told him? *He must have done, surely?*

"We'll have to see. Adam won't be here much longer."

"Why?"

"Because he only agreed to work here until the end of August." She needed to get out of the kitchen to avoid any more questions. "I'm just going upstairs, I'll be back in a second. When you've finished your trifle, go and find Uncle Philip and ask him to show you the video he took."

She made her way upstairs which was out of bounds to the guests. As she approached the bedroom door, she stopped as she heard Max talking, obviously on the phone to someone. She stood still and put her head closer to the door, straining to listen to what he was saying.

"Monday, I promise. I'll have it all sorted by then. I'm going to have to dash, we're in the middle of her party."

Her party? Who was he talking to? Whoever was on the other end must have been referring to her by name, or why else would he say *her?* Anyone that mattered to them was already at the party, and those that couldn't make it had sent apologies. So who could be talking to Max?

She reached for the handle and opened the door. The tone of his voice changed, "I can sort that out for you in the week. Not at all. Okay, will do. Bye."

He cut the call. "Alright love?"

"Yes, I've just come to touch up my make-up. Who was that on the phone?"

"Nobody. Wasn't Freddy the star of the show tonight?"

"Yes, he was. Who was ringing you on a Friday evening?"

"Just someone from work. Right, I'd better get back." He

walked towards the door, "Don't be long will you, the dancing will be starting shortly, and don't forget to save the last dance for me," he smiled and closed the door.

The dressing table stool saved her as she slouched down in a heap with her heart racing. *What the hell just happened?* The call could only mean one thing. He must have been speaking to someone he was intimate with.

Her face stared back at her in the mirror. Max was having an affair, deep down she knew it. Maybe she'd always known it but buried her head in the sand. They'd been here once before and she'd forgiven his indiscretion, as he'd referred to it, and given him a second chance because she loved him and he was sorry and still loved her. But she'd told him categorically, there would never be a third chance. She'd made that abundantly clear.

She went through the motions of applying some fresh face-powder and lipstick. It was going to take all her strength to rejoin the party. But she would do. She was going downstairs to play her part, but as soon as every guest had left, she was going to have it out with Max. Fortunately, Freddy was going back with her mum that evening to spend the weekend with her brother and do some fun activities. The irony was, that was exactly what her and Max were supposed to be doing – having a fun weekend together. What a joke.

If he was having an affair, it would be the end of their marriage.

Chapter 40

Annabelle

Little did Max know, while he was speaking on the phone to her, she was in the car outside his house . . . watching. She'd seen every single guest arrive. Even her therapist George Grey in his BMW turned up and made his way down the drive. He'd explained the night before that he needed to case the house out to ensure their plan would work. They'd formed quite a pact each night, as he talked about death through smoke inhalation, and how she would be free of clingy and her pathetic excuse for a child. She would fall asleep smiling and dreaming of sex in the sun with her new husband. Tonight, George was at the house so he could produce a map of the layout for the arsonists. It made her heart race just thinking about it.

She ached to be with Max. She had to keep telling herself it wasn't long now. She shouldn't have rung him in the middle of clingy's party. She just couldn't help it – she needed to hear his voice. They were so close to beginning their life together and all she wanted was the reassurance he was as happy as she was. She had to know he was going through with his promise to tell clingy this weekend that they were over. It was silly watching the party goers arriving as she could only hear the noise of the party in full swing, she couldn't see anything, and it tortured her. The thought of Max playing happy families with clingy and their spawn was like a knife twisting in the gut.

Of late, she'd fantasised more and more about the fire and the whole charade going up in smoke. Fortunately, George Grey was as enthusiastic as she was. He'd started popping into her office during the daytime to see her too, applauding her efforts to secure a great future for herself.

She reached in the glove compartment for her self-medication. Her reliable gin was disguised in a water bottle. She took a gulp and enjoyed the warmth as it trickled into her stomach. She was becoming quite dependent on alcohol but as soon as her and Max were living together, she planned to cut back.

The wedding was all sorted, Max was as attentive as ever, all she had to do was wait until the party was over. Then Max would be hers for the rest of their lives. All was well.

She took a deep breath in and another swig before returning the bottle to its hiding place. The alcohol was relaxing her but it also tended to make her reminisce. And some of her past she didn't like being reminded about. She thought back to the night of the accident that killed her husband and how fast she'd been driving. It had been one of her *episodes*. She'd been driving like a madwoman, not caring if they both died – she just wanted blackness. When she woke up in the hospital with an unresponsive battered body, she knew that despite everything, she did want to live. When the doctor explained her husband had been killed outright and hadn't suffered, she made all the right noises of a grieving wife. It had been a blessing; divorce would have been costly and he didn't deserve a penny of her hard-earned fortune. Her daddy would turn in his grave.

The lawyers worked hard to ensure she escaped manslaughter charges. How could they prove she set out to kill her husband by driving so fast? It was too ridiculous to contemplate. Why would you set out to kill yourself if you wanted your husband dead? You wouldn't and that was the prosecutor's dilemma. She paid handsomely to the lawyers and the newspapers who reported that her husband had tragically died in a car accident and she was to undergo months if not years of extensive therapy to mend her fragile body.

There had been little evidence to prove intent, but there had been an insistence she underwent psychiatric assessment and the report suggested there were some issues that needed resolving. The court had ruled she was to undergo the work with the psychiatrist, Dr Stead to deal with the clinical diagnosis and medication, and work with George Grey in relation to behaviours and coping strategies. If it kept her out of prison, she was happy to go along with it. But she needed to draw a line under all that now. Once this weekend was over, and Max was truly hers, then the first day of her new life would begin. She might even start trying for a baby before the wedding. What a joy that would be.

It was time to go. She reached for a mint and placed one in her mouth. She was close now to having everything she wanted. Max would leave the marital home, and the house would be torched. End of clingy and her brat. And if that didn't come off as George Grey assured her it would, she had a back-up plan. One way or another, by the end of the week, clingy would be well and truly gone. End of.

She started the engine, put the car into gear and set off home. Only a couple more nights on her own and then she'd have Max with her permanently. She stopped at the junction, checked left and right, and eased the Nissan Juke into the main stream of traffic.

Chapter 41

Claire

The party was over. The guests had all gone. She'd packed an overnight bag for Freddy and, along with her brother and Mum, she'd cheerily waved them off, painting on the brightest smile, telling them it had been the best birthday she'd ever had when in fact it had turned out to be the worst. Now it was just her and Max, stood facing each other in the kitchen.

"I want to know who you were talking to on the phone earlier. And don't give me that crap it was about work. You know it wasn't and I know it wasn't. Tell me the truth," she glared at him, "are you having an affair?"

"Can we talk about this tomorrow?" he shuffled uncomfortably. "I've had a lot to drink. If we sleep on this, I can tell you the whole story in the morning. It's not what you think, I promise."

"I doubt that very much. I reckon it's exactly what I think and you're stalling so you can come up with a legitimate story. Well that isn't happening. I don't care how trashed you are, I want to know who you were talking to?"

"If you must know, it's the woman I'm going into business with. I'm on the edge of that deal I spoke to you about. I'm merging her company with mi . . . ours."

"Really? So it's her you've been seeing all this time? All

these late-night business meetings and overnight stays in London, it's her you've been with?"

"No. Well, not like that. Of course I've had meetings with her, but it's been purely business. Sometimes it's easier to do the talking away from the bean counters in the office."

"Oh, I bet it is. Tell me, is this woman fat and over fifty, or is she fit and under forty?"

He didn't answer. Max being lost for words was definitely a first. She knew the answer anyway so carried on, "What do you do, go over contracts in bed while your wife waits patiently at home?"

"Don't be stupid," he scowled, "it's not like that at all. Why would I cheat on you? You know how much I love you and Freddy."

She raised a hand, "Don't you dare bring his name into it. This is about us and your infidelity yet again. You promised me, Max."

"I haven't done anything, I give you my word. Yes, Annie and I have had a few dinners."

Her head felt fuzzy. Where had she seen the name Annie before? Recently. She'd seen it somewhere.

"And where have these dinners been? Name the restaurants and then I can check with her, because that's exactly what I'm going to do." She paused giving him chance to reply. But his normal astute and charming personality evaded him. Because there were no restaurant meetings – not that he'd care to tell her about, anyway.

"I'm guessing by your silence, you've been meeting at her house?" She focused directly into his eyes, waiting for him to deny it.

"I have been to her house once or twice for a meal, yes. But that was all. There were caterers around and I always left at a respectable time and stayed at the flat."

Annie . . . Annie. Where had she heard that name?

"Look," he grimaced, "why don't we talk about this in

the morning. We've both had a lot to drink. There's no point in going over this anymore tonight. Our perspectives are cloudy."

"Mine isn't," she snapped. "And I don't want to wait until tomorrow, I want to know now."

He sighed heavily, "After we've slept, we can discuss this more rationally. I promise you, I know what it looks like but nothing is going on. You have to trust me on this."

"I don't trust anything you say. Not anymore."

"Please, Claire, let's do this in the morning." He drew himself a glass of water and drank it down.

As angry as she was, she couldn't think straight. He was having an affair, she knew that now. It all fitted into place. What a fool she'd been to trust him again. She needed to put some space between them both for her own sanity. It would still all be there in the morning. And some time away from him would give her chance to think.

"Okay then. Tonight, tomorrow, whenever. Do you know what, I don't really care, Max. You'd better go in one of the spare rooms, 'cause you're not sleeping with me. I dread to think where you've been."

Despite everything, it still hurt to see the pain on his face. But she had to be strong. She'd listen to his lies tomorrow. There wouldn't be any forgiveness though, not this time.

He didn't say any more. She watched him leave the kitchen. Her head throbbed and she turned to the sink for a drink and glanced out of the bi-fold doors at the empty marquee. Only hours earlier it had been buzzing with all the people that mattered in her life, who had come to celebrate with her. She downed two glasses of water in quick succession.

Happy sodding birthday to me.

She lay alone in the huge bed she normally shared with Max and remembered the happy times when they'd made love, and how they used to spoon together each night to settle down to sleep. He always said he could only sleep properly that way. *Yeah right.*

What an idiot she'd been. It was all so obvious now. She closed her eyes desperately wanting to block the pain out, but sleep was elusive. Her mind was working overtime. The black cloud that had been hanging over her head must have been some sort of premonition. Deep down she must have subconsciously feared the end of her marriage. Tears rolled down her cheeks, she couldn't stop them. There was no Dad around this time to persuade her to give Max another chance.

Finally, the alcohol must have kicked in as she felt herself drifting off to sleep. But not before she remembered where she'd seen the name Annie before. It had been at Pippa's. She'd glanced at a personal card while Pippa went to fetch her jacket. It was a printed romantic verse which she hadn't had chance to read fully, but she remembered the dedication. It was *to dearest Annie.*

Pippa? Annie? – she didn't get it. Her head throbbed relentlessly trying to piece things together. Was Pippa somehow Annie? She couldn't be. Max wouldn't be having an affair with someone disabled, surely? Max was all about image and attractiveness. And what man would be daft enough to move his mistress round the corner, and conversely make friends with his wife? No, that was too ridiculous. His Annie must be in London. But what about Pippa? Why would she have a card in her possession addressed to dearest Annie?

It couldn't wait. She got out of bed and headed for the spare room, opened the door and slammed the light on. Max looked startled and eased himself up on his elbow, "For Christ's sake, what now?"

She glared from the doorway. "Do you know Pippa, that new friend I have in Frogmore Close . . . the blonde-haired woman in a wheelchair?"

"What? No."

"You're sure?"

"Course I'm sure. I don't know anyone in a wheelchair."

"So your Annie, isn't in a wheelchair?"

He sighed, "I've told you, there is no *my* Annie. The woman you're referring to lives in London and she most definitely isn't in a wheelchair. Now can we try and get some sleep and sort this out tomorrow."

"Have you ever been to Red Chimneys down Frogmore Close?"

"No, I haven't." He scowled. "Why are you asking all this about some random woman in a wheelchair?"

"Because *Pippa*," she emphasised her name, "or whatever she's really called, has a card with to dearest Annie written on it, and a verse. Something to do with *if being loved by someone gives you strength and loving someone gives you courage* . . . did you give her that?"

She wasn't entirely sure if she imagined it, but staring directly at him, it appeared as if something was registering. But only for a split second, he was soon back to being dismissive. "No, I didn't."

"Well, she's definitely your type, apart from the wheelchair. Slim, blonde, pretty, oh, and she has a tiny mole above her lip. Is that ringing any bells?"

"I'm not answering any more of these stupid bloody questions tonight."

"No, I bet you're not. Tomorrow will be better for you. Then you can think up a pack of lies. I know something isn't right, so I'll be going round to speak to her myself tomorrow. And I'll find out from her exactly what's going on."

"And what do you reckon she'll think about you making up these ludicrous allegations?"

"Believe you me," she said through gritted teeth, "I'm well passed caring about what anyone thinks. I can't trust you to tell me the truth, so I'll get it from her. Most of it is fitting into place, anyhow. The bit I don't get is, however hard I try to picture it, I just don't see you with someone in a wheelchair."

"I told you. I am not having an affair and I don't know this woman you're talking about."

"I think you do," she sneered, "I think you know exactly what I'm talking about." Her mind was working fast considering she'd been drinking. "Does she drive a Nissan Juke?"

"Who?" he seemed almost distracted.

"You know who. Annie, aka Pippa."

"Claire, this is stupid. I don't know this woman."

"Tell me what car she drives."

"Why? What does it matter?"

"Because someone has been following me in a red and black Nissan Juke, the same as Dad had."

"What do you mean, following you?"

"Foll-ow-ing-me. What don't you get? Turning up at the places I go to so she can spy on me."

"Then why the fuck haven't you said anything before now?"

"Because you're never here. You're too busy shagging Annie to be bothered about my welfare, that's why."

"For the last time, I have not been having an affair."

"I don't believe a word you say," she spat. "But one thing is certain, I'll find out tomorrow when I go round to Pippa's, and if I get no joy from her, then I'll speak to the Annie you say you've been seeing in London. So I'm telling you now, I will find out exactly what's been going on. I'm certainly not trusting anything that comes out of your mouth anymore."

She slammed the door shut and headed back to her room. He might be able to sleep, but she couldn't. Her mind was in too much of a scrambled turmoil.

It was too bizarre to think Max could be having an affair with Pippa. Was she being totally ridiculous? None of it added up. The one thing that she was certain about, though, was Max had been having an affair with someone. And she vowed she'd find out once and for all either from Pippa, or this Annie woman in London. She wasn't going to rest until she did.

Then she'd sort out ending their marriage.

Chapter 42

Annabelle

Something woke her from a deep sleep. Was it glass smashing? She wasn't quite sure if she was dreaming, until she heard another crash. Someone was breaking into the house. Could it be George Grey? Something told her it was. And he wasn't doing it quietly. She quickly lifted her eye mask. It was still dark as she reached towards the bedside table for her phone. It wasn't there. She must have left it downstairs after too many glasses of wine the previous evening trying to drown her sorrows about Max. She'd crawled into bed almost paralytic, missed her night time chat with George, and now he was angry.

Loud footsteps were running up the stairs as if the person was taking them two at a time. She could hear the doors systematically being opened, one by one. Fear rushed through her as she attempted to jump out of bed. Her intention was to barricade herself in the ensuite, but she wasn't quick enough. The door to her room flung open and slammed off the wall. But it wasn't George Grey stood in the doorway, it was Max. His face contorted with rage. She pulled the covers up as if somehow they might save her.

"What the fucking hell's going on?" he spat.

"What? What's the matter?"

"What's the matter?" he screeched. "What the fuck are you doing here at Sandbanks with all this disabled stuff in the house? The wheelchair, the stair lift. What the hell do you think you're playing at?"

She kept her eyes on his as she got out of bed and took a few tentative paces towards him. She had to try and calm him down. In the state he was in, he could hurt her.

"Nothing's going on. I'm here with a friend. She's gone away for a few days."

She could see the cogs moving in his mind.

"What friend? You're a lying bitch. You've been posing as disabled to get close to my wife," he snarled. His eyes were full of fury. Her heart rate accelerated further, if that was possible.

"Don't be stupid. Of course I haven't." She had to try and pacify him. "I admit I came here so I could be close to you, but that's all. The person that owns all this stuff has gone away for a few days."

"What without her wheelchair? I don't think so. Why, Annabelle?" he never called her by her full name, "I don't get it. Why? Why go to all this trouble? This is crazy behaviour!"

"Look, can we go downstairs and talk about it. I need to tell you some bits you don't know about me. Health things. It'll explain about some of the stuff I do." She moved a step closer not taking her eyes from his, "I just wanted to be close to you, that's all, and to have an idea where you live and what Claire is like. It's only because I love you. You know that." She rubbed her forehead. "I've just lost my way a bit. All this disabled stuff is from my accident before I met you. I couldn't walk for months. But none of that matters, does it? It's our time to be together now. Have you told Claire about us?"

"Are you completely mad?" he tapped his forehead with his fingers. "I haven't told Claire anything. And I'm not going to after this crazy stunt. It's over between us. End of, after this fiasco. It's going to take me all my time to convince Claire to stay with me."

An explosion erupted in her head, like a grenade going off. "You can't stay with Claire, your future's with me. It's all sorted. We're going to be married, have children together. It's all arranged."

He started to retreat towards the landing. "Nothing's arranged," he snarled, "it's over. I'm going back to my wife. This isn't right what you've done. You need to get some professional help."

The look of disgust he gave her was enough to make her sob. She couldn't let him go. She loved him so much. She rushed after him as he made his way towards the stairs.

"What do you mean, you're staying with your wife!" she screeched, "*I'm* going to be your wife, the wedding's all arranged. December the 6th at the Ritz."

He paused at the stairs and looked at her with wide eyes. "What?"

"December the 6th, at the Ritz. I've arranged everything. You're going to love it, Max."

"You've arranged our fucking wedding?"

"I wanted it to be a surprise."

"Jesus Christ," he said, shaking his head at her, "you're even more deranged than I thought. It's over between us. And if my wife does come round here, you'd do better to keep your crazy mouth shut and carry on pretending to be this Pippa woman who she thinks you are, or so help me God I'll have you arrested for stalking."

"Arrested? No, Max please, you don't understand. Please don't go, I love you. We need to talk about this together. I'm sorry, truly I am. It's all got out of hand. I haven't done anything really that wrong. I've only rented this place for two months. We can leave right now, together."

"You're barking mad if you think I'm going anywhere with you. I never want to see you again. Get some help. You're sick."

"I'm not sick," she spat, "she is, hanging onto you when

you don't love her. And what about the businesses, we're on the verge of merging them?"

"Not any more we're not. Especially not with someone as warped as you. You have something seriously wrong with you. And just so you know, I never was going to marry you. I love my wife, and I'm not going to divorce her. Not now, not ever."

Rage thumped in her head. Her tummy was tight with anger, almost as if it might burst open. Her hands were clenched tightly at her sides. In her peripheral vision, George Grey appeared on the landing. "He never loved you," he said. "He loves his wife."

She looked back at Max, shaking his head at her as he approached the first stair. Her hands reached out to him. "Please, Max, please . . ."

George Grey's voice was relentless in her head. *He never loved you, he loves his wife, he never loved you, he loves his wife.* Max didn't want her. All her dreams of a future with him were over.

With as much strength as she could muster, she lunged forward and gave Max one almighty push. He reached out to stop himself falling, but there was no level floor to save him. She grabbed the hand rail to balance herself, and as if she were seeing it in slow motion, she watched the man she loved tumble head first down the stairs, bouncing forcibly on each step. He cried out as he headed downwards – his fall at the bottom broken by the stair lift, which only served to contort his neck at an acute angle from his torso.

Silence.

He was still.

His bulbous eyes were open and staring at the ceiling.

The position of his neck from his body indicated it was broken.

She tentatively took the stairs one by one towards him, as if she was expecting him to wake up and attack her. On the bottom step, she reached down and gave him a gentle shake. He didn't move.

Max was dead.

She looked around for George Grey but he'd vanished.

What now?

There was no point in calling an ambulance. What could they do?

Should she call the police?

She headed into the lounge and found her iPhone on the sofa where she'd discarded it the night before. She scrolled through the contacts and found the number she was looking for. She pressed, call.

"Yegor, is that you? Something terrible has happened. I need you to come."

Chapter 43

Claire

She opened her eyes, suddenly remembering the confrontation from the night before, the angry words, and amazed she'd slept at all. She reached for her phone to check the time. It was 9 a.m., which surprised her. She grabbed her robe from the back of the door and headed downstairs determined she was going to carry on where her and Max had left off. But she needed coffee first.

The kitchen was empty and a hastily scrawled note from him said he'd gone out and to wait for him. She crumpled it up and stuck it in her robe pocket. He'd be trying to work out a plausible story and no doubt contacting his Annie to get her to substantiate it.

She filled the coffee maker and switched in on, all the time thinking about the events of the previous day. The marquee stood empty on the lawn. The evening had been quite perfect until she'd heard Max on the phone to Annie whoever she was. She'd got it in her head that Annie was her friend Pippa but in the cool light of day, she wasn't quite so sure. Max wouldn't be having an affair with a woman in a wheelchair. He was all about appearance and definitely not the carer type, which you would undoubtedly be if you were the partner of a disabled person. Not that Pippa wasn't able to care for herself, but no matter how hard she tried, she couldn't visualise Max with her. It just didn't fit, even though she was particularly attractive.

A thought started reverberating in her mind. Maybe she should go round to Pippa's house just to see if Max's car was there? If he was there right now, then it would be proof they'd been cavorting about together. If he wasn't there, she'd come straight home.

She finished her coffee and headed for a quick shower. She was experiencing the morning after the night before in terms of alcohol consumption. Her head throbbed and her breath felt sour. She wasn't entirely sure if she might actually be over the limit to drive the car, so thought it best to walk round the corner to Pippa's. Her priority had to be finding out exactly what was going on. She barely dried herself before slipping on a pair of jeans and a tee shirt, grabbing a jacket and her bag and heading off on foot to Frogmore Close.

She paused outside Red Chimneys and scanned the immediate area. No sign of Max's car, which made her think she was being ridiculous. What evidence did she have really? A card she'd spotted in Pippa's house with the endearment of Annie on it, and Max whispering to whoever it was on the phone the previous evening. That didn't mean Max had been just round the corner screwing Pippa all those times he should have been in London.

But doubt festered as she recalled one of their conversations when Pippa had questioned her about Max having an affair. Was that to find out if she suspected anything? Were they planning to be together? Was this the so-called woman Max was going into business with? If this was indeed her, why would she want to meet her lover's wife? It just didn't add up.

The overwhelming urge to knock on the door was pushing her forward, but the cautious side of her was wondering what she would say? '*Have you been having an affair with my husband, and are you really called Annie?*' It sounded daft.

But so what? Pippa was reasonable. If there was another explanation then she'd have the grace to apologise. And Pippa would completely understand, surely? Okay, it might be the end of their friendship, but was she bothered? No, she wasn't. After this fiasco, her life would be moving in a different direction anyway. She took a deep breath in. What had she got to lose?

She made her way up to the front door, surprised to find it was slightly ajar. She stepped into the hallway and walked forward towards the kitchen area. "Pippa, are you there . . ." she called.

A noise behind her caused her to turn around. Utter astonishment was the only word to describe the vision in front of her.

It was Pippa – standing upright.

Every time she'd seen her she'd been confined in a wheelchair. But not any longer. Right now she was standing on both legs and walking towards her with a manic look on her face.

"You can walk?" Claire reeled back, astounded and not quite believing what she was seeing in front of her.

"Of course I can walk," Pippa snapped.

It looked exactly like Pippa, but she was different. Her friend had warm, kind eyes – this one's eyes were murderous. Fear rushed through Claire's veins.

"But I've only ever seen you in a wheelchair. What's going on?"

"You in the way, that's what's going on."

Claire had been right all along. "You've been having an affair with my husband," she spat, "I know that. But why the wheelchair, what the hell is all that about?"

"Does it matter?" What matters is Max and I would be together now if it wasn't for you."

Claire had no idea now about her future with Max, it was still such a shock. But right now, she was frightened. Perspiration began running down her back. She shouldn't have come. Her eyes were jumping from the hallway to the stairs. Where was Max? Had he been there earlier? He didn't appear to be right now.

Adrenaline spurred her on. "Max has had affairs before you know, you aren't the first."

It wasn't strictly the truth but she felt it was important to keep Pippa talking. Her frenzied eyes were raging, as if she was on drugs or something. Certainly not the docile woman in the wheelchair she knew.

She tried to pacify her. "Look, he can't be trusted. I think he's led us both on. I've only just found out about you. And he's still denying it. We're victims, you and I. Where is he, by the way? Has he been here this morning?" She was talking quickly because she was scared. She wanted to get out of the house but Pippa was blocking the front door.

"You've spoiled everything," Pippa said, agitation evident in her ferocious eyes, "Max was going to leave you after your stupid fucking party, to make a life with me. But you wouldn't let him go, would you. You've hung onto him like the clingy whining wife you are."

Claire shook her head, "I'm not entirely sure what lies he's spun you. If he's led you to believe he's leaving me, it's not true. He isn't leaving . . . not by choice anyway. Only last week he booked a luxury holiday for us at Christmas."

Rage flashed in Pippa's eyes. She looked unhinged.

She had to get out of there . . . right now. She could smell the danger.

"Anyway, I'm going to find Max and have all this out with him."

She moved forward, prepared to use violence if necessary to get past Pippa.

But she sensed someone behind her. Before she had

chance to turn around, a huge blow struck her on the back of her head.

And then darkness.

Chapter 44

Adam

He turned the corner and continued walking towards Claire's house. Just a few hundred metres and he'd be there. This was his final week working for the Marics, and the way he saw it, it was a good thing he was finishing really. Against his better judgement, he'd developed feelings for Claire that he shouldn't have. And as far as he could see, she was happily married to that arsehole, Max. It was evident she loved him, which made his situation all the more difficult – there wasn't a smidgeon of a chance for him.

It was becoming more obvious each day he had feelings for her. He couldn't completely hide them, as hard as he tried. She must have guessed something. He remembered the first time she'd come to the door when he'd knocked. She was rushing to go and pick her mother up from the hospital. He was blown away at how attractive she was but put that down to just being released from prison and anything with breasts and a skirt was appealing.

But each time he saw her, he got a tiny bit more excited, until his whole day consisted of desperately hoping to catch a glimpse of her. He hated the weekends when he didn't see her. They dragged endlessly. He'd taken up with a few friends and gone out on the social scene, flirting with women, having a couple of one-night stands, which suited the women as well as himself, but all he really wanted was Claire, even though he knew categorically she was out of bounds.

She was a kind woman and extended her friendship to him. She wasn't the type to be leading him on in anyway. Not one of these rich types that would screw any bloke to satisfy their ego. Claire wasn't one bit like that. She was just a strikingly attractive woman with a huge heart. And such a great mum to Freddy too. If she was his wife, he'd want her to be pregnant with more kids. Being a mother suited her. She was beautiful inside and out.

But in just five more days, he'd be out of there. The thought of never seeing her gorgeous face again with the cute impish haircut which only she could pull off, or hearing her gentle voice, bloody well hurt deep within him. There was no point in asking if he could stay on, though. He'd done loads of the work, and while it would need a gardener to keep on with the rest of it, it couldn't be him. It would be torture every day seeing her but never having her. And as much as he'd enjoyed the interactions with Claire and her son Freddy, he couldn't live a life wanting to be part of theirs, but never having the opportunity.

He turned into the drive. Her car was parked there so she'd be in. The thought he'd see her excited him. Every day he fantasised about telling her exactly how he felt, even though it would embarrass her. His emotions ranged from eagerly expecting to see her each day, to hoping he didn't. Because each time he did see her, he only wanted more and he'd never have that.

He spotted Julia, Claire's mother approaching as he continued down the drive. She was clutching her mobile phone and looked dishevelled. Anxiety was etched all over her face.

"Oh, Adam, thank goodness you're here."

"What is it?" He moved towards her, concerned, remembering her recent stroke. "Are you alright?"

"No, I'm not, I'm worried sick. I can't get hold of Claire or Max. They were having the weekend to themselves after Claire's party but something is wrong. I took Freddy to school this morning as planned, but Claire never called him last night. The poor little mite is beside himself. Claire would always ring to speak to him before bed when he's staying with me. I had to tell a white lie and say she called very late when he was asleep and there was a signal problem. But she didn't. I haven't heard from her." Her eyes were filled with worry. "I'm not sure what to do," she said sniffing back the tears. "I think I'll have to call the police."

He took her gently by the arm, "Why don't you go inside, sit down for a minute and have a cup of tea first of all. It won't do your blood pressure any good getting worked up. There could be a load of reasons why she hasn't made contact."

`"Like what?"

He paused at the kitchen door. "Erm . . . maybe Max has been taken ill or something and she's at a hospital with no signal."

She considered what he'd said, "Do you think?" then shook her head, "not that I'd want Max to be ill. But that could be an explanation." She looked at him stood outside on the patio. "Come inside, Adam. I'm not messing about with all that not being able to, business. This is serious."

He stepped inside the kitchen but stayed close to the door. He didn't want another rant from Max when he did turn up.

"But surely, if she was at a hospital, she'd go outside and ring. This isn't like her at all. And Max for that matter, he's always contactable."

"What happens when you ring their mobiles?" he asked.

"Nothing. They don't ring, it's like both their phones are dead."

"Here, let me try." He pressed Claire's number on Julia's

phone, but she was right, it appeared to be switched off. "Is it the same with Max's phone?"

"Yes. I've even rung his work, but he's not there. Seemingly he'd planned to take today off anyway. As I said, they were both going off to do something together yesterday, that's why Freddy came to mine after the party. They were picking him up today from school at five o'clock after football practice."

"What about Claire's friends? Do you think her and Max could have had a row or something and she's gone to stay with one of them?"

"That wouldn't be beyond the bounds of possibility but she'd still ring Freddy, I know she would. Something's wrong," her bottom lip quivered, "like a car accident or something. The fact I can't get either of them is even more frightening."

Julia was right. Claire wouldn't miss speaking with her son. She was the perfect mother and Freddy was her life.

"There is Emma who I know well," Julia continued, "she lives in Bournemouth, she's Claire's closest friend. I could give her a ring I suppose, just to see if she knows anything."

"Yeah, maybe do that first of all and if no joy, then, yes, I think you should ring the police. At least they can find out quickly if there has been a major accident involving a married couple."

"Yes, that's what I thought. Oh, Adam, I'm terribly worried. Claire is the most reliable person in the world. She wouldn't worry me like this."

"I know that. Look, you ring Claire's friend and I'll make some tea. If she doesn't know anything, I'll stay while you contact the police."

"Would you? I'm so sorry burdening you with all of this. I just don't know what else to do. My son Philip and his wife left for their flight home yesterday," she looked at her watch, "they'll be back in Canada now. We all went to the airport together so Freddy could see the aeroplanes. We had no idea then of course that this might happen. I only started worrying last night when she didn't ring Freddy before bedtime. I've not slept a wink."

"It's not a problem, I can stay. Is there anyone I can ring to come and be with you?"

"Not really. You're sure you don't mind staying?"

"Of course I don't mind. I'm going to make the tea, you do the phoning. You'll have to speak to the police though, I can't do that for you, I'm afraid."

"No, no, I don't expect you to. I'll try her friend Emma first of all."

He moved to the sink to fill the kettle. He could hear the anxiety in Julia's voice on the phone to Claire's friend. It didn't sound as if she'd seen her, either. While he'd done his best to reassure Julia, he'd not done terribly well as he shared her anxiety that something had happened. Claire would always contact Freddy, her mother knew it, and so did he.

He made the tea but didn't sit down, even though a rant from Max was now becoming desirable.

At least that would mean Claire was safe.

Chapter 45

Claire

Was she dreaming? She was laid down, so must be. But the pain in her hip and head told her no, it was real. It was terribly cold. And dark – she had no idea where she was. An acute pain throbbed in her head. She raised her hand to it and felt something crusty stuck to her face. She ran her fingers along her cheek. Was it dried blood? Her eyes were darting around the area she was laid in. Where was she? Was it a cellar? She could make out some steps . . . yes, it appeared to be a cellar. An ache reverberated in her head as she tried to piece together what had happened. She'd been at Red Chimneys. Pippa had been stood in front of her, blocking her way out. As she tried to make her way towards the front door, the last thing she remembered was a blow to the back of her head. How long ago had that been?

An excruciating pain was relentlessly throbbing in her hip. She tried to move it but it hurt, terribly. Maybe it was fractured? Her chest felt tight, her breath was catching. A noise interrupted her examining herself for more injuries – footsteps. A narrow strip of light appeared at the top of the steps. Shadows moving. A lock being turned.

The door swung open, and a woman stood there. Pure panic set in. Dear God, it was Pippa, staring down at her as she lay in a crumpled heap on the cold floor. Fear snaked through her veins as her breathing quickened. What now? Was she going to hurt her? There was no way of fighting her off, she could barely move. *Please God, no.* Adrenaline surged so fast she wanted to vomit. Hadn't she done enough to hurt her?

Pippa stood completely still, as if checking if she was alive or dead. Claire's muscles were out of power so she had no option but to remain motionless. If she'd have been quicker, she maybe should have closed her eyes and played dead. Now, paralysed with fear, her heart rate increased.

"You stupid fucking bitch," Pippa snarled, "you've spoilt everything. You and your whining brat."

Beads of sweat trickled down Claire's brow. Her jaw became tight. She had to try to reason with her, even though she was clearly mad. She had to fight. She had to stay alive.

"Please, listen, you can have Max for all I care. I don't want him."

"I don't want him," Pippa mimicked.

She had to try a different tack, anything to stall from whatever was going to happen next. "I'll go away," Claire said, "you never have to see me again. You can make a life with Max. Just let me out of here, please. Don't do something you'll regret. If anything happens to me, you could end up in prison."

"Will you shut the fuck up! You're not going anywhere, you stupid bitch. My future's gone because of you," her voice went up an octave, "the only man I've ever loved is *gone* because of you."

What did she mean gone, had Max broken it off with her? Her whole body was trembling, she couldn't stop the shaking.

"I can speak to him for you," Claire said trying desperately not to cry. Surely Max was out looking for her? Maybe he'd called the police.

She carried on. "If he loves you, he'll come back. I'll tell him his future is with you. He doesn't love me anymore. I know that now."

"Yeah, too fucking right, you stupid clingy waste of space. He never loved you. He loved me. He was happy with me. We were getting married . . . but you spoilt everything, you dumb bitch."

She started walking down the steps. The closer she came, the greater Claire feared for her life. *Please God, help me. I don't want to die.*

Claire couldn't see her eyes, which was a good thing. Her manic voice was enough for her to know she was in danger.

"Please, just leave me. Go find Max. He's probably at home now. I can just disappear from your lives. You never have to see me again."

"You're right about that. You are going to disappear. For good. And nobody will mourn you, you insignificant clingy bitch."

She cowered, petrified now. "Please don't hurt me. I've never done anything to you. It's Max that's caused all this, not me. Have him, have your life with him. But you won't get it if you do anything to me. I'll be found and they'll come looking for you. Then you won't have the life you want with Max. Please, I'm begging you."

"Shut up! Shut up! Shut up! How can I think with your constant whining, ay? No wonder Max came looking for me."

Tears rolled down Claire's cheeks. Freddy's face flashed before her. She had to keep her talking. Where was Max? Where were the police? The pain was excruciating in her hip. And the cold, she was shaking so badly, it was becoming unbearable.

"Why harm me? What have I done to you? It's Max you want. Go now, leave me here. Someone will eventually find me but you'll be long gone by then."

"Nobody is going to find you," Pippa snarled, "you stupid

fucking fool. I'm going to burn this house down. You won't be found. All that'll be left is your clingy bloody ashes."

"Please don't . . . I'm begging you. I have a son." Her fingers were curled into a fist, her nails digging into her palms. "He needs me. Just go and leave me," she pleaded, "I won't say anything, I promise. You can have your life with Max, just let me live so I can have mine with my son."

"Too late. You've wrecked everything," she spat, "you and your whining kid. You've wrecked my future, you deserve to die."

She turned towards the steps and started moving back up towards the cellar door.

"God, please, no," Claire cried, "don't do this. Max won't want this. He won't want me to die."

Pippa stopped at the top of the steps and took one last look at her lying on the floor.

"I had my life all planned out, but you've wrecked everything . . ."

Claire heard a male voice far in the distance calling. Maybe outside? Was it Max? Was it the police? Please, let it be. Whoever it was caused a degree of urgency. Pippa quickly exited through the door and it sounded like she locked it behind her. Was it her accomplice calling her, the one who'd hit her over the head?

Claire was hyperventilating. She'd long since stopped going to church but she had an overwhelming urge to pray for her life.

"If you can hear me . . . " her teeth chattered due to her quivering jaw, "please let her be gone. Don't let her set fire to the house . . ." she clenched her teeth in an effort to keep her jaw still. "I want to live. I want to see my son . . . and my mother." The tears flowed freely, "Please help me," she sobbed, "I don't want to die. Please . . . somebody."

* * *

Her eyes, becoming more accustomed to her surroundings, scanned the floor and walls. Her teeth were chattering with the cold, her misted breath visible in the darkness. There were some random storage boxes covered with dust sheets, which she could use to try and keep warm.

Where was Max? She felt for her wristwatch but it wasn't there. It hurt too much to try and recall if she'd been wearing it. Probably not, as she'd left home in a hurry.

Max must be wondering where on earth she was by now. Surely he'd come and look for her?

She called out, "Help," then louder, "help, is anybody there?" But all she could hear was dripping water, which sounded like rain outside.

Her mouth felt crusty and dry.

You have to get some water, she heard and turned her head to the side. "Dad?" she squinted, trying to see who had spoken to her, but nobody was there. Was it in her head? Maybe. He was right though, she had to get some water until she was found. It wouldn't be long. Max surely would have called the police by now.

Her thoughts drifted to Freddy. How long had she been there? Her eyes scanned around again. There wasn't much she could see that could save her. A few boxes scattered around and a large chest freezer. It must be on as she could see the light from the plug. Maybe the freezer would have some ice? That's what she needed to do – somehow get some ice.

"I'm going to try and get some ice," she croaked out loud. Nobody was there to listen but she felt better hearing her own voice. It was comforting.

How long had it been since she saw Pippa standing without the wheelchair, with the manic look in her eyes as if she was going to hurt her? She'd pieced together she was Max's Annie, and she got that Pippa had tried to get close to possibly extract information which in itself was weird, but what she couldn't understand was why she would fake being disabled. She'd have to be pretty sick in the head to do that. Thinking about it made her head hurt more – she had to put Pippa out of her mind. Right now, her focus had to be on getting out alive. She needed water and warmth. Tears welled up in her eyes. "Stop it," she chastised herself out loud, "don't cry. Push yourself towards the dust sheets. However long it takes, crawl towards them."

She hoisted herself onto her good hip and slowly started to move forward on her tummy. She was close to losing consciousness, the pain in her injured hip was so acute. "Keep talking, Claire," she spoke to the emptiness, "you have to stay awake."

To spur her on, she started to recite The Owl And The Pussycat, the rhyme Freddy had been learning for choral speaking. "The owl and the pussycat went to sea," she used the strength of her arms to project herself a tiny bit forward, "in a beautiful pea green boat." She managed to move a little further. She was perspiring, which would only dehydrate her further, but she had to keep going. The effort caused excruciating pain and sweating. Her hip most certainly had to be fractured.

Eventually, she was within leaning distance of the dust sheets. She reached out with her fingertips and managed to grab the edge of one and dragged it towards her. It smelled fusty, but she didn't care. She quickly wrapped it around herself as best as she could, tucking it tightly under her body and placing it over the top of her head for a few seconds to try and get some warmth from her breath. Another dust sheet would help for extra weight and warmth, but she was too exhausted to reach for it.

Her breathing laboured, her eyes felt heavy. And as much as she tried, she couldn't control them closing.

"You still need water," she said to the air. But not right this minute, she thought. The pain would be too much to try and crawl towards the freezer. Perhaps after a sleep she would think about it.

Max would be looking for her, she reassured herself. By now he'd have called the police. He might be having an affair but he wouldn't abandon her. Or their precious son, he'd find her for Freddy.

He'd come soon, she was sure of it.

She felt slightly warmer.

Her eyes had a will of their own and closed.

Chapter 46

Adam

"Would you like a drink, Adam?" Claire's mother, Julia called from the patio. He was busying himself weeding and sweeping up. He'd kept well out of the way while the police officer was inside the house. The last thing he needed was anymore dealings with the law. He approached the bi-fold doors.

"Come in," Julia nodded to the kitchen table, "and have a seat. I've made a pot of coffee. I could do with the caffeine. Would you like one, or maybe a cold drink?"

"Coffee's fine. Black please."

Julia handed him a mug and took a seat opposite him.

"The officer was ever so nice. He said he'd make some enquiries about any accidents but wasn't unduly worried." She shook her head, "You can't believe it, can you? I'm worried sick and he's going to *make some enquiries*. No urgency whatsoever. They don't know Claire I suppose," she shrugged, "they must be used to this. I told him it was completely out of character."

"I agree. I don't know her terribly well, but I do know she wouldn't leave Freddy."

"No, she wouldn't. That's exactly what I said."

Adam noticed her hand shaking as she lifted her mug to her lips. He remembered she'd been ill herself when he first came to the house. It might be an idea for her to have something to occupy her. All the worry wouldn't be good for her. Freddy would need her.

"Do you know any of Claire's friends in London? She must have loads of contacts there, I would have thought? One of them might know if she had anything planned."

"I do know there's a lady who used to babysit for them when they went out. Marjorie somebody or other."

"Maybe give her a quick call then, you never know."

"I'll do that if I can find her number. These days everyone has telephone numbers stored in their mobile phones."

"Yeah, they do. What about Max's work?" he asked, "he must have a secretary. She might be able to help in some way. It might be worth a call?"

"I suppose so. I'm not keen on worrying people, but I might have to. I do wish the police would use a bit of urgency. The officer did say he would ring me back today but I'm not good at all this waiting."

Her lip wobbled and he wished he could say something to reassure her. The fact was he was worried himself. He took a sip of his coffee, wondering if Claire had any local friends. He'd not seen any women visiting the house, but she must have girlfriends.

"Do you know of any friends Claire has in Sandbanks? Maybe you could try and make contact with one or two of them?"

She shook her head, "I don't to be honest. That was one of the things she struggled with. She joined the choir though, but I have no idea where she goes for that. It's on a Wednesday night, but that's all I know really."

"I know where choir is. I've actually been myself." He felt he needed to explain. "Claire invited me when she found out I could sing. I've only been once; it's not really my thing."

"You have? Can you contact anyone there?"

"I'm not sure until Wednesday. I don't actually know

anyone personally, and to be honest, I'm not sure if she's particularly close to anyone there."

"No, I think it's more for company with Max working the hours he does."

She banged her mug down on the table. "I've just thought. She has that local friend she's made recently. A disabled lady – she's been to visit her a few times. I think she met up with her when her dog went missing."

He remembered finding the dog collar and giving it to Claire when he first started working for her and Max. It had the dog's name on it but he couldn't for the life of him remember the address on the back.

"Yeah, that's right. What's her name, do you know?"

"Erm . . . I don't. My memory is not what it once was since the stroke, I'm afraid. It will come to me, it just takes time." Julia shook her head, "She won't be able to help though, I wouldn't have thought. Claire hardly knew her."

"She might know something. It's worth a try. Do you know where she lives?"

"No, I can't say as I do. It's round here somewhere though. Claire walked round there a few times while I was here, so it can't be far."

"That's right, I remember now. When you fell in the kitchen and we rang her, she was back within minutes, wasn't she?"

"Yes, she was. I do know it's an adapted disabled house. Claire said it had ramps and all sorts. Said that was one of the reasons . . . Pippa, that's it, that's her name. Claire said that was why Pippa had rented it. Seemingly the owner that rented it out had been disabled, or his wife. Someone was anyway."

"Well maybe this Pippa knows something. It can't be hard to find a house that caters for a disabled person if it has ramps at the front. I could go and have a scout around."

"But you could end up wandering around for hours."

"Yeah, but what else can we do?" he shrugged. "I walk here in a morning and I reckon I'd have spotted a house like that and I haven't, so I'll set off a different way. If anyone is about, I'll ask them. Someone that knows the area might know the house."

"I guess it's worth a try. Claire may have confided in this lady, you never know."

"That's what I thought. I'll go now and look around. Don't get your hopes up, though."

"I won't. Thank you, Adam," she squeezed his arm, "you're a good man, helping when you don't even know us that well."

"I know Claire and she's a decent lady. I want to help. And I want to find her for Freddy. He's a good kid."

"How long do you think you'll be?" she asked wearily. He didn't like the look of her. He was no medic but she looked flushed, like her blood pressure was up.

"About an hour or so maybe? Who knows? Give me your phone and I'll put my number in, then ring me if you hear anything."

"I will do. And likewise could you let me know." She reached for a notepad and scribbled her number down. He put it into his phone and put his number in her contacts. Julia walked alongside him as she made his way towards the door.

"I've got to fetch Freddy from school at five," she said, "I'm praying we've found her by then. He's upset enough as it is. I've said by the time he comes home today, his mummy will be home. It was the only way I could get him to school."

"She might be," he reassured with a confidence he didn't feel. "I'll do my best to find her friend and hope she knows something. I'll not be long."

Julia's hug shouldn't have surprised him. That's where Claire obviously got her caring nature from, unlike that dickhead husband of hers. He wasn't bothered one bit about finding him. But Claire mattered. She was a beautiful person inside and out, and even though she didn't belong to him, he wanted her home and safe.

Chapter 47

Claire

She opened her eyes. Nothing had changed. It wasn't a dream. She was still laid on the cold and gritty floor, covered in a stinking dust sheet. She was marginally warmer with the sheet she'd managed to shuffle over and get, and the pain in her hip was throbbing, but right now she needed water. She'd have to get to the freezer. Maybe crawl a bit and rest, crawl a bit and rest. That's what she'd do. Once she'd got some ice, she'd be able to think. It might be worth trying to call out first though in case anyone was around. Pippa, or Annie, or whatever her real name was, was most likely long gone. Why wasn't Max looking for her?

"Help," she called, "help." She wanted to scream louder at the top of her lungs, but she couldn't. She hadn't the strength. "Please somebody, help me!" she shouted again.

Nothing.

Where was Max? Freddy would be beside himself by now not hearing from her. And her mum, bless her. They'd be frantic wondering where she was. Surely they'd call the police?

A lump formed in her throat like she'd swallowed a marble. "Oh no you don't, Claire Maric. You need to drink." Her dad's face flashed in her mind. He'd tell her to get to the freezer, to push herself forward through the pain. She thought about a documentary she'd once watched about an earthquake in New Zealand where a woman had lived for days underneath the rubble because she'd had access to water. Water had saved her life.

She attempted to crawl again, with the chest freezer in sight. It was a slow process. She managed to shuffle along the floor but had to keep stopping. The pain in her hip was excruciating and wouldn't allow her to move freely, but she kept going. She had to.

Her hand touched something small and hard. Picking it up, she could just make out that it was a little red whistle. There must have been a child in the house at some stage, which reminded her of Freddy. Her heart was torn apart. He'd be distraught. She was always there for him. She'd vowed when she had him that she'd always put him first. She purposely became a stay at home mum. That's all she ever wanted to be. That's probably why Max felt the need to have an affair – maybe he found her boring? No, that wasn't true. Despite his infidelity, she knew Max loved her. She never doubted that, but obviously she hadn't been enough for him. Where was he right now?

Why wasn't he looking for her? Thoughts came of him and his ... lover, speeding away in his car, laughing together. And then horror as she realised it could have been Max that hit her over the head. They'd left her here to die.

"Stop!" she said loudly. "Thinking like that will get you nowhere. First things first. Now move yourself!"

She tried to breathe through the pain as she shuffled on her tummy towards the freezer. It made her think of being in labour, with Freddy, breathing through the contractions. Freddy, dear little Freddy. She paused for a rest and took some more deep breaths in and out. Maybe she had a fractured rib or two also, as her left side pulled as she crawled. It could be the excessive use of the muscles though, she wasn't sure. All she knew was that everything hurt.

"Keep going," she said, "crawl through the pain. You must get some water. Do it for Freddy."

She had to keep alive to get back to her son. An image of him with his cute, curly and unmanageable hair and his lopsided smile came into her mind.

"I'm coming, sweetheart, I promise."

Salty tears escaped down her cheeks, but she kept on crawling, breathing through the agonising pain. Finally, she was close to the freezer. She paused again, needing to rest and think of a way to somehow get up to open the lid. She wasn't a heavy woman – but would it take her weight if she pulled herself up on it? She'd have to try, but not just yet. Not when the pain was so bad.

She breathed warmth into her hands, told herself to take the pain, to make the adrenaline work in her favour. All she had to do was hoist herself up, lift the lid and try and get some ice.

In the shadow at the side of the freezer, she spotted a trowel next to an old shovel, leaning against the wall, and next to those was a small child's three-legged milking stool.

"I could use the trowel to chip away some ice," she said out loud. A flicker of excitement rushed through her. She moved towards the trowel. Adrenaline spurred her on. "Deep breaths, in and out, in and out," she told herself, "you're doing this for Freddy."

She reached across and grasped the trowel. Next was the stool but she had to pause for a while. It wasn't far away, but the smallest movement was hard. Eventually, she had them both.

"You did good," she said getting her breath back, "you're nearly there."

With her remaining energy, she crawled towards the freezer. Once there, she lay in front of it to catch her breath – she'd made it. She shoved the stool in front of the freezer and with one almighty push, she hoisted herself up. She'd never felt so much pain in her life. The sitting position aggravated it more than crawling if that was possible. She was sweating profusely, which she could ill afford. The final task was to get the freezer lid open and chip off some ice.

With a phenomenal effort she managed to raise the lid of the freezer and toss it back against the wall, praying it stayed upright. It did. "Breathe. You're nearly there. Get some ice and you can rest," she told herself.

She reached gingerly for the trowel on the floor, wincing at the pain as she straightened back up. All she had to do now was hoist herself up and rest her arms on the edge of the freezer and scrape some ice.

"Do it now. You have to stay alive for Freddy."

She hoisted herself up and cursed as the agonising discomfort gripped her, but she pushed on. She placed her arms inside, and leant in so the edge of the freezer was supporting her armpits. She was worried it wouldn't take her weight and topple, but it didn't.

In and out she breathed, desperately trying to manage the unbearable pain. She closed her eyes for a second and waited for the adrenaline to kick in. "You can do it, quickly, now."

She leaned forward and reached inside, clutching the trowel. One last hoist and she peered inside, ready to chip away some ice. Her eyes were drawn to something bulky . . . it took a second to register exactly what she was looking at.

The trowel dropped out of her hand.

Staring back at her from inside the freezer was Max.

Chapter 48

Adam

He'd wondered around most of the streets in the close vicinity of Claire's house but couldn't see one with ramps leading up to the front door. He spotted a man walking his dog and thought it was worth asking if he was from the area.

He approached him. "Excuse me, mate, bit of a funny question I know, but you don't happen to know of a property in this area that a disabled person lives in do you? It's a long story, but I'm trying to locate a woman that lives somewhere round here. To be honest, I can't even see any bungalows, all I see are houses."

"It's a bungalow you're looking for, is it?"

"Er . . . well I was, yes. It's a female in a wheelchair. I think she's only here as a short-term let but it's definitely an adapted place."

"Well, there aren't any bungalows round here, the nearest are on Chestnut Lane but that's a good ten minutes away in the car."

"Right, it won't be there, I wouldn't have thought. It's definitely within walking distance from around here. Sorry to have bothered you."

"No problems, sorry I can't help. Haven't you got a phone number for whoever it is you're looking for?"

"No. I wish I had. As I said, it's a long story, which I won't bore you with."

The man nodded as if he understood. No doubt making his own story up in his head. Adam walked away. He cursed. He'd have to go back and tell Julia he'd not had any luck.

"Hey," the man called him back. "Richard Davis has a house that he had adapted as he's in a wheelchair. I know he's gone away for the summer. Maybe your friend could be stopping there? It's a house though, not a bungalow."

"Is it close by?"

"Yes, it's just left at the bottom of this road. It's about half way down, Frogmore Close. You can't miss it. Big bay windows and a huge ramp leading up to the front door. Might be worth a knock, you never know."

"Cheers mate, I'll give it a try."

"Good luck," the chap smiled as if it was some sort of lost love he was searching for.

He certainly would be close. Claire was his love and she was lost to him.

No point in dwelling on that right now though. He needed to find that house.

* * *

He soon found it. A large house with the bay windows; it was called Red Chimneys. He made his way up the ramp and knocked on the front door. He waited but there was no answer. It was doubtful anyone was in, the length of time he waited, but he decided to go round the back of the house, wanting to make absolutely certain. Even if it wasn't this Pippa friend of Claire's, he'd be honest and explain.

He squeezed past the garage and around to the back of the house. "Hello, hello," he called, "anyone at home?"

He peered in through the patio windows at a large living area with low kitchen units. It all appeared tidy but it was evident nobody was home. The thought of going back to

300

Julia's with nothing made him feel uncomfortable. She was going to be upset. Should he wait for whoever lived in Red Chimneys to come home? It might be a while and it was a long shot anyway. And even then they might not know anything. If it was Claire's friend, she might not have confided in her. And who was to say Red Chimneys was even the right place?

He went back down the side of the house and peered in the garage. It was empty. Maybe she didn't drive if she was disabled although one of the chaps he knew at uni was paraplegic and he had a specially adapted car.

He took a few paces forward and faced the huge sweeping garden. He couldn't help but admire it. The lawn was short as if it had recently been mowed, all the roses were pruned and the shrubs trimmed. There wasn't a weed in sight so somebody was an avid gardener. He glanced at the paved areas, sympathetically prepared for a disabled person with the ramps, rails and seating area suitable for a wheelchair user. The overall garden was stunning.

It was peaceful and he could see the attraction for anyone let alone a disabled person. There were a few blackbirds singing, but apart from that, it was deathly quiet. Although he could hear a faint whistle in the distance.

He sat down on the wall and checked his phone. No call from Julia. He stared at the imposing house thinking he should have bought a pen and paper to leave a note. Maybe he should come back and put a note through the door asking whoever the owner was to ring his mobile? Anything was better than doing nothing. He no longer cared what Max thought. If they came back now with some explanation they'd been away for a few days, that was fine. The main thing was Claire being safe. That's all he cared about. He was in love with her, which was stupid when they hadn't even had a relationship. But the feelings he had for her were completely different to Lucy who he was engaged to before he went into prison. Claire had the ability to make his heart race, literally, which he thought only happened in fiction. Working on the gardens at her house initially gave him a boost as he loved gardening, but it was Claire that was the attraction. Each day seeing her brought him joy, even though he knew there could never be a future for them. She'd never leave Max, not in a million years. Claire wasn't the type to do that. And even though he thought Max was a dickhead, she clearly didn't. He couldn't stay around waiting for her, he had to move on. His job was almost finished anyway and he couldn't see Max keeping him on. So there was absolutely no chance of a future with Claire. He knew that. But he had to see her one last time. He wanted to know she was safe.

He decided he'd return to Claire's house, write a note and then come and push it through the door. Unless Julia had some news when he got back. It could well be Max and Claire were already there.

He made his way down the drive. As he got to the gate, he heard the faint whistle again. His eyes were drawn to the bay window and upwards to the bedroom.

Nobody was there, though.

Chapter 49

Claire

Someone had been knocking, she hadn't dreamt it. Someone had been there at the house as she lay in the cellar. She sobbed until she had no tears left. Max was dead. She remembered his eyes, wide open, cold and staring. The shock had sent her tumbling to the floor. The pain from her hip enough to make her pass out. And then the knocking. Loud enough to rouse her. Trembling. Cold. Shaking so much, she could barely move. Barely breathe. She'd reached for the whistle she'd placed in her pocket and she'd blown it until she was gasping for breath, willing whoever was out there to come and find her. But nobody came.

Her throat felt like a dozen razor blades had cut it. Any saliva she had left had dried up hours, or was it days ago? She gripped the whistle tight, taking steadying breaths against the burning pain in her hip and awful trembling. She had to move. Had to keep warm. Had to do something to stay alive for Freddy. His father was dead, curled up in a freezer right next to her. Crazy. This was crazy. Why kill Max? What sort of person could do that? Max couldn't have had any idea what Pippa was like. He couldn't possibly have known how unbalanced she was. And to pose as a disabled person – she was clearly mad. What was it all for? If Max wanted to leave her and make a life with this woman, he could have.

He didn't deserve to die, whatever he'd done. She realised there must have been an accomplice. Someone hit her over the head and it wasn't Max. Max was dead. He was gone and now it was just her and Freddy. Tears came again, wracking sobs that did nothing to help the pain. The heartbreak. Yes, her heart was breaking. Not just for Max, but for Freddy. She had to do something. Keep moving. Keep warm. Keep blowing that damn whistle.

"Mum will have called the police," she said to the cold damp air, "they'll be here soon."

She lifted the whistle to her crusty dried lips and blew it again – vowing she'd keep on blowing until there was no more breathe left in her.

Chapter 50

Adam

He walked out of the drive and down Frogmore Close, away from Red Chimneys. He could still hear the high-pitched whistle and looked around for any children playing but couldn't see any. It was becoming fainter the further he moved away from the house. He walked a few paces on, and as he crossed the road, a Citroen drove past, indicated and turned into the house of the drive next door to Red Chimneys. Was it worth going back and asking them if they knew if their neighbour was a young female? If they said it was a bloke or a family, there wouldn't be any need to bother returning and leaving a note. But if they said it was a youngish female, he could ask to borrow a pen and paper and put a note through the door.

He backtracked towards the house. As he got closer, the whistle became louder. It was almost as if it was coming from Red Chimneys. But nobody was there so it couldn't be. He hesitated, undecided about speaking to the neighbour. It was an awkward situation. But the whistle was still there. Short blows, but it was definitely there. Was someone stuck in the house? Maybe Claire's friend had fallen and couldn't get up? He really shouldn't walk away.

He approached the house next door and spotted an older lady unloading shopping bags from the back of her car, which was a relief. It seemed easier somehow than knocking on the door and disturbing her.

"Excuse me for interrupting," Adam said from his standing point at the gate. He didn't want to appear intrusive and venture down the drive. The woman turned.

"Hi," he gave a friendly smile, "sorry to disturb you. I'm looking for someone who I believe might be temporarily living next door, but each time I call she appears to be out. I'm wondering if she's actually left now, to be honest."

"As far as I know," the woman replied, "I think it might be rented to a young woman but she isn't here very often."

She walked a few paces towards him. "Are you a friend of hers?"

"Yes. It's a bit of a long story. I was just trying to make contact again. It may not be her, but it's worth a try."

"Well, normally I'd say I'll pass on a message, but like I said, she's hardly ever here. And I've never actually spoken to her to be honest. The neighbours round here keep themselves much to themselves, really."

"I see. Would it be possible to borrow a pen and piece of paper? I'd like to leave her a note."

"Of course you can," she turned toward the house but stopped, "Oh! Now I remember, there was a bit of activity during the night though, but it all seems quiet now. Although, if you listen hard," she stopped speaking, "there's a faint whistle coming from somewhere, but there aren't any children around as far as I can see. So I have no idea where that's coming from. But I keep on hearing it."

Adam's antenna lifted. "Yeah, I can hear it. It's odd I'll grant you that. Anyway, it sounds like if it was my friend, she might have moved on." The woman looked puzzled so Adam continued to probe, "With you saying there was some activity during the night."

"Oh, I see what you mean. No, I don't think it was her moving on as such. It was more one car arrived, and then another. I thought it was odd about three this morning. I only noticed as I was up to use the bathroom and saw the cars down the drive. I wasn't being nosey or anything."

"No, I didn't think that for a minute. We need to keep a careful eye out these days. I'm all for these Neighbourhood Watch schemes."

"Me too," she agreed.

"I don't suppose you know the make of any of the cars that arrived, do you?"

"No, I can't say that I do." She thought for a minute, "I could tell one of them was expensive, though. It was big . . . and black. My husband calls them Chelsea tractors."

"Oh, yes, I know exactly what he means." Could it somehow be Max's car? He drove a black Range Rover. But why would he be visiting Claire's friend's house during the night? It didn't add up.

"I'll get that pen and paper." The old woman went into the house.

Adam listened. There it was again, a short whistle, followed by another.

"Here you are, dear."

The woman was holding out a pen and a notepad, but Adam didn't take it.

"Bear with me," he said.

He headed back to the adjacent Red Chimneys and went directly round to the back of the house where he was drawn to the whistle sound. It was much weaker now, but he could still hear it. Although he knew that nobody was in the house, he knocked forcibly on the back door with his fist and paused, listening all the time with his ear close to the door.

He heard a faint whistle.

He thumped hard for a second time with his fist clenched.

The whistle blew again . . . louder this time.

Someone was inside. They needed help.

"Claire!" he shouted as loud as he could. "If you can hear me, blow that whistle!" Adrenaline kicked in as he bellowed again, "Blow it, Claire, blow the whistle!"

One continual blow came back . . .

Chapter 51

Claire

Early morning was her favourite time of the day. That quiet and calmness before all the morning rush, when she liked to sip her freshly made black coffee, stood in front of the bi-fold doors that when opened fully, almost brought the garden into the house. As she watched the two resident, collared doves scrambling around the lawn for crumbs, the events of the last months were still at the forefront of her mind. It was like déjà vu. Only months earlier, she'd stood in the exact same spot, overlooking the garden. She'd watched the doves on that particular day, too, and recalled the foreboding feeling she'd had; a premonition that something dreadful was about to happen.

How right she'd been.

Although it had been much worse than dreadful.

It wasn't hard to bring to mind the most horrendous time in the cellar at Red Chimneys as it was constantly at the forefront of her thoughts. Thanks to her dear late father though, she'd survived. He'd promised faithfully on his deathbed he'd be with her forever, and she believed he'd been watching over her – *'Those we love don't go away, they walk beside us every day.'* And sleeping upstairs was the man who'd saved her. The man who'd broken down the door and raced down the stairs into the cellar to find her lying in a shivering heap, desperately dehydrated and blowing hard on the only hope she had – a child's whistle. He'd gently extracted it from her hand when she wasn't sure if she was dead or alive, but kept blowing anyway.

He'd stayed with her in the ambulance as the paramedics pumped fluids into her. He held her hand and his calm voice told her she was going to make it, comforting and stroking her, reassuring that Freddy and her mum knew she was safe, and promising her he wouldn't leave her. And he didn't. He slept in the chair by her bedside until she was ready to be discharged days later, following surgery to repair her hip. Once home, he moved into one of the spare rooms and, along with her mother, looked after her. She needed rest as several of her ribs had been fractured, too. She deduced she'd been thrown down the steps into the cellar and left for dead.

Eventually, her mum returned to her own home, but Adam stayed. He took her hand one evening as they were sitting outside watching the last of the sun go down, and told her he was prepared to wait for her, however long it took, he wanted her to have the time and space she required.

He'd been right. It took weeks to come to terms with what had happened. She'd even had to see a therapist to discuss the ordeal. That wasn't what she needed though. She only needed Freddy and her mum. And as the weeks turned into months, and the stronger her body became, the closer she became to Adam. Their friendship gave her time to analyse her marriage to Max. She quickly came to the conclusion Max was most probably a serial adulterer. He was a handsome man and worked in a female dominated industry. She was sure now, on reflection, he'd had other lovers. But she had loved him and knew he loved Freddy, and her too. Sadly, he'd picked the wrong woman with Annabelle Claybourne. The police had confirmed she was a schizophrenic and had killed her first husband although it hadn't been proven conclusively. She'd got behind the wheel of a car and driven at such speed, that the outcome most definitely was a fatal accident. But fate had intervened and she'd lived. Initially, she spent some time in a wheelchair, but once her body healed, she gradually started to walk again. She went through a trial for attempting to kill her husband, but it was difficult to prove. How would anyone set off on a journey with the intention of killing someone and themselves? It most likely was the case, but it was concluded she wasn't of sound mind. The courts had recommended that she undergo regular psychiatric assessments and therapy, and she'd been prescribed drugs to combat the schizophrenia. Seemingly, she hid it extremely well – she'd certainly fooled Max and he was no pushover. But she was a beautiful woman, adept at stroking a man's ego, and as with most men, often their thinking was done in their trousers. Claire concluded that most probably Max had been using Annabelle to get at her leisure business. He had been a ruthless and driven businessman, so she wouldn't put it past him. She doubted very much he was intending to be with Annabelle Claybourne long term. She couldn't be sure of that, but she thought it unlikely he would leave her and Freddy.

Annabelle Claybourne was definitely not of sound mind. To pose as the disabled Pippa was macabre. She'd certainly fooled her. Her ability to be able to pull it off was largely down to having actually spent a period of time following the car accident that killed her husband, in a wheelchair. For some bizarre reason, she'd rented Red Chimneys with a view to getting close to her. There hadn't been a dog called Tiny that had gone missing, the flier was fake. And she'd placed the dog collar in the garden hoping it would draw Claire in, which of course it had. She'd stupidly taken the collar back and become embroiled in the fabrication. Did Max know? – Claire thought that unlikely. Annabelle Claybourne was devious, and not really at Sandbanks that often, most probably spending her time with Max in London and then travelling up to Red Chimneys to spy on her. The police confirmed she'd hired a red and black Nissan Juke.

She was currently being held in a psychiatric unit, and her accomplice, the giant of a Russian, was in custody pending the trial for attacking her and throwing her down the stairs to the cellar, and as an accomplice to Max's death by disposing of his body.

Seemingly, the night of Max's death, he'd gone round to Red Chimneys demanding to know what Annabelle was playing at posing as disabled, and it appeared he had met his death falling down the stairs, or was most probably pushed. The post mortem had concluded his neck had been broken. The Yegor character had hid the body in the freezer in the cellar, no doubt planning to move it at some stage. Her turning up that morning hadn't helped the situation. While she argued with Pippa/Annabelle, he must have hit her from behind and thrown her down the cellar, probably believing she was dead. The police concluded his intention would be to come back and remove both the bodies at some stage. Claire believed her time spent down the cellar was much longer than it actually was. It had felt like days, but it was actually thirty hours.

Max's funeral had been an ordeal. The press were there. She'd played the part of the dutiful wife, mainly for Freddy. She'd got through it with the support of her mother. Adam had kept a respectful distance away, but knowing he was there silently supporting her, helped.

Anthony Gorman, who it seemed was a manager in the Claybourne Hall group, had tried to purchase Maric Leisure, which was quite an irony. He was standing by Annabelle Claybourne, and for that reason there was no way she could allow her to benefit from the company Max had built up from nothing. He'd offered a good price, far more than she did eventually get when she sold it on. It was unlikely

Annabelle Claybourne would have benefitted, anyway. She'd not be out of incarceration for many years to come. She'd remain in a secure unit, no doubt.

The flash-backs and nightmares had been hard to erase. Max's dead eyes still haunted her, especially while she slept. One of those nights, she'd woken up screaming and Adam was quickly there, rushing into her room and holding her while she cried. And one memorable time, in the dead of night, as he held and comforted her, the crying turned to something else. They'd made love. The time felt right. Since then, she'd moved into his room with him and stayed there. Her and Max's marital bedroom lay dormant.

The house had been on the market for only two weeks when the Sold board went up. A buyer had snapped it up – Sandbanks was a prestigious area and there was a waiting list for luxury houses. They were going into rented accommodation for a short while, near to Freddy's secondary comprehensive school.

Adam never tried to rush her. He said they had the rest of their lives to make decisions about their future. They both knew wherever it was, it would be together. But something had happened that particular morning which would mean they'd have to expedite making some plans sooner, rather than later.

As if he knew she was thinking about him, Adam came into the kitchen in just a pair of shorts. She never tired of seeing his virile body. He stood behind and wrapped his arms tightly around her.

"I wondered where you'd got to." His warmth breath on her neck was comforting. "Are you alright? I missed you."

"Yes, I'm fine. Do you want some coffee?"

"Please. And let's watch the sunrise before Freddy descends on us. He's harassing me about coming into his class. Apparently, all the children are inviting parents and relatives who have something of interest to share with the other children."

313

"Hey, good for you. That's lovely."

"Yeah, I thought it was sweet. Quite what the children will make of me talking about gardening, I don't know. It's a bit boring."

"They'll love it. And you'll be fab, I know you will. And I'm proud he's asked you, bless him."

"Me too. I must say, it made me feel good."

She tilted her head and kissed his cheek. "I can't thank you enough for how you've supported him since he lost his dad."

"You don't need to thank me. Freddy's a great kid. And he's yours so I'm a bit biased."

"Yeah, well you are a natural, that's for sure. Which brings me onto the next thing I want to say."

She extracted herself from his arms so that she was facing him and kept her eyes directly on his. "I did a test this morning and . . . I'm pregnant."

It took a second for it to register exactly what she was saying.

"Pregnant," he stared hopelessly. As if he had no idea how babies were made. "Are you sure?" He stared intensely at her, almost as if he thought she might be kidding.

"Yep, I'm sure."

A grin spread across his face and she let out the breath she was holding. He was smiling from ear to ear, clearly thrilled.

"And you're okay about it?" he asked with an incredulous look on his face.

She reached up and kissed him softly. "Yes."

He wrapped his arms around her. For the few seconds he held her, they didn't speak, revelling in the miracle that had happened.

He pulled away but kept his arms on her shoulders. "You've made me the happiest man in the world. I love you, you know that don't you?"

They'd never said they loved each other. It was another first for them.

"I know you do. And I love you too." She glanced down at her tummy, "And our little one."

After the hideousness of the last few months, she smiled adoringly at the man who'd not given up and found her.

She had a future to look forward to with Adam.

He'd saved her life – with help from a tiny red whistle.

Epilogue

Annabelle

She walked toward the psychiatrist office accompanied by a member of staff. Confinement in the secure unit sucked. Anthony had been his usual devoted self and visited regularly, updating her on the spa. As always he was loving and concerned about her welfare, and Della had been to visit her but she couldn't stand to see the sympathy written all over her face, as if she'd been a naughty child and deserved pity.

She'd been taking her medication for several weeks and her sharpness had returned, hence asking to see the psychiatrist. They'd be surprised as she hadn't spoken to any of the medics since she'd been there. Initially, she couldn't remember exactly what had happened, but gradually each day, the detail of that terrible night became clearer. Max, her only love, was now gone and she mourned him. It was going to take time to come to terms that he wouldn't be part of her future. But she couldn't dwell on that anymore. Her focus now had to be to somehow get out of the wretched incarceration she'd found herself in. And today was the first part of the journey to do exactly that. It would take a while, but she was confident her plan would eventually facilitate it.

The warden tapped on an office door.

"Come in."

A flash of adrenaline surged through her as she made her way into the office.

Let the journey to freedom begin!

The same old psychiatrist who'd tried to engage with her previously when she was first admitted was sitting behind the desk.

"Come and take a seat, Ms Claybourne."

She felt drab as she took her seat opposite him. Despite having all her cosmetics with her, she used little. For the next few weeks, months or even years, drab was what she'd strive to be. She was supposed to be in shock after all.

"Now," the psychiatrist smiled kindly, "what is it you wanted to see me about?"

"I've remembered exactly what happened."

"You have?" he peered over his glasses.

"Yes. It's taken a while, I know, but I can see it all now as clear as day."

"That's interesting. I think possibly it's because you're calmer now and the medication has helped steady your thought processes."

"Yes, you could be right. I certainly feel much calmer."

"That is as I expected."

"I feel now more able to speak to the police. I know you've protected me from that, but I need to explain exactly what happened on that dreadful night."

"Yes. You will need to do that, but maybe not quite yet."

"But I want to. I think it's necessary and sooner rather than later."

"Why is that?"

"Because the police have got it all wrong. It wasn't me that pushed Max Maric down the stairs . . . it was Yegor, the caretaker at the spa. I'd made a mistake and we had what I thought was casual sex, I now realise it meant more to him than me. I did speak to him on the phone that terrible night, but he wouldn't take any notice. He came charging round to Red Chimneys in a rage. I remember it all clearly now. He was the one that killed Max and attacked his wife."

317

She took a huge, exaggerated breath, as if unburdening herself had been a relief. She'd got away with murder once before, she was confident she would do so again.

"That's why I must speak to the police. I'm completely innocent ..."

The End

Acknowledgements

As always there are people to thank when producing a book. I come up with the story, but I need to make it desirable to readers. In that respect, I'm fortunate to be surrounded by people who want me to succeed, and for that I am truly grateful.

Firstly, and always top of my list is my excellent editor, John Hudspith. Brilliant insightful editors are a gift to any writer and I thank my lucky stars each day I have John guiding me. He is constantly pointing out ways to improve the story, but at the same time making sure I keep my voice as the storyteller. He just has that innate ability to see how the story can be improved which is what I'm striving for always.

I am fortunate to have the fabulously talented Jane Dixon-Smith designing the gorgeous cover – and she never disappoints (JD Smith Design). To attract a reader to a book you need a special cover, and Jane delivers every single time. Thank you Jane for turning my clumsy first thoughts into something special.

To my diligent beta readers, Sally and Sue, I'm always appreciative of your input. Your beady eyes are so valuable pointing out all the pesky typos I miss. I'm constantly astounded in how many little idiosyncrasies you find – I must strive to do better! I do also love your encouragement about the story. It's always a nerve wracking time waiting for feedback on your precious cargo when you first write it.

To my closest and dearest friends, you know who you are.

I can become a bit of a book bore (don't you dare agree!), but I love you all and your encouragement which makes me feel I'm the best writer in the world. What a tough year it's been not having our regular meet ups. I have missed you all this past year (and the beer and gin!).

Special thanks to the bloggers who enthusiastically share my books when they are released. These wonderful folk are out there industriously helping and directing readers towards my book and for that I want to say a huge thank you. With you, more people will read my stories and that's all I want.

Thanks must go my family who are so easy to love. Each day I appreciate how fortunate I am to have you in my life. Thank you for being there and supporting me.

Finally to all my readers – I couldn't do it without you. Every email, review or message I receive saying you've enjoyed reading one of my books makes all the blood, sweat and edits worth it. Thank you most sincerely. While you continue to take pleasure from them . . . I'll continue to write them (God willing!).

If you have enjoyed the story, and are able to write a review on Amazon or Goodreads, I would be grateful. Each review gives the book greater exposure which I hope will attract new readers. Any author will tell you, that is primarily why we write. We just want readers to enjoy our stories and I'm no exception. So thank you in advance if you are able to write a few words about the book. And please do get in touch directly if you so wish. My email is joymarywood@ yahoo.co.uk – I love hearing from readers.

Lightning Source UK Ltd.
Milton Keynes UK
UKHW010647050422
401078UK00001B/23

9 781839 459719